THE DRAGON'S LAIR

"Ah, how long it has been since a young fool has come calling at my door," a terrifying voice said. "And a Nain, at that. What are you doing here, boy? Can youth no longer find less painful ways to die these days?"

"I did not come to die, unless you insist—"

"Yes, if I do, you will."

"—but rather with a gift instead," Ven said into the large opening. "May I come in?"

The dragon laughed an extremely ugly laugh.

"Oh, yes, by all means, come in. I love delivered food."

Ven stepped over the threshold and into the cave.

FROM STARSCAPE BOOKS:

The Lost Journals of Ven Polypheme
by Elizabeth Haydon

The Floating Island
The Thief Queen's Daughter
The Dragon's Lair
The Tree of Water (forthcoming)

→ The Lost Journals of Ven Polypheme ←

THE
DRAGON'S
LAIR

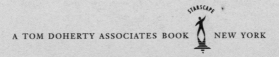

Text compiled by

ELIZABETH HAYDON

✳

Illustrations restored by

JASON CHAN

A TOM DOHERTY ASSOCIATES BOOK   NEW YORK

This is a work of fiction. All of the characters, organizations, and events portrayed in this novel are either products of the author's imagination or are used fictitiously.

THE DRAGON'S LAIR

Copyright © 2008 by Elizabeth Haydon
The Tree of Water excerpt copyright © 2008 by Elizabeth Haydon
Reader's Guide copyright © 2008 by Tor Books

Illustrations copyright © 2008 by Jason Chan

Map by Ed Gaszi

A Starscape Book
Published by Tom Doherty Associates, LLC
175 Fifth Avenue
New York, NY 10010

www.tor-forge.com

ISBN: 978-0-7653-4774-9

First Edition: July 2008
First Mass Market Edition: July 2009

Printed in May 2009 in the United States of America by Offset Paperback Manufacturers, Dallas, Pennsylvania

0 9 8 7 6 5 4 3 2 1

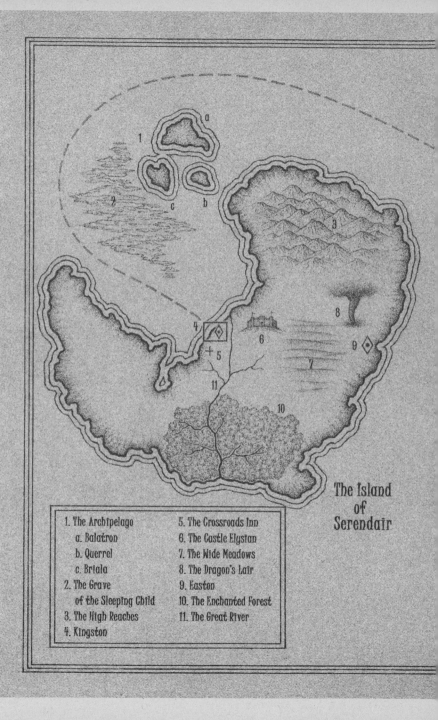

The Island
of
Serendair

1. The Archipelago
   a. Balatron
   b. Querrel
   c. Briala
2. The Grave
   of the Sleeping Child
3. The High Reaches
4. Kingston

5. The Crossroads Inn
6. The Castle Elysian
7. The Wide Meadows
8. The Dragon's Lair
9. Easton
10. The Enchanted Forest
11. The Great River

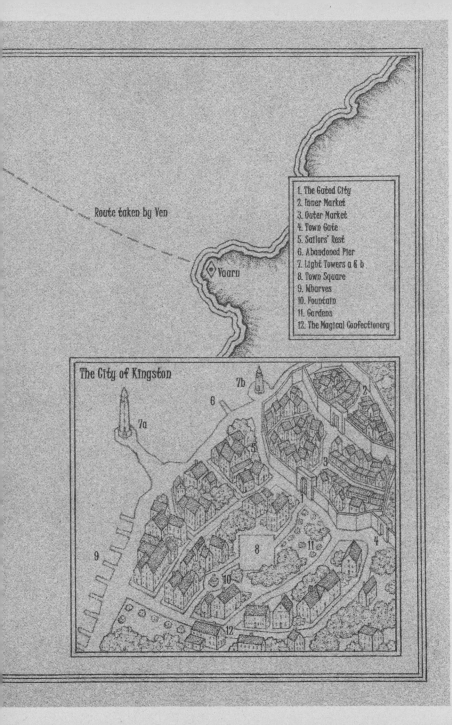

Route taken by Ven

Vaarn

1. The Gated City
2. Inner Market
3. Outer Market
4. Town Gate
5. Sailors' Rest
6. Abandoned Pier
7. Light Towers a & b
8. Town Square
9. Wharves
10. Fountain
11. Gardens
12. The Magical Confectionery

The City of Kingston

7b

6

7a

5

3

2

9

8

11

4

10

12

PREFACE

Long ago, in the Second Age of history, a young Nain explorer by the name of Ven Polypheme traveled much of the known and unknown world, recording his adventures and the marvelous sights he witnessed. His writings eventually formed the basis for *The Book of All Human Knowledge* and *All the World's Magic.* These were two of the most important books of all time, because they captured the secrets of magic and the records of mythical beings and wondrous places that are now all but gone from the world.

The only copies of each of these books were lost at sea centuries ago, but a few fragments of Ven's original journals remain. Recently discovered by archaeologists, some of those diary entries are reproduced in this book, in Ven Polypheme's handwriting, as they were originally written. Some of them are little more than a few words, or a sentence or two. A number of sketches from his notebooks also survived and are reproduced here as well. Great care has been taken to reconstruct the parts of the journal that did not survive, so that a whole story can be told.

A separate notebook containing only sketches of dragons, plus drawings of what appear to be cards made out of dragon scales, is still being restored. It was found, buried with the journals, in a waterproof chest lined in gold. In this, the third of the journals discovered in the dig, a reference to this book of dragons finally appears.

It is perhaps the most deeply magical book of all time.

The dragon scales appear to be cards in an ancient deck that allowed a special reader to see the Past, know the Present, and predict the Future. They apparently had older, deeper powers of magic, which we are just beginning to learn about. This journal contains the first account of Ven encountering a live dragon. Because it is the last of the journals found at this site, we cannot be sure whether he survived that encounter or not. Our archaeological dig is continuing in other places Ven was thought to have visited, but so far we have not turned up any more journals.

So this may be the record of Ven's final journey.

These few scraps of text and sketches provide a map back in Time to hidden places, where pockets of magic might still be found.

Contents

~ 1 ~

A Surprising Guest

I was sort of hoping to have a moment to rest before my next adventure began.

I hope for a lot of things that never happen.

Don't get me wrong—I love adventuring. Unlike most people of my race, I go to bed at night dreaming of faraway lands and all the magical things waiting to be found there. It's only been recently that I discovered adventures can be less than magical, and very dangerous.

My name is Charles Magnus Ven Polypheme. Most people just call me Ven. When I say "most people of my race," I'm referring to the Nain, an old race of people who live in dark mountains, far away from the upworld. I am fifty years and a few months old, but that makes me about twelve or thirteen in human years, because Nain live about four times longer than humans. Even though I am Nain, I have lived around humans all my life, and have never been downworld to see how Nain really live.

I began life the youngest of the thirteen children of Pepin Polypheme, a shipbuilder of note back in my homeland of Vaarn, which is a city, not a mountain range. Now I live at the

Crossroads Inn in the beautiful countryside just east of the city of Kingston on the Island of Serendair, far from my home and family.

Even though Nain don't like to travel, I do. They don't know how to swim, either, but I do. They generally try never to leave home, but I did. Most Nain are suspicious and grumpy about trying new things, but I was born with a driving curiosity that burns so hot in me that sometimes I feel like my head is on fire or my skin is being eaten by ants when something new and adventurous comes along.

Even though they are highly superstitious, the upworld Nain I know don't believe in magic. I imagine that's even more true for the downworld Nain I've never met.

But I know it exists, because I've seen it with my own eyes.

I guess in many ways I'm sort of a fish out of water. That's fairly odd, since most Nain don't even know what a fish is.

Anyway, I have a brand new journal, bound in purple leather with crisp, blank parchment pages inside. I am supposed to be keeping track of all the magical things I see in the world, especially those that are hiding in plain sight. I was asked to do this by the ruler of this land, His Majesty, Vandemere, high king of Serendair. When the king gave me my first journal a short time ago, I thought it would be many years before I had filled all the pages with notes and drawings of the magic I had seen.

This purple journal is my third one in only a few weeks' time. I've filled up so many pages with notes and drawings that I have worn an inch off the albatross feather I am using for a quill pen. Fortunately, the feather is as long as my arm, but at this rate it will be worn down to the size of a chicken feather in no time.

Which is why I was hoping to give adventuring, and my fingers, a rest for a while.

But that is not going to happen. My next adventure is beginning less than one day after the last one ended.

And it's just as well, because it seems that if I don't get started on my next adventure—and out of here—quickly, the job of recording the world's magic may have to be finished by someone else.

Because I may no longer be alive, having met my end in what is sure to be a very painful and unpleasant way.

VEN'S BEDROOM IN THE BOY'S DORMITORY KNOWN AS HARE Warren was still dark when he heard the first *thump*, followed by horrifying sounds of snarling and screaming.

He had been sleeping soundly, so at first his head was fuzzy. His heart began to beat wildly as he fumbled for the lantern on his bedside table. After a few seconds he removed the hood of the lantern and light spilled into the room.

The snarling and screaming turned into hissing and moaning.

"Gah! Ven, douse the light, you're stabbin' my eyes!"

Ven looked down at the floor between his bed and that of his roommate, Char. Char was lying on the floor, covering his eyes with one arm and rubbing his shin with the other. Ven scrambled out of bed and helped him stand up.

"What happened?" he asked woozily. "What's all the noise?"

"Blimey, I dunno," Char replied, still rubbing his leg. "I just came back from the privy. I got to get to work, it's almost dawn. I was headin' for the lookin' glass when I tripped over somethin'. And it *stabbed* me."

Ven looked around the floor. "Spice Folk, maybe?" he asked. The invisible fairies who lived at the Crossroads Inn, behind which Hare Warren stood, loved to torment Char, but they weren't usually violent.

"Criminey, I hope not," Char said. "Never known a spice fairy to draw blood before." He raised his ragged pant leg. Three long red stripes were dripping down his shin, forming what looked like an *M* slashed into his leg. "Besides, it was bigger, like a pillow."

"Uh oh," said Ven. "Murphy, is that you?"

From under the bed he could hear the sound of a throat clearing.

"Murphy, what are *you* doing out here?" Char demanded. "And what the *heck*?" He pointed to his bleeding shin.

Slowly the head of a large orange cat emerged from beneath the bed. Murphy was an old tabby, a famous ratter who had caught rodents on the ships of Captain Oliver Snodgrass, the husband of the innkeeper. He looked annoyed.

"I'm on an errand for Mrs. Snodgrass," he said testily. "I was sent to wake Ven up and tell him to come in with you when you report to the kitchen for work. Mrs. Snodgrass wants him to help you unload some of the supply wagons that are making deliveries this morning. I'll have to let her know that your response was to boot me across the room."

Char's mouth dropped open in horror.

"I did no such thing," he insisted. "I'd no idea you'd be on the floor. It was dark in here—I try not to wake Ven up when I go to work." He glanced sourly at his roommate. "He needs his beauty sleep."

Murphy came all the way out from under the bed. He stretched lazily, allowing his front claws to extend all the way out.

"That's no excuse for kicking me," he said, yawning. "I've been keeping the Spice Folk busy and out of your room for days, and this is the thanks I get. Well, I'd be sure to watch myself from now on if I were you. They've been cooking up all kinds of interesting tricks to play on you. I think I'll just let them. Now, if you'll excuse me, I'll be on my way back to the Inn, where no one would dare to trip over me. Next time you kick me, I'll write my entire name on your leg."

Char sighed, and limped to the door of the room. He held it open for the cat, who strolled out regally, then shut it behind him.

"Well, this day is off to a *lovely* start," he said. "At least it will leave an interesting scar. Come on, Ven, we better hightail it to the kitchen." He checked himself in the mirror, ran his hands through his straight black hair, then hurried from the room and closed the door behind him.

Char never leaves our room without trying to make himself look presentable, because the girl he has a terrible crush on works with him in the kitchen of the Crossroads Inn. Her name is Felitza, and she's very shy and quiet. When I first met her, I wondered what it was that Char saw in her. She has rather large teeth, and neither her hair nor her skin has much color in it. But there is something about her that has appealed to Char from the moment he met her. At first I thought it was that she is a wonderful cook, and he was named Char by the men he sailed with because he burns everything. But now it's clear that he just really likes her, and he does his best to look good and behave properly when she's around.

This isn't easy for him, because Char is an orphan, like many of the other kids who live in the dormitories behind the Inn. But unlike them, Char was sent to work on the sea when he was too young to remember any other life. So his clothes are more ragged than everyone else's, and he learned his manners from sailors, so it's sometimes either comical or disturbing to watch him eat. But he is the best friend anyone could ask for, and I'm really glad he's mine. He is smart, resourceful, and more loyal than anyone I've ever met. He follows me everywhere, because Captain Oliver once told him to look out for me. He's even saved my life a couple of times.

So if he says Felitza is beautiful, he must be right. Now I think of her that way, too.

Ven climbed out of bed and got dressed quickly, then left Hare Warren and hurried up the path to the back door of the Inn. The air around him was cool and heavy with vapor, and the sky was still dark. The edge of the horizon was the faintest shade of gray, meaning the sun would not be up for almost another three hours.

Inside the Inn the fire on the enormous hearth was burning, as it did year-round. Sitting in front of it, as he always seemed to be, was McLean, the Inn's resident Storysinger. He smiled and waved from across the vast room, and Ven waved back, even though he knew that McLean could not really see him.

Most of the other people in the Inn, including Char, have no idea that McLean is blind. McLean is a Lirin Singer, a race of people who have a special understanding of the vibrations of the world, especially music. While his eyes do not work, he's able to see things in other ways. Once he showed me how to see the Spice

Folk the way he does, and it was amazing. Sometimes even I forget what I know about him.

Which I'm sure is the way he wants it.

"Good morning, McLean," Ven called as he headed for the kitchen.

"Morning, Ven," the Singer called in return. "Enjoy your big day."

Ven stopped where he was. "What big day?" he asked.

The Singer shrugged and went back to tuning his instrument.

"You just have the feel of a big day about you," he said idly. "Like something important is about to happen to you."

"That's interesting," said Ven. "Important good, or important bad?"

"No way of telling," said the Singer. "Sorry. I hope it's good."

Me too, Ven thought. He pushed open the door that led into the kitchen.

Unlike the main room of the Inn, which was quiet except for McLean's soft music, the kitchen was bustling with noise and activity. Mrs. Trudy Snodgrass, the innkeeper and Captain Snodgrass's wife, was walking rapidly around the cabinets, sorting and moving containers as she gave orders to the kitchen staff. Her brisk manner reminded Ven a lot of her husband calling orders to the sailors on his ship, the *Serelinda*. The *Serelinda* had rescued Ven when he was floating, helpless, on a piece of wreckage in the middle of the sea, so Ven felt he owed both the Snodgrasses a large debt.

"Get those sacks of dried peas and beans out of the cupboards, Char, and move them to the pantry," Mrs. Snodgrass was saying. "We need to make space for the fresher fruits and vegetables. Felitza, make sure the sausages and porridge are started. We can't let breakfast be overlooked just because we're getting deliveries. Ciara, you wipe the cupboards down inside and out." She spun around and came within inches of bumping into Ven. Even though she was human and Ven was Nain, a race generally a head shorter than humans, Mrs. Snodgrass was a Knuckle or two shorter than he was. Her eyes twinkled, but her expression remained stern.

"Ah, you're here too, good," she said. She looked over at Char, who had already completed his task. "You two boys go out and wait at the crossroads for the wagons. One has already dropped off a load of cheese, which will need to be taken to the icehouse. While you're waiting, you can move some of it in. But keep an eye and an ear out for the wagons. Some of the drivers won't wait if there's no one to meet 'em because they'll think we don't need anything this week. I've got a full house for the first time in a long while, and I don't want to get caught short on food. Hungry guests are grumpy guests. The only one allowed to be grumpy around here is me."

"Yes, ma'am," Char said quickly. Char was terrified of Mrs. Snodgrass. So was every sailor that had ever served on one of her husband's ships. Even though she barely came up to Ven's chin, her temper was legendary and known in every port across the seven seas.

The boys hurried back into the main part of the Inn and headed for the front door. They were within a few steps of it when it opened. Otis the barkeeper was just coming in for work, carrying a pile of clean dishcloths.

"Mornin', Otis," Char said.

"Hmmph," snorted the barkeeper. "Not for a few more hours, lad."

"Hope your day goes well," called Ven as they hurried past him and out to the crossroads.

"Sure," said the barkeeper, closing the door behind them.

The sky had not grown any lighter since he had first come into the Inn, but Ven was beginning to hear the occasional twittering of birds and could feel the mist getting thinner. Dawn was still a long time away, but at least he could tell the morning was coming.

By the side of the road lay three large wooden wheels of cheese in different sizes. Ven looked down the road leading east to the Great River. In the distance he thought he could hear the clopping of horses' hooves and the rattling of wagons.

"Do you want to start moving the cheese now?" he asked Char. "It sounds like we have a few minutes before the first wagon gets here."

His friend looked at the cheese wheels. "I think I could prolly take the smallest two by myself," Char said. "You wait here for the wagons. Then, once all the deliveries are done, we'll move the big one together."

"Sounds good," Ven agreed. He helped Char stand the two smallest wheels up and watched as his friend rolled them toward the icehouse shed near the stable. He could see a tall figure come out of the stable in the dark as Char approached, and realized it was Vincent Cadwalder, the house steward of Hare Warren. Cadwalder took one of the wheels and held the icehouse door open for Char.

As he was watching the two boys store the cheese, the sound behind him grew louder. Ven turned to see three wagons approaching, though he could not make out what they were carrying in the dark. He waved his arms, feeling a little foolish, but not wanting to miss the deliveries.

By the time the first wagon slowed to a stop at the crossroads, Char had returned.

"Gah, look at all those apples," he murmured. "That should take a while to unload."

"Not all of them are for the Inn, I'd bet," Ven said. "I'm sure he's taking the rest of them to Kingston."

Char nodded as the farmer stood up, pushed his straw hat back and pointed into the wagon.

"Those ten bushels are for Trudy," the man said crisply. "Make haste, young'uns, I want ta be to town before daybreak."

"Yes, sir," Ven said as Char climbed into the wagon. The two boys unloaded the bushels as quickly as they could, then waved to the farmer as he started west. Char picked up two bushels and headed into the Inn while Ven waited for the second wagon. That one was full of corn, and just as they were finishing unloading Mrs. Snodgrass's order, a third wagon pulled up, full of parsnips, with one man driving the horses and a second following behind on a mule.

"Give us just a moment, please," Ven called to the man driving the third wagon. Beneath his straw hat, the farmer nodded. The boys finished quickly, then waited for the third wagon to replace the second in front of the Inn.

"Thank you for your patience," Ven said to the driver, who nodded again. The second farmer came down from the mule and walked over to the wagon. He reached inside, gave Char a large sack of parsnips, handed another to Ven, and then hauled two more up onto his shoulders. He turned and started for the Inn.

"Want these in through the front or at the back kitchen door?" he asked. There was something vaguely familiar about his voice, but Ven could not see him clearly in the dark. Besides, all farmers and people who worked outdoors wore broad-brimmed straw hats in the summer, making it hard to see them anyway.

"If it's all the same to you, the back would be great, thanks," said Char. "We appreciate the help."

"Always happy to lend a hand," said the farmer. He trudged around behind the Inn, with the two boys following him, lugging their sacks of parsnips. When he got to the door, he held it open for Char, who went through first, then nodded to Ven to go next.

"Thank you," Ven said as he struggled with the heavy sack.

The man chuckled. "Not at all," he said. "How are you this morning, Ven?"

Ven stopped in his tracks. He stared up under the broad brim of the man's hat and saw two blue eyes twinkling at him in return. His mouth dropped open.

"Your Majesty?" he asked, thunderstruck. "What are you doing here?"

-2-

The Big Day Begins

KING VANDEMERE PUT A FINGER TO HIS LIPS.

"Shhh," he whispered. "I'm delivering parsnips."

"Well, yes," said Ven quietly in return. "I can see that. But why? I just saw you yesterday. I thought you couldn't even get out of the castle without all of Westland and the entire Castle Elysian knowing about it."

"That's usually true," said the king. "But first things first." He followed Char into the kitchen, with Ven coming a moment later, dragging his sack of parsnips.

Mrs. Snodgrass was still bustling around the kitchen, unpacking the apples. She didn't even turn around as Ven and the disguised king came in. "Put those over there," she ordered, pointing to the corner. "And don't bruise them, you oafs." The king complied, then touched his hat respectfully before leaving the kitchen. Ven followed him, but paused at the door.

"I'll get the rest of the deliveries, Char," he said. "And I'll put the last cheese wheel in the icehouse. You and Felitza can get started on breakfast."

"Thanks, mate," Char said. Ven grinned, then caught up with the king.

Vandemere stopped in the middle of the main room and looked around in wonder.

"It's just as you described it," he said. "There's magic everywhere in this place."

"Did you just want to see the Inn? Is that why you're here?" Ven asked. His scalp was burning like wildfire.

Ever since the day I left my father's factory to do an Inspection of the new ship he had just finished, my curiosity has been raging almost non-stop. I am an odd Nain, like my great-grandfather, Magnus the Mad, who left the mountains of Castenen to set up the shipbuilding factory centuries ago.

The Nain consider this a sign of madness, by the way, hence Magnus's nickname and the strange looks people give me.

In the course of having my wish for adventure come true, I have had my ship attacked by Fire Pirates and blown up, been shipwrecked, arrested, thrown in jail, captured by assassins, lost in underground sewers, chased by thugs and all sorts of other dangerous things.

Maybe this proves the Nain are right after all.

But I still haven't gotten the itch of curiosity out of my head.

Fortunately, King Vandemere understands this.

He has the itch, too.

For a brief moment I was officially his Royal Reporter, searching for magic left over from the dawn of Creation that is still alive in the world today, much of it hiding in plain sight, just as the king had done when he was my age. The king fired me almost immediately so that I would not become a target of people *who might be looking for that magic themselves for evil purposes. But I still am out in the world, being the eyes of the king. Nobody knows this but the king, my friends and me, but I am willing and happy to do it for him.*

Because I understand how much the curiosity itch can drive a person crazy.

"Seeing the Inn is wonderful," the king said, "but I would never risk leaving the castle just for the sake of curiosity, especially these days. Let's move your cheese to the icehouse and I'll tell you more." He took a final look around the Inn, sighed contentedly, and made his way to the door, with Ven close behind him.

As they passed the hearth, McLean, who had been playing a soft windy-sounding song to a group of invisible Spice Folk, stopped in mid-note. His head turned in the direction of the king. He bowed slightly, then returned to his song.

"Well, McLean knows you're here," said Ven once they were outside the Inn. "If you were hoping to remain totally in disguise and have no one notice, I think that hope is dashed."

"We have far more pressing worries, Ven," said the king, taking hold of the largest wheel of cheese and standing it on its end. "You need to leave Westland immediately, as soon as humanly possible." He started to roll the wheel toward the icehouse. "Or Nainly possible, if there is such a thing."

Ven helped him push. "Because of the Thief Queen?" he asked nervously.

"Yes. Grateful as I am that you were willing to go into the Gated City to discover the story of my father's lightstone, I fear that you have made a very powerful and very vengeful enemy because of it. From the time that penal colony was established, no one has ever escaped from the Queen of Thieves, as far as anyone knows. The Raven's Guild in that market of thieves is all-powerful—or at least it was until you got in, then got out again, taking the Queen's daughter with you. Felonia does not forgive—*ever*. And she seems to be intent on finding you."

"When we were in her chambers, she said that every exit, even the secret ones out of the market, had been sealed, at least temporarily, so that we couldn't escape. Of course, we did, er, escape, but I thought I had a couple more days before anyone could get out of the Gated City to come after me."

The king shook his head. "I doubt that," he said. "You have less time than we originally thought. There have been huge flocks of ravens flying across Westland and even the open fields past the river all the way to Castle Elysian all night."

"Ravens at night? I thought ravens only flew by day."

"That's true most of the time," said the king. He stopped in front of the icehouse, lifted the latch, and opened the door. "But there is a breed of bird known as the night-hunting raven. They are very rarely seen in Serendair because they live in lands north of the equator. It seems that the Raven's Guild is using them as spies.

"Additionally, the fishermen in Kingston have been reporting a large amount of noise and underwater disturbance off the shore outside the walls of the Inner Market. It has long been rumored that tunnels exist into the sea below the ground there—if they were sealed quickly, as you say, it now seems as if the thieves of the Raven's Guild are trying to get them reopened. They are looking for any exit they can find. The harbormaster has ordered all the fishing and shipping vessels away from that area, to keep them from danger."

"Felonia can even threaten the *harbor*?" Ven's throat went suddenly dry.

"The Thief Queen has eyes *everywhere*, Ven, and will stop at nothing to get what she wants. From what you told me of your adventure within the Gated City, I am certain that her anger is raging, especially toward you. You escaped from her prison—and you took her daughter with you. You cost her an important alliance, since the marriage Felonia planned to force her daughter into is now ruined. She may be angry enough to make use of every tool she has to find you both. I am sending you away, out of Westland, across the Great River, to the eastern lands, long enough to escape her clutches. This is imperative, Ven—I fear for your life if you don't leave quickly. I want you out of Westland by sunset.

"While you're gone, we can make it seem as if you've left the island on a ship. I'll make all the arrangements to have that rumor released into the Gated City. I'll also get Captain Snodgrass to bring back word from the sea that you have been sighted in a far land. If you can stay away for a month or more, I believe that Felonia will think you got away and she will give up the search. Then you can come quietly back from the eastern lands to the Crossroads Inn."

The prickling excitement in Ven's scalp was fighting with a hint of anxiety.

"I don't know anything about the lands to the east of the river," he said, trying not to sound nervous. "The only place I've ever been past the river is your castle."

The king slammed the icehouse door shut and reset the handle.

"I know," he said, heading back to the wagon. "I have everything arranged—well, almost. We just need a few more provisions, and Tuck will take care of that this morning."

"Tuck?"

"Polypheme, you idiot—make certain that door is closed!" Cadwalder's voice rang out from inside the dark stable.

The king glanced over his shoulder, then looked back at Ven.

"That would be your house steward?"

Ven groaned. "Yes. Vincent Cadwalder."

"The one who framed you for theft?"

"Again, yes."

"He's still here? Why?"

"Mrs. Snodgrass has a kind heart," Ven said, "and an iron fist. She knows he has nowhere else to go—his parents were killed by brigands at the crossroads when he was just a baby. But she is getting extra work out of him, and it's smelly, unpleasant work to boot."

"Hmm. Seems like all things point to this being an excellent time for you to be leaving for a while. When you come back, be careful of that young man, Ven. These days it's important to know who you can really trust. And you're about to be introduced to someone you can." The king returned to the wagon with Ven at his heels, trying to keep up with him in the dark.

The king stopped in front of the other driver, removed the hood of the wagon's lantern and leaned up against the buckboard.

"Ven," he said, "meet Tuck."

The driver lifted the brim of his hat and nodded politely.

I knew immediately there was something different about him, even though I could barely see him in the shadows of the small flickering light. He also seemed familiar somehow, though I was certain I had never heard his name before.

Tuck seemed to have a very pleasant face, oval with high cheekbones, and not a tremendous amount of hair underneath the straw hat. His eyes were both bright and piercing, a light color that I learned was green once I saw him in daylight. They twinkled merrily, and he was smiling slightly. Then he dropped the brim of his hat and faded back into the shadows again.

"Good day, Tuck," Ven said. "Have I met you before?"

"You may have seen him in the gardens of Castle Elysian," King Vandemere said. "Tuck is my chief forester. He is in charge of all the new plantings you saw last time you were there. He designed all of the topiary hedges shaped like dragons and griffins and such."

"Oh yes," said Ven excitedly. "They're quite beautiful."

Tuck chuckled. "They might be when they grow," he said. "Now they're just plantings with wire cages around them." His voice was clear and low, his words clipped. It sounded as if he did not speak very often, and when he did each word was important.

"In case you can't tell in the dark, Ven, Tuck is Lirin," the king continued. "I know you have met very few Lirin, and there are lots of kinds of them. There are Lirindarc, the kind of Lirin who live in forests, and Liringlas, who live in open fields. There are even Lirinpan, who live in cities. Tuck's people are known as the Lirinved, the In-between, who are equally at home in forests and fields, but live in neither. They wander, a little like Rovers. Tuck knows the lands east of the Great River better than any man I know. I would trust him with my life, and I think you're safe trusting him with yours, and that of any of your friends you feel might also be in danger."

Ven thought about Ida, the daughter of the Queen of Thieves

who lived in Mouse Lodge, the girls' dormitory behind the Inn. He had no doubt that her mother was looking for her as well as for him. Then he thought about how interested the Thief Queen had been in Saeli, the little Gwadd girl who also lived in Mouse Lodge and had an almost magical way with flowers and plants, as all Gwadd did. The Thief Queen loved poisonous plants, and was very happy to have Saeli to tend her collection of them. Saeli's escape probably made her as angry as Ida's had.

Finally, his mind went to Char. Felonia had taken an instant dislike to him, instructing her soldiers to shoot him first if any of them tried to get away.

"I think we have to get everyone who went into the Inner Market of the Gated City out of Westland," he said at last. "We all managed to make the Thief Queen angry in our own ways."

The king held up his hand, and Ven fell silent. "Tuck knows the plan, Ven. It's not safe to talk too much more about it out here in the wind. Even though we're standing at the blessed ground of the crossroads, I don't want to take any chances. He's on his way to town now to get the rest of your provisions and supplies. Then he will return to pick up you and your friends, and off you'll go. Are you ready?"

Ven exhaled. The excitement of adventure was dancing in his brain along with the urgent need to get out of Westland. His thoughts were jumbled, so he shook his head to try and straighten them out.

"Let me tell my friends to get ready," he said. "If it's all right with you, sire, I'd like to go to town with Tuck. I have some things to take care of there before I leave."

The king looked solemn. "If you do, stay low in the wagon and keep away from the Gated City," he said. "There's no sense in tempting fate. The Raven's Guild is doing the best it can to find you while they are still trapped within the walls of the city. You don't want to make their work easy for them."

"No," Ven agreed.

"There is one thing more," said the king. "The last time we spoke I believe I mentioned to you that a dragon was burning the Nain settlements in the foothills of the High Reaches."

"That's right," Ven said. "You did. I forgot about that."

"It's early in the morning still," said the king, looking at the dark fields around them. "You are probably still partially asleep. You need to wake up, though, Ven. I'm not sending you out looking for hidden magic this time. I'm sending you away for your own safety. Your parents are far away—someone needs to look out for you. And even though you are a wise young man—er, Nain—it's still very easy to be overwhelmed by new sights and mystical places. You must keep your head about you now. It's very important."

"I'll stay alert," Ven promised. "But I assume if I see any magic hiding out there, you will want to know about it, won't you?"

The king chuckled. "Always," he said. "But first and foremost, stay safe. Listen to Tuck, and keep your head down." He glanced around him again, and leaned closer.

"I do, however, have a task I would like you to accomplish if you can do so without putting yourself or your friends at risk."

"Yes, Your Majesty!" Ven blurted. "What is it?"

The king sighed. "First, you must understand that each of the kingdoms over which I am high king has its own ruler, its own set of laws. I may be in charge of all of them, but only loosely. Some of the kingdoms don't get along very well. There has been an old grudge between the kingdom of the Lirin and the king-dom of the Nain for a long time, something that may soon lead to war if it's not settled. Apparently the Nain have something belonging to the Lirin king that the Lirin want returned to him. And the Lirin have something *I* want. How to make all that happen, well, it's a tremendous puzzle—and you know how I love a good puzzle."

"Yes indeed, sire," Ven said. His favorite room in the king's palace was filled with nothing but puzzles and thinking games in all sorts of sizes and colors, made of every material imaginable.

"You are the perfect ambassador to send to the Nain. Do you speak their language?"

Ven flushed with embarrassment. "I do," he said. "But my family has been upworld for four generations—more than six centuries. This means we speak our version of the Nain tongue—but I'm not sure it's what real downworld Nain speak. I'd hate to say the wrong thing and start that war you're trying to prevent by accident."

"I wouldn't worry about that," the king said. "Downworld Nain also speak the common tongue, so you can converse in that, if nothing else. The Nain ambassador to my court says he doesn't know why the dragon is attacking them. If you meet with the Nain that live where the dragon is burning settlements, you can ask them questions that might help puzzle out the reason. Remember the puzzling rules I taught you, and you might be able to find the solution. The only other thing to do would be to ask the dragon directly, and somehow I don't think that's a good idea."

"Right."

"If you can help figure out why the dragon is so angry with the Nain, without putting yourself or your friends in harm's way, you might be able to trade that information to the Nain in return for them giving back what the Lirin want. And if you can give the Lirin back what *they* want, the Lirin king may give you what *I* want. You can bring that to me, and in return I will give you something *you* want."

"I—I don't really want anything, Your Majesty," Ven stammered.

The king smiled. "Of course you do," he said. "You've told me about your quest for the Ultimate Adventure, the thing that is so amazing, so inspiring, so wonderful, so *magical* that it satisfies your endless curiosity once and for all. While I can't give you that, since neither of us knows what it is, I can at least give you the tools to help you find it. I'm working on one of them right now, as a matter of fact."

"You *are?*" Ven's head felt like it was going to explode.

"Yes. I'll tell you more about it after you come back. It might be ready by then. We'll see." The king's smile faded. "Here's one last thing to remember. The king of the Lirin who live in the great Enchanted Forest far to the southeast is a proud, great man. His name is Alvarran. He's occasionally known as Alvarran the Intolerant, because he does not have a lot of patience and he does not suffer foolishness well. It is he, and he alone, who has what I want in the Lirin kingdom.

"If you reach the Enchanted Forest in the course of your journey, say this to him: 'I am the herald of His Majesty, Vandemere, high king of Serendair, and as such I claim his protection. King Vandemere states that if you will send him the greatest treasure in your kingdom, he will swear fealty to you and ever after will call you "sire."' Can you remember that?"

Ven's eyes opened so wide that his eyelids hurt. *The king is willing to give up his throne?* he thought. *For a piece of treasure?* "Uh, yes, but Your Majesty—"

"Memorize it just as I said it to you, please, Ven." The king's voice rang with an authority that made Ven stop breathing for a moment.

"I am the herald of His Majesty, Vandemere, high king of Serendair, and as such I claim his protection," Ven repeated. "King Vandemere states that if you will send him the greatest treasure in your kingdom, he will swear fealty to you and ever after will call you 'sire.'"

The king nodded again. "That's it exactly. Very good. Now, Ven, listen to Tuck at all times, keep your head down, and remember that the most important achievement in this mission is for you and your friends to stay alive. Nothing else matters if you fail in that."

"Yes, Your Majesty."

"Best of luck to you," the king said. He took one last look at the Inn. "How I wish we could trade homes someday, Ven."

"No, thank you, sire," Ven said. "The basement of the Inn is a little scary and damp, but nowhere near as scary as your dungeons. Having spent some time in those, I think I'll stay here if it's ever safe enough for me to again."

The king laughed. "Good enough." His blue eyes twinkled, and he looked Ven up and down one more time.

"Your beard is coming in nicely," he said. "It's a sign you are growing up into a fine man. Perhaps by the time I see you next you'll have added another whisker."

Ven smiled, but he wanted to sink into the earth. "Perhaps." *Two whole whiskers*, he thought. *That's pathetic. I should have grown my entire Bramble before I was forty.*

The king turned back to the wagon and motioned to Tuck, who bent down, and whispered something in his ear. Then he went to the mule and mounted, waved to Ven, and started back east toward the Great River, beyond which Elysian lay.

"You ready?" Tuck asked.

"Just a moment, please," Ven said. He hurried inside the Inn, ran to the kitchen and pulled Char aside.

"After breakfast, be ready to leave and be gone for a long time," he told his roommate, who was struggling to carry a large pile of plates to the table.

"What? What are ya talkin' about?" Char demanded.

"I've got to leave here right away, and so does Ida. I've learned by now that anywhere I go, you're going too."

"Darn right," said Char. "'Bout time ya stopped arguing about it."

"Then finish serving breakfast and get packed."

"I *am* packed," Char said. "I'm always packed. I don't own anything."

"Tell Ida to do the same."

Char groaned. "You want me to talk to *Ida*? It's not even light outside yet. Are ya *tryin'* to ruin my day?"

"If we get caught by the Raven's Guild it will be a lot more ruined," Ven said. "We need to hide out for a while. While you're at it, ask Nick, Clemency, and Saeli if they want go, too. They were in the Gated City with us, so they may be in danger as well. We'll all fit in the wagon. I'll be back before noon-meal. Anyone who's ready then can come. Anyone who's not stays behind. Understood?"

"Aye, sir," Char said, grinning. "Faith, you're startin' to sound more and more like the Cap'n."

"If only I could think like him," said Ven. "See you in a few hours."

He ran out the front door of the Inn and climbed aboard the wagon next to Tuck. Tuck clicked to the horses, and the wagon rumbled off into the west toward Kingston.

Ven was too excited, and it was too dark, to see the long line of black birds perched atop the roof the Inn, watching them as they went.

-3-

The Merrow

WHEN THE SUN CAME UP BEHIND HIM VEN WAS SITTING AT THE
end of an old abandoned pier at the north end of Kingston's harbor. It was a place he had sat several times before, waiting for a
friend to show up. His stomach was boiling with excitement and
nervousness.

The tide was coming in, and frothy white waves rolled under
the pier. Ven watched them bubble through the holes in the
wooden decking. He knew that if he had been home in Vaarn and
his mother saw him sitting on such a rickety structure she would
be very nervous. She would probably drag him off it by the ear.
But he had tested each of the boards of the pier carefully, and
knew where all the solid ones were.

*I've certainly had plenty of time to do so. Amariel usually keeps
me waiting a while, so there's else nothing to do.*

*Full-sun is what sailors call the moment in the morning when
finally the whole ball of light rises above the sea's edge. The sun
rises on the other side of the Island, but you can still tell that it's*

full-sun by the way the color of the sea changes. It's very rare to see Amariel before full-sun. Maybe she's sleeping late, but I would never ask her. She can be a little touchy and gets offended pretty easily.

I'm not sure exactly how she sleeps in the first place. Being a merrow, what humans call a mermaid, she may look for a floating piece of debris or a rock off shore to rest on. Or perhaps she swims down to the darkest depths and sleeps there, because she has gills that let her breathe under water. Maybe she just floats between the waves. I've never actually seen her do it.

I'll have to remember to ask her about it. But I will be sure not to imply that she's being lazy. Girls don't appreciate that, at least the human girls I know. When Char accidentally greeted Ciara the other day with "Good afternoon" when she came in for breakfast, she almost pulled every hair from his head.

But however I have to say it, whether it offends her or not, I have to get her away from this place, now that the Thief Queen's thugs are breaking open the tunnels beneath the sea.

Finally, when Ven was beginning to wonder if he would see her at all, the merrow's head popped up in front of him, just behind the breaking edge of a white-capped wave.

"Good morning," she said.

"Well, hello," said Ven. "Are you feeling adventurous today?"

Amariel snorted. "Of course. Merrows are *always* adventurous. Does this mean you want to come with me and explore the depths of the sea? Because you keep promising to do that but you never actually come. I'm starting to believe you are just teasing me."

Ven stood up. "I would never tease you. At least not in a mean way like that."

"That's a good thing, because you *owe* me," Amariel said, floating backwards into another oncoming wave. It broke over her head, making her long, dark hair drift all around her like seaweed. "Merrows don't forget their friends. But more important, they don't forget when their friends are rotten to them. What happens as a result is not pretty."

"I would think not," Ven agreed. "But I'm not teasing—I'm here to invite you to come on an adventure with me." He sat back down again on the rotting dock.

"An adventure? Out of the sea? In the dry world?"

"Yes."

"When?"

"Today."

Amariel's green eyes blinked. "Today?"

"Yes," Ven said quickly. "I have to get out of this part of Serendair—er, the dry world—right away." *And so do you*, he thought. *Your family and your school, if they're still out there, need to leave as soon as they can.*

"Why?"

Ven thought back to something the merrow had told him when they first met.

My father knows that if he tells me not to go to a place, I sometimes don't listen.

Can't risk that happening now, he thought. *Amariel already knows about the tunnels into the harbor. If her curiosity gets the better of her, and she goes to investigate—*

"Well, it's gotten very dangerous for me here," he said. "The king thinks it's important that I leave today, before the people I made angry in the Gated City come looking for me. And he gave me an important mission."

Amariel's eyebrows drew together suspiciously.

"Is this the same king who set you on fire?"

Ven thought for a moment, trying to guess what she meant. Amariel saw the world through a sea-dweller's eyes, and sometimes that led to misunderstanding of the language of the human world. "Set me on—oh, you mean *fired* me? Yes. I mean no. I mean—that's a long story. But if you come with me, I will have lots of time to tell it to you. And you have said in the past that I owe you stories, since you told me so many merrow tales when I was floating on that wreckage in the sea."

"Hmmmm," said Amariel.

"Please come," Ven said. His excitement was growing, squashing his nervousness. "It will be so much fun! You'll finally get to explore the dry world, and meet some of my other friends."

The merrow's face went white in alarm. She blinked, her eyes wide, then disappeared below the surface.

It took Ven several seconds to recover from his surprise. He scrambled to the edge of the dock on his knees and leaned as far over as he safely could.

"Amariel!" he shouted over the breaking waves. "Amariel, come back!"

Farther out in the harbor he could see a red cap encrusted with pearls pop out of the water, followed a moment later by hair and eyes. The rest of the merrow remained below the surface.

"What's wrong?" Ven called anxiously. "What did I say to upset you?"

More of her body emerged. Ven could see the beautiful multicolored scales that came up to her armpits glint in the light of dawn beneath her gown of bubbles.

"*Other* friends?" the merrow shouted back. "*What* other friends?"

Ven nervously wiped the salty grime and sweat from his hands. "Er, just a few people I know, mostly my mates from the Inn where I live."

The merrow's head disappeared again. It resurfaced a few moments later in the waves in front of him, wearing a frown.

"Like that boy you were fishing for birds with?"

"Yes!" Ven said, relieved. "That's Char." He and his roommate had flown a kite on this very pier on the night he landed in Serendair. Amariel had been hiding beneath the water, watching them. She had thought the kite string looked like fishing line in the sky, and told him so after Char had gone away.

A cold blast of salt water hit him directly in the face. Ven shut his eyes just as the merrow's tail slapped down on the waves again, drenching him a second time.

"Are you *crazy?*" the merrow said angrily. "These friends of yours are *humans*!"

"Uhmmm—yes, most of them."

"Didn't I tell you about humans and merrows?" Amariel demanded. "I'd rather be in the company of *Megalodon* than a human."

Ven shuddered. He had seen Megalodon when he was aboard the good ship *Serelinda*, after Amariel had saved him from drowning. The *Serelinda* was one of the biggest ships Ven had ever seen, a four-masted schooner more than 150 feet in length. Megalodon, an ancient deep-sea shark, had appeared beneath the ship's hull, a ghostly black shadow that rose from the depths.

And was longer than the ship.

"Humans really aren't *that* bad," he said, wiping the salt from his eyelashes. "Some of them aren't to be trusted, for certain, but most of them are good, many of them are very kind. And they definitely won't try to swallow you whole."

Amariel had floated back and was swishing the multicolored scales of her glorious tail around in the foam. "I don't think I believe you," she said. "My mom says that merrows should *never* trust humans, or even talk to them. We're allowed to save them if they're drowning—that's only proper, of course—but other than that, we should keep as far away from them as possible. I only stayed with you because you told me you were Nain. Otherwise you would still be floating on that broken piece of ship somewhere in the sea."

"No, I would be dead," Ven said seriously. "The only thing that kept me from falling into the depths and drowning was the fact that you stayed, and kept me awake, and told me stories. I can never repay you for everything you've done for me. You're my friend, Amariel, the one I've had the longest—at least here in this place. I wouldn't introduce you to anyone I thought might hurt you."

"Hmmph," Amariel said. She did not look impressed.

"Besides, if you want to grow legs and come explore the dry world, you would be giving your cap to me." Ven pointed to the delicate circle of red thread and pearls on top of her head.

The merrow did not seem to be paying attention to what he said. Instead she was staring at his hands. "How do you make them work?" she asked curiously.

"Make what work? My hands?"

"Yes."

"Uh, like anyone else's, I guess." Ven stole a quick glance at the merrow's hands to see if perhaps she had fewer fingers than he did, but they seemed about the same as his own.

Amariel peered into his palms. "They're all wiggly and loose," she said. "You'd never be able to keep up with a school of merrows with hands like that. This is what hands are *supposed* to

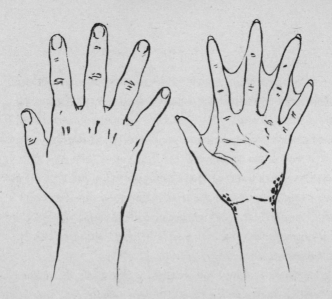

look like." She held up her own for him to see, and Ven noticed
that in between her fingers was a slight webbing. "Ours make for
much better swimming."

"I imagine so," said Ven. "Nain don't usually swim. In my
family, my mother and I are the only ones who can."

"And why do you have a picture on one of them? That's very
odd."

Ven blinked in astonishment. "You can see that?"

No one has been able to see it before except me. McLean knows
it's there, but he only feels it, since his eyes don't work.

When I went into the Gated City on an errand for the king, I
had my fortune read by a woman named Madame Sharra. She is
probably the strangest and scariest person I've ever met. She is
tall and thin and gold-skinned with eyes that look as if they can
see your thoughts. She has a deck of dragon scales that are very
old, and each of them has an image on it that tells her
something about you.

Madame Sharra let me choose three scales in my reading. The first one had a picture of a windmill on it. She told me this showed where I was in life right now, changing all the time. The second was the Thief Queen scale—and that accurately predicted what is happening to me now.

But the third scale I chose would give me a gift of great power, Sharra said. She warned me that most people did not choose a third scale in their readings, because great power is backed by great consequence, and most people are not willing to risk it.

Of course, I am not most people.

Which may be why I am frequently in trouble like I am now.

Madame Sharra called the third card I chose the Time Scissors. It had a picture of an hourglass with a pair of scissors in front of it, a thread in between the blades. When I chose that card, the picture on it appeared in my palm, and hasn't washed off or disappeared since. She said having it gave me a magical second chance, the opportunity to undo one thing I had done in the Past. She also warned me how dangerous it would be, because everything that happened in the Past after whatever I changed might be changed as well.

Her warnings about the use of this gift left me pretty sure I'm never going to use it. If I don't, no one will be the wiser, because aside from McLean and Madame Sharra and me, no one even knows it's there.

Except Amariel, apparently.

The merrow's eyes narrowed.

"Of course I can see it," she said indignantly. "Do you think I'm blind?"

"No, no, certainly not," Ven said. "No one else has been able to see it before, that's all. What does it look like to you?"

"Is this a trick question?"

"Not at all."

The merrow did not look like she believed him. "Sort of like this," she said after a moment. She touched her two fingers together and made a triangle in the air, its long side on the top, then another beneath it, its long side on the bottom.

Ven nodded. "That's supposed to be an hourglass."

"What's an hourglass?"

"Something humans—er, people—use to keep track of time," Ven said. "It's made of glass and the bottom is filled with sand. You turn it over and the sand starts running from the top to the bottom. It lets you measure time."

"You are making absolutely no sense," the merrow said. "How can you measure *time*? No one can even *see* time, let alone get it to stand still long enough to measure it. And running sand? Please. Even I know that sand can't run, and I don't have feet."

Ven smiled. "Not yet, anyway," he said. "Do you see anything else?"

The merrow eyed him suspiciously, then took his palm and looked into it again.

"There *is* something else, but it's quite strange. I think I saw one of those once in a sea dragon's lair. It's a human thing, and my mom would not let me look at it up close."

"Can you describe it?" Ven asked. His curiosity was rising inside him, making his face feel hot.

Amariel made two circles with her fingers, then a V. "Like this," she said.

Ven nodded. "Those are scissors. They are very sharp tools used for cutting things."

The merrow dropped his hand in alarm and moved away from the dock.

"Don't worry—it's just a picture," Ven said. "It can't hurt you."

"You know, you keep saying that," Amariel said. "But between kings that set you on fire, and angry people looking for you, and pictures in your hand that can cut you, and worst of all, *humans*—I'm not sure the dry world is even the slightest bit safe to explore."

"You do have a point," Ven admitted. He could see in her eyes the same gleam of interest that he saw in his own whenever he looked into a mirror. Amariel had the same gift, or curse, of curiosity that he did. "And if you're worried and don't want to go, I understand completely. It sounds like your mother won't let you, anyway."

The merrow's face lost some of its shine. "My mother is on the other side of the sea, very far away," she said sadly. "When I followed your ship, I had to leave my school and my family behind."

"I'm sorry," Ven said. "I didn't know." *Just like me, and the other children at the Inn*, he thought. *But that means she's alone here—and she would have to swim north past the Gated City to get home. An even better reason for her to come overland with me.*

"Well, that's because I didn't tell you," Amariel said. "Merrows don't go around telling their business to just *anyone*." She looked up and down the beach, and when she looked back at Ven, her eyes were beginning to sparkle once more. "When she kissed me goodbye, my mom said I should stay away from humans, but to have fun and see as many exciting things as I could before I came home. So I guess she wouldn't really mind if I went exploring the dry world, so long as I don't give my cap to a human."

The top of Ven's head began to itch fiercely.

"So you'll come, then?" he asked hopefully.

"Well, it sounds like you're going to be gone a long time. If I don't come with you now, I might never see you again."

"That's possible. So will you come?"

The merrow glanced around again. "It's going to be morning soon," she said. "Even though no one uses this pier anymore, there will be people around here."

"Then we'd better hurry," Ven said. He tried to sound calm, but his voice cracked with excitement. "How do we do this? Do you just give me your cap and that's it?"

The merrow shrugged. "I don't know," she said. "I've never done it before. I suppose we can start with that." Her smile faded. "Don't lose it, and don't you dare let anyone else touch it. Especially a human—if a human touches it, I'll start going human, too. And if *that* happens, I think I only have a turn of the moon to get back to the sea before it's permanent." She shuddered. "Uggh. My scales get itchy just *thinking* about it."

Ven unbuttoned the pocket in his shirt. "I promise I won't let anyone touch it," he said. "Not even my human friends. I would never want anything bad to happen to you."

"And *don't* tell anyone I'm a merrow. Especially boys. My father told me to be especially careful of human men, because they're the ones who want a merrow to be their household slave. If they know the legend, they might try to steal the cap from you. I don't want to be doing anybody's chores—I hate chores, especially cleaning. Once when I got in trouble, I had to peel seaweed off rocks every day for a turn of the moon—my fingernails are *still* green from it. If it even looks like that might happen, you are in *so* much trouble."

"I promise. I won't tell them—they'll think you're human."

"There's no need to be insulting."

"Actually, I only have one human male friend who I think will be going overland—his name is Char—and he would never want you to do chores. He likes doing them himself—because it gives him a chance to be around a girl he likes."

"He *likes* chores? More proof that there is something *seriously* wrong with humans." Amariel looked around one last time. Then her eyes met Ven's, shining so brightly that they looked like starlight on a green sea.

"All right," she said. "Let's try it."

Ven put out his hand. It was shaking violently.

Amariel's eyes were locked on his for a long moment. Finally she reached up, her hand shaking almost as much as his, and gently took the lacy red cap from her head. She stared at it, then slowly held it out to Ven.

I was almost afraid to touch it. I wasn't sure what it was made of, but it seemed very fragile. As much as I wanted her to come with me, I suddenly was worried that something bad might happen to her outside the sea where she has lived all her life. It probably wasn't the best of ideas to take this chance when a whole market of thieves was about to come looking for me.

But I didn't think about that until the moment after the red pearl cap was resting in the palm of my hand.

The cap felt very strange. It was cold and wet, as I expected it to be, but not very soft. It didn't have the suppleness that lace has, but instead appeared to be some sort of sea plant, delicate but hard. It was as intricate and fine as a spider's web, and looked a lot like one, the tiny pearls glistening the same way dew does in the morning on the nets that spiders build. I could have stood there and stared at it all day.

But if I had, I would have missed seeing something much more amazing.

And terrible.

~ 4 ~

The Transformation

At first, nothing seemed to happen.

The merrow continued to float in the water off the pier. She looked around her, then back at Ven.

"I don't think it's working," she said after a few moments. "I guess it really does have to be given to a *human* man after all. Oh well. This is stupid. Give back my cap."

"Wait," said Ven. He thought he had noticed a difference in the color of the water surrounding her, more than just the change of full-sun. He kept watching as the waves swirling around her went from blue-green to a paler aquamarine to yellow to gold.

An intense light swelled beneath the surface, gleaming brighter than the morning sun. A few seconds later, an explosion of bubbles rose up in great rolling streams, turning the water white, as if it were boiling.

"It's happening!" he shouted.

"Uhmm—yes," said the merrow uncertainly. "I—I'm not sure I like this—"

Like a giant snake shedding its skin, great peels of multicolored scales, now white and lifeless, began rising to the surface of the water on the bubble stream. Amariel's face went similarly white as she struggled to push them back down, but it was no use.

She was beginning to unravel, like a piece of cloth with a thread snagged, or a fruit being skinned.

Amariel winced as if in pain. She rubbed her shoulder against her neck, then her hand, as the tiny flaps of skin that served as her gills began to seal shut. Her mouth dropped open in horror.

"Ven," she gasped, "help me!"

Ven lunged to the edge of the pier and bent down.

"Here!" he shouted. "Give me your hands!"

"Give it back!" the merrow screamed. "Give me back my cap!"

By now coils of dead scales were floating away from the merrow and flipping around, lifeless, on the waves. Ven held the brittle cap out to her, struggling to keep from dropping it into the sea. Amariel tried to reach it, but she was being dragged farther and farther from the pier by the storm of bubbles. Ven dropped to his stomach and reached as far out over the water as he could with his free hand.

"Give me your hand!" he shouted again.

Fighting panic, the merrow stretched her arm out toward him.

Ven made a grab for it, and caught hold of the webbing between her index and middle fingers. It was slippery and cold.

And then, suddenly, the webbing slid back into her hand and disappeared.

The rolling clouds of bubbles began to slow their boiling.

The merrow, no longer in Ven's grasp, disappeared below the waves.

"*Amariel!*" Ven screamed. He looked around desperately for a few more seconds, but there was no sign of her.

He put the cap down on the pier, pulled off his boots and dove into the water.

Even though it was summer, the water was cold. Ven was stunned by the impact at first, but let his body straighten out as the waves rolled over him. He opened his eyes, which stung from the salt. Before him was a moving wall of green and white, cloudy with seaweed and sand and sunlight.

Below the surface, the water was still swirling with strands of discarded skin and scales. Ven could see nothing else, so he swam away from the pier and tried to get beyond the churning mess. He held his breath as long as he could, but he could still see nothing in the murky green waves.

His head popped up at the water's surface. He shook the water from his face and looked around, but aside from the pier behind him, he could see nothing.

"Amariel!" he shouted. "Where are you?"

My stomach cramped so hard that I almost bent in half. I was thinking of the sight of the gills in her neck sealing shut, and realized suddenly that she could no longer breathe beneath the waves. Apparently she could no longer swim without her tail, either, and had sunk like a rock.

I should have known this would happen.

I should have made her sit on the dock before she gave me the cap.

I should have left well enough alone.

But my bloody curiosity made me forget everything I should have kept in mind.

And now I'd probably killed her.

High above, a harsh cry rang out.

Ven looked up.

Circling in the air was an enormous white bird with webbed feet, its wingspan wider than the pier.

Ven's heart leapt. *The albatross!* he thought, watching the bird dive toward the surface of the waves as if it were fishing. Then it banked up into the air again and returned to flying in low circles, just as it had when he was floating on the wreckage of the *Angelia*, his father's new ship that had been destroyed when the Fire Pirates attacked.

He swam quickly for the area above which the bird was flying.

"Amariel!" he shouted. "Amari—" He caught a wave in his mouth, sputtered and gagged. He spat out the bitter water, then looked up at the albatross again.

The bird was diving from above, a terrifying swoop that skimmed the surface a few feet in front of him. Then it rose up into the sky once more.

Even though he could see nothing, Ven took a breath and dove himself. He swam through the gloomy green water, feeling his way through the floating weeds, until his hands felt something similarly long and flowing but smoother and less slippery. He gave it a yank, and could tell it was attached to something heavy.

It's her hair, he thought desperately. *It must be her hair.*

He tugged again and swam to the surface, pulling the weight along with him.

When he broke through to the air, he pulled as hard as he could.

A fisherman's buoy popped to the surface next to him, slimy and criss-crossed with weeds.

Panic exploded inside him. Ven made another dive, kicking hard to get down to the sand at the bottom as quickly as he could. He searched blindly through the weeds until he found more smooth strands. This time he felt along them until he found that they were attached to what felt like a ball at the other end. He gave the strands a jerk, and immediately the weed patch began swirling as whatever he was clutching began to thrash around inside it.

This must *be her*, Ven thought as he kicked back toward the surface. *If it's not, whatever I'm pulling up is going to beat me to death.*

He dragged the slippery strands, and pulled with all his might.

The merrow's head popped above the water, her hair full of kelp. She was gasping for breath, her arms flailing wildly around her. Ven pulled harder to try and keep her mouth away from the breaking edge of the wave rolling toward them.

Amariel's arms stopped flailing. She reached out and punched him in the face, rocking his head back.

"ARRRGhhh!" she screeched. "Let go of my hair!"

Ven dropped it quickly, then seized her arm instead. He pulled her onto her back and helped her float.

"Calm down," he said quietly in her ear. "Don't panic—you're all right now. Just lie on your back and I'll get you to shore." He looked down into the merrow's face. It was gray, her lips blue and trembling, her peg-like teeth chattering, and he felt his throat start to close. "I'm sorry about everything. I never should have suggested this. Don't worry, I'll get you to shore."

"G-g-g-ive me m-m-my c-c-c-ap," the merrow whispered.

"It's on the pier," Ven said. "I didn't want to lose it in the water. Stay calm—we're really not that far from the beach. We'll be there in a minute."

"I w-w-want to g-g-go h-h-home," Amariel said, struggling to keep her eyes open. "I think I'm g-g-going to d-d-"

"Don't even say it," Ven said. He was only using his feet to swim now, holding Amariel steady with both hands and letting the natural direction of the waves carry them closer to shore. "You're not going to die—I won't let you."

The merrow's green eyes, glassy from shock, cleared. She turned her head and stared coldly at him.

"As if you have anything to say about it," she said scornfully. "You won't *let* me? Shut up. I'll die if I want to. And I was going to say 'drown,' thank you very much."

I have to admit, when she said that I had to work hard to keep from chuckling. Amariel is the most stubborn, independent person I have ever met. She tells me all merrows are like that, and I believe it. Her biggest fear about giving me the cap was that she would "go human," which the stories say is what happens to merrows and selkies, creatures like her mother, when they let human men take their pearl caps. They grow legs so that they can walk on the land, but "going human" means that they lose their fiery natures, their stubbornness, and become wishy-washy and mealy-mouthed, doing whatever they are told. It's almost impossible for me to imagine that happening to her, cap or no cap.

But if it does, I have promised her I will take her back to the sea myself, put the cap on her head and toss her in.

I guess I won't get the chance to find out, though, since she wants it back already and I haven't even seen if she actually grew legs or not.

"Well, I'd prefer if you didn't drown *or* die," Ven said. His foot touched the bottom and dragged along the broken shells and sand. He glanced back over his shoulder and saw the abandoned pier was almost within reach. He kept kicking gently until he was at the edge of the shoreline, then stood up in the frothing waves, still holding on to the merrow's arm. "Can you stand up?"

"Stand up?"

Ven looked into the froth. Amariel was lying on the sand in the shallows, her formerly exquisite tail in tatters around her like a torn skirt.

Peeking out from beneath the shreds of what had once been scales was a pair of human legs. They looked like any other legs he had ever seen, except there seemed to be a small amount of webbing in between the toes.

"Try and put your feet on the ground," he said. The sand was slipping back into the waves beneath his own toes, making it hard for him to stand still.

Amariel shook her seaweed-tangled hair violently.

"No, I'm just going to lie here while you get my cap." She stretched out on the rippling sand. "I don't even want to try, I just want my tail back and to get out of here as fast as I can."

"That seems like a bit of a waste, don't you think?" Ven said. "After what we just went through, don't you at least want to see what it feels like to walk on human legs? You did take the trouble to grow them, after all."

"No, thank you," said Amariel firmly. "This does not feel at all nice—in fact, my stomach feels like it is going to be sick. So unless you want me throw up ambergris on you, I suggest you get me my cap *right now*."

"What's ambergris?"

"Whale vomit. Sailors are always looking for it floating on the sea. My mom says humans make perfume out of it. Yet one *more* reason not to trust them. Who on earth *wants* to smell like *vomit*?"

Ven was watching the tide pulling out. The albatross was gone.

"I don't think I can leave you here safely, Amariel," he said nervously. "I think you might get pulled back out with the waves. Stand up just for a moment and walk to the edge of the sand where the waves can't reach. I'll help you. Then you can wait while I run up on the pier and get the cap."

The merrow eyed him suspiciously.

"This had better not be a trick," she said. She was shivering, her skin still gray.

"Not at all," Ven said. "I'm very sorry this happened. Let me help you up."

The merrow glared at him one more time, then seized hold of his forearm.

"Ugh," she said, staring at her hands. "Wiggly fingers. Yuck."

"You get used to them after a while," Ven said. He pulled smoothly, helping her rise out of the foaming waves.

"Hmmph," said the merrow. "Not if I can help it." She opened her mouth and took several deep breaths. "I don't know *how* you breathe this way," she said, sounding disgusted. "I miss my gills already."

Once she was standing, Ven took the opportunity to get a

better look at her. The scales that had once covered her body from her armpits to the fin at the end of her tail now resembled a colorful and somewhat ratty dress. The gown of bubbles that she usually wore seemed to have vanished, but the black cape that hung down her back was still attached to her shoulders. Ven remembered how she had told him that she had gotten the cape from her mother, and that when selkies wore them they resembled seals in the water. The one time Char had caught a glimpse of Amariel following the *Serelinda*, he had thought she was a seal.

Her legs wobbled at first, but after a moment the merrow was able to stand steadily.

"All right, I'm *standing*," she said. "Now go get my cap."

Ven nodded. He took hold of her hand and walked her a few steps toward the dry sand. Amariel's human legs buckled at each step, but she did not fall.

"You're doing great," Ven said encouragingly as her knees quivered and sprawled awkwardly.

"Shut up, Ven." The merrow gripped his hand until his fingertips turned white. Ven struggled to keep from gasping in pain. "I hope none of the seabirds can see me—they have such big beaks, they're sure to tell the seals, and then the whole *ocean* will be laughing at me. Ugh! I look like a *crab*. This is *so* embarrassing."

"You look fine. Nobody walks gracefully on wet sand—not even humans."

"Oh, goodie. So now I have something else in common with humans. Just stop talking, Ven—you're making it worse."

Ven held onto her until she seemed to get her balance. Once her webbed toes were touching the warm, soft dunes and she was standing steadily Ven let go of her hand.

"I'll be right back," he promised. "Stay here, don't move."

Quickly he ran over to the rotten pier, pulled himself onto it, and jogged to the end where his boots still remained. The cap was lying beside them. He pulled the boots on, then picked up the lacy, pearl-encrusted red sea plant and was surprised to find that it had gone limp and soft, like actual fabric. He trotted down the pier and back to where Amariel was still standing, staring at the city of Kingston in the distance.

"Here," he said, holding out the cap to her. "I am *so* sorry. I hope you'll forgive me."

The merrow nodded absently. "When do the people wake up?" she asked.

Ven looked back at the streets.

"Some of them are already awake," he said. "The shopkeepers and the merchants are cleaning out their stores, getting ready for morning. The baker's been working all night, and he's probably getting ready to go to bed. The fishermen are long gone, out on the sea already. After breakfast—that's when most of the noise starts. The fountains begin splashing, the ships start coming into port, the music begins. It should start any time now, in fact."

"That might be interesting to see," the merrow said.

There was a change in her face, Ven noticed. The sallow gray that had been there a moment before had been replaced by a healthier color, and her cheeks had turned pink. Even though the seaweed still clung to her hair, her skin had dried a little, and she now looked a lot more like a human girl than she usually did. But what was most noticeable was the look in her eyes. They were bright and glistening, the way his own did when his curiosity was itching.

He thought back to what she had said to him when he was floating on the wreckage, trying to stay awake.

Do you want to hear what happens to merrows who want to walk on the land? It is a deep and sometimes irresistible desire.

"Amariel?" Ven said, trying not to spook her. "Do you still want your cap?"

The merrow did not answer, but continued to stare at the wakening city.

"Of course," she said finally, still looking into the distance. "Of course I want it. But—well, maybe it wouldn't hurt to look around a bit. I mean, after all, it *was* quite an ordeal getting here in the first place. It seems a little stupid not to see *anything* in the dry world."

Ven looked down at her feet. She was rubbing them in the sand, as if to clear the webbing between the toes. *She said something about that desire getting stronger when merrows finally set foot on dry land,* he thought, not sure whether to rejoice in her possible change of heart or to be worried by it. *Maybe now that she has, the call to see it is stronger than the horror of what just happened.*

"Do you want to come exploring, then?" he asked hopefully. "You know, go overland beyond the Great River with my friends and me?"

"Of course not," said the merrow, still looking off into the city.

The bells of the clock tower began to chime, filling the morning air with sweet music. Almost as if by magic, the noise of children playing, fountains splashing, and the clopping of horses' hooves began floating toward them on the sea wind.

Ven sighed and held out the cap again. "So what do you want me to do with this?" he asked.

The merrow did not say anything for a long time. Finally she ran her hand up and down her arm.

"Hold on to it for the time being," she said. "Let's go have a look at the city." She did not take her eyes off Kingston, but extended her hand to Ven. "Just for a moment. Then you can give it back to me and I'll go back to the sea."

"Whatever you want," Ven said, happy to have her on land for a little while at least. "I can only stay for a moment longer—I have to meet up with Tuck and get underway. But if you want to take a peek, I guess I could help you do that. Put one foot in front of the other and just keep moving. I won't let you fall." He took out one of the three clean pocket handkerchiefs his mother insisted he carry with him at all times, wrapped it around the cap, put it carefully into his pocket and buttoned it securely.

"You better not," said the merrow, still watching the city.

"Hold still a minute," Ven said. He picked the seaweed out of her hair, then took her hand again. Together they started across the dry, soft dunes to the packed sand that led to the cobbled streets of Kingston, sprawling and wobbling a little less with each step.

They were almost to the first row of shops when a rainbow flash caught Ven's eye.

A blazing streak of shimmering light.

That he had seen before.

In the fortune teller's tent.

Deep inside the Gated City.

-5-

Madame Sharra

VEN'S HEAD TURNED TO THE LEFT, FOLLOWING THE FLASH.

In the light of the morning sun, a long dark shadow clung to the side of a nearby building where the cobblestone streets began. Ven saw the rainbow glimmer again as the shadow took shape and stepped into the cobbled street.

Standing there in the light was a tall, thin woman with golden skin and eyes that matched. She was watching him with a steady gaze that he remembered from the first time he had seen her, deep within her dark tent in the Gated City.

"Madame Sharra?" he asked in wonder.

The golden woman continue to watch him but said nothing.

Ven turned to Amariel. She was still fascinated by the buildings of Kingston, where the doors were now beginning to open and the streets starting to fill with people.

"Amariel, wait here, please, and don't move," he said. The merrow nodded distantly, still watching the waking city. He took a few steps closer to the golden woman.

"How did you get out of the Gated City?" he asked.

The Reader's eyes narrowed slightly. Ven knew immediately he had asked the wrong question.

"Why are you here?" he asked, trying again. He looked back at Amariel, who had not moved. Behind her, the people of the town, the farmers' carts, the merchants, even the fountain seemed to be moving very gradually, as if Time had slowed down around them.

Madame Sharra's gaze remained steady.

"I came to find you, Ven Polypheme," she said. Her voice had a strange dryness to it, an old, ancient sound that felt like magic in Ven's ears. "I wanted to see if you were still alive."

"Oh. Well, thank you," Ven said awkwardly. "I'm fine, thank you."

"For now," Madame Sharra said. She looked deeply into Ven's eyes. "I also came to find out how long that will be true."

Ven glanced back at Amariel again. She seemed frozen in place, like the rest of the world around him. "Should I be worried?"

"Look at me," the fortune teller directed. "My time here is short. As yours may be."

Not knowing what else to do, Ven obeyed.

Madame Sharra stared down at him. She was more than a head taller than he was, and her golden eyes were hypnotic. Ven found himself staring back, feeling warm and cold at the same time. He had no idea how long he stood there, his gaze locked with Madame Sharra's, but finally she looked away, breaking the lock.

"What do you see?" Ven asked.

The Reader of the scales shook her head. "When I look in someone's eyes, I can often see the footprints they will leave in the sands of Time in the course of their lives. Even when they are no longer in my presence, I can occasionally see their paths. Sometimes those paths go on for great distances, into almost endless horizons, because their lives will be very long. Sometimes those paths are very short, because death waits beyond the next hill."

Ven swallowed. It felt like a cobblestone from the street was lodged in his throat.

"And? What do you see for me?"

The golden woman exhaled.

"From within the Market, when I looked for your path, I could see nothing," she said. "But the Gated City is under a cloud at the moment, a cloud brought about by your actions, I believe." She smiled slightly. "For the first time in a long while, the walls actually hold the residents in."

Except you, Ven thought.

"It is the prison it was meant to be, at least for a moment. Many of those who dwell in the deepest recesses of the city are not pleased with this change. Perhaps the cloud of their anger kept me from seeing your future clearly. I wanted to know for myself—so I have come to see if I can get a better look."

"Why?"

"Because your destiny, and that of the dragon scale cards, seem to be entwined."

Ven's face flushed hot. "What does that mean?"

"I'm not certain," said Madame Sharra. "But the gift you received from the scale you chose, the one that you carry in your palm, has never been given to anyone in the history of the Deck. For thousands of years, people have sought answers from these cards. The cards seem to favor you for some reason—a scale known as *The Endless Mountains* in particular. You did not select this scale in your reading within my tent—but it tried to get your attention, humming and vibrating on the table beneath the glass where your hand rested. It has continued to hum with the same vibrations since, as if it were calling to you. I need to know why."

The tall golden woman bent down and scooped up some sand from between the cobblestones of the street. She curled her long fingers into a fist, then stood up straight again and held it out over Ven's right hand.

"Your palm," she directed.

Ven opened his hand. It was shaking, either from nervousness or excitement.

It could have been either one.

The last time we met—which was the first time we met as well—Madame Sharra had used sand to read a little bit of my fortune. But she had poured it from a tall hourglass onto a glass table and passed her own hand over it. The sand had taken on shapes. First it looked like an eye, which she said meant someone was watching me from afar. Then she passed her hand over it again, and it took on the shape of a bird, the sign of the albatross. She said the albatross was acting as the eyes of someone who was watching me, which made me very nervous.

But she had never put sand into my hand before.

The long fingers opened. The sand sparkled gold as it fell into the picture of the hourglass in Ven's palm.

And passed right through it onto the street below.

Ven blinked in surprise. He stared at his hand, which seemed as solid as it had always been.

On the cobblestones the sand had taken on the shape of a crown.

Madame Sharra's golden eyes went from the street to Ven's face.

"Though you were born to a common family, you are destined to be in the company of royalty all your life, Ven Polypheme," she said. Her voice was as sandy as the cobblestones. "Before that life ends, you will have met several different kings and queens, some who will trust you, some who will not. Some will seek to protect you. Some will seek to avoid you. And some will seek to destroy you."

Ven sighed. "I know."

"Whether you live to see another birthday will depend on your ability to correctly determine the intentions of any king or queen you may encounter," Madame Sharra said. "Remember, not every king wears a crown."

She stared into his palm a moment longer, then shook her head. Ven thought he saw a flicker of sympathy in her eyes, but when she looked back at him it was gone, replaced with the steady gaze.

"Alas, I do not see anything for you beyond the next horizon, Ven Polypheme," she said. "I hoped that coming here to you would clear the clouds from your future, but it is not to be. I fear for the future of the Deck, since its fate is tied in some way to your own."

Ven felt cold run through him like an icy river starting at his head and seeping through his veins to his feet.

"I'm going to die, then?" he said. His voice cracked as he spoke the word *die*.

Madame Sharra smiled slightly.

"We are *all* going to die. That is the waste of a question. If I had demanded a goldpiece of you for this reading, it would have been an expensive mistake. Questions worth paying for are *when*? Or *how*? Or *where will I die*? But these answers I cannot give you, because I do not see your path. I only know that soon you will be lost to the sight of the world."

Ven's face was growing hotter. "Do you have any suggestions? Any advice?"

The Reader smiled more broadly.

"Live as much as you can in the time you have left. It is the same advice I would give to anyone whose fate I was reading, no matter how long or short the path of their future footprints."

Ven inhaled deeply, then nodded.

Madame Sharra opened her hand. In it was what looked like a piece of thin black stone in a smooth oval shape. She held the black stone over his palm, then tapped the picture of the hour-glass with her index finger.

"Here's another suggestion—use the power you have been given wisely. It would be far better to waste a magical gift than to misuse it. But when you believe the moment is right, do not hesitate, lest you lose the opportunity." She placed the black stone in his hand.

"Yes," said Ven, his curiosity itching fiercely. "Thank you. What's this? And can you tell me how to—" He stopped speaking. Madame Sharra was looking behind him over his head. He turned quickly.

Time was moving again.

The merrow was gone.

Every question that had been tumbling over itself to get out of his mouth dried up and disappeared.

"*Amariel!*" Ven shouted.

He dashed across the cobbled alleyway to the main street where the shops stood. He looked both ways, and, not seeing her, ran into the town square where the mongers' carts were beginning to gather with the morning's wares.

After a few moments of looking around desperately, he spied her standing on the other side of the fruitmonger. He hurried around the melons and cherries in the large wooden cart and came up beside her. She was staring into a wagon, her face white with horror, her hand in front of her mouth.

Ven followed her gaze. He found himself looking into a fishmonger's cart, filled to the brim with flapping, gasping bass and cod, their silver and white scales glimmering dully in the morning sun, their eyes cloudy and dull. Cats of all colors and sizes were rubbing up against the monger and his cart, while the man pushed them away, counting his wares.

"Amariel, don't go off like that without me," Ven scolded. "You could get hurt." His mouth snapped shut. Amariel looked like she was going to be sick.

"Is this how humans treat all seafolk?" she asked, trembling.

"No, no, of course not," Ven said. He took her by the arm and led her gently away from the fishmonger. A number of the cats left the wagon and followed them as they walked away, rubbing up against Amariel's ankles and meowing hungrily. Ven pushed them away with his feet to keep her from tripping over them.

"I thought merrows ate fish, too," he said, heading back toward the abandoned pier. The cats continued to follow them, chasing the merrow, their voices growing louder.

"We do," said Amariel. "But one at a time—and under the water, where their spirits can go back to being part of the sea. We don't take a whole school of them and leave them, *alive*, to dry out in the sun and smother to death—it's *barbaric*. I feel ambergris in my throat." She looked down at the cats, then wiped her nose. "Can you make them stop?"

"Shoo!" Ven said, but the cats would not be chased away. He looked around the square for Tuck and the supply wagon. The forester was approaching from the south, the wagon loaded with sacks and barrels. To the west, more cats were coming in from the beach, heading for them.

Or, actually, straight for Amariel.

The merrow was beginning to panic. She grabbed Ven's arm.

"What are these horrible animals, and why are they chasing me?" she gasped.

"They're cats," Ven said, wading through the pack and shoving them away with his feet. "And normally they're perfectly harmless. I don't know why they are being so obnoxious." He could see the townsfolk beginning to stare, first at the feline parade, then at the strange girl with the dress of tattered scales. "And I don't know if we can get back to the pier without being seen, Amariel—everyone's watching now."

The merrow looked around, then nodded.

"I don't want to go back yet, anyway," she said. "If we can get away from these howling land-beasts, I would like to go exploring a little more. While you were gone I saw a fountain that sprayed water in different colors, and beautiful anemones growing in boxes attached to the dwellings, and so many other odd and wonderful things. I think it would be a horrible waste not to look around at least before I go back to the sea."

Ven's heart leapt. He looked back to the south and saw that Tuck and the wagon were at the closest street corner.

"Then let's go," he said excitedly. "This is our wagon, and it will get us out of here and away from these cats."

"*Lovely,*" said the merrow.

Ven looked over at the alley where he had seen Madame Sharra, but the golden woman was gone.

Along with his chance to ask her anything else.

Ven looked down at the thin black stone in his hand. He turned it over curiously, but his attention was drawn away by the merrow's pinching fingers as Tuck and the wagon approached. Amariel backed away behind him as the horses clopped nearer.

"How awful," she whispered in his ear. "What happened to those poor hippocampi?"

"Hippocampi?"

Amariel pointed at the team of horses. "Where are their tails?"

Ven hid his smile. "Those aren't sea horses, they're *land* horses," he said. "That's what they are supposed to look like. They have legs, not tails—er, well, they have tails, too, but not like yours—their tails are more like your hair."

"Hmmph," said the merrow. "That's just plain *unnatural.*"

"And just like hippocampi, you can ride them in races, too,"

Ven continued. "Didn't you tell me you want to be a hippocampus rider when you grow up?"

"Maybe," Amariel said. "I'm not so sure now that I've seen those things. I might want to teach a dolphin school instead. The dry world is very strange."

Her words were lost in the rumble of the wheels as the cart rolled to a stop. The Lirin forester pushed the brim of his hat up and looked down in surprise at the cats swarming around Ven's feet.

"You ready?" he asked.

"Yes, thanks," Ven replied. "Tuck, this is my friend Amariel." He felt her shrink down behind him, and turned around.

"Don't worry," he said quietly. "He's not human—he's Lirin."

Amariel peeked out from behind him and looked up at the forester.

"Hold still," said Tuck to the two children. He clicked to the horses, and they stomped their feet in unison, rattling the sides of the wagon and vibrating the cobblestones.

The cats scattered.

"Hop aboard," Tuck said.

Ven took hold of the merrow's arm and helped her climb into the back of the wagon. When he reached out his hand, he realized he was still holding the black stone Madame Sharra had given him. It was almost as if he had forgotten it was there.

He held it carefully and clambered in beside her, then settled down next to her amid sacks of carrots, oats and potatoes. He nodded to Tuck, who whistled to the horses again, and the wagon lurched forward over the cobblestones and northeast through the waking streets toward the main town gate.

Ven crouched low at they passed the massive walls of the Gated City, pulling Amariel down with him. He looked back to the place where he had first seen the rainbow flash that seemed to be a sign of Madame Sharra's magic, but there was nothing there but sunlight on the wall.

It was not until they had passed through the gate and were well away from Kingston that the thin black stone in his hand exploded with color in the light of the rising sun.

- 6 -

Black Ivory

IN THAT INSTANT, BOTH HORSES REARED AND SCREAMED IN FRIGHT.

The wagon rocked violently from side to side, spilling carrots and apples over onto the roadway, and sending Ven and Amariel up into the air. They landed heavily on the floorboards with a *thud*.

Tuck was up on his feet on the wagon board immediately, speaking quietly to the horses, gentling them down. It took him a few moments to calm them, but once they were settled and standing steadily again in the road, he sat back down, turned and leaned over the seat board into the wagon bed, where the two children were trembling.

"Well, Ven, that was certainly a lot of fun," he said acidly. "What was *that*?"

"I—I don't know," Ven stammered. He held out the oval of thin black stone. "I—I got this in town, and when the sun hit it, well, it sort of exploded with color." His face grew hot and his stomach weak as he realized he was telling his secrets to an almost total stranger.

Tuck pushed his straw hat back and eyed the stone. In the

morning light Ven could see more of his face than he had in the darkness of foredawn. It was wizened and slightly wrinkled, like an old apple, but pleasant, as if the lines had come from laughing a lot, even though he seemed to be very quiet. His eyes were green as summer leaves, and thin silver hair fringed his head. There was an angle to his face that was definitely not human, a lot like Amariel's. He held out his hand for the stone.

"Let's have a look," he said.

I sat there, staring at his hand, feeling my heartbeat in my ears. From the moment I left home I have had to make choices about who to trust with secrets, or things that might be secrets, that could save or end my life. I usually try to keep most things I am not certain about to myself, or sometimes I tell Char.

Amariel, for instance. I told Char while we were on board the *Serelinda* that I thought I had seen a merrow. But I never told him I had actually met her, and that she had saved my life.

So here I was with the king's forester, who I met in the dark and have only known for a few hours. He is about to take me and my best friends in the world into unknown lands past the Great River, on the run from the Thief Queen's thugs and spies. I don't know anything about him, except that the king trusts him.

Then I thought about what he had said to me.

Tuck knows the lands east of the Great River better than any man I know. I would trust him with my life, and I think you're safe trusting him with yours, and that of any of your friends you feel might also be in danger.

So even if I don't know Tuck that well yet, if the king trusts him, I guess that is good enough for me.

And even if it wasn't, I don't know what other choice I have.

Nervously Ven handed over the oval stone.

The king's forester's eyebrows arched, but he said nothing. He took the stone and turned it over in his hand, examining it carefully. He rubbed his forefinger along the top edge, then handed it back to Ven.

"Black Ivory," he said. "Where did you get it?"

"In—in Kingston, in an alleyway," Ven said. The pit of his stomach was boiling. As much as his curiosity was raging, he was certain that Madame Sharra would not want him to tell the whole world about their meeting. "What's Black Ivory?"

"The tusk of a narwhale," Amariel whispered. She looked like she was going to cry.

"A narwhale?" Ven asked.

"A whale with a horn," the merrow said shakily. She put her hand up to her forehead like it was a unicorn's horn.

Tuck shook his head. "No, not at all. Ivory's a bad name for it, because normally ivory comes from an animal. This is not the same. Black Ivory is a piece of stone that was once alive but now is past dead. All of its magic, its lore, has been stripped from it, leaving it totally without life."

"Isn't all stone lifeless?" Ven asked.

Tuck chuckled. "I cannot believe a Nain just uttered such words. Clearly you have been upworld all your life." His eyes took on a look of sympathy as he saw Ven's face flush with embarrassment. "All stone still has some kind of life within it, I've been told—all except Black Ivory. It's so dead that it makes a great hiding place from anyone or anything that can feel vibrations on the wind."

Ven nodded. "Like a Lirin Singer," he said. "Or a Kith, like Galliard, the king's Vizier. His Majesty once told me that Kith were an ancient race even older than the Nain or the Lirin. Kith have the power of wind in their blood, and can hear what is being spoken on it."

"Or even those who just have normal senses," Tuck said. "Black Ivory is so good at masking vibrations that it's almost invisible. Even if it's in your hand, you can almost forget that it is there."

Like I did, Ven thought.

"Black Ivory is extremely rare," Tuck said. "Because of its properties, it is usually made into a box or a sleeve and used to hide something very important, something magical that gives off vibrations of power. Inside a sleeve of Black Ivory, even the most powerful item would be impossible to find unless you know it's there."

"So you think there is something inside it?" asked Ven.

"Look at it carefully. Then you decide."

Maybe Madame Sharra's news that my footprints in Time seemed to be coming to an end soon had made my brain race. It made me hear a lot of words of wisdom that I had heard before. The king's comments about Tuck cleared out of my head, and now I was hearing something my father had said to me on my last birthday. Even though it was not that long ago, it seemed like a lifetime had passed since I heard them. He said the same thing in a letter the albatross brought me a week or so ago.

This was your great-grandfather's jack-rule. Now it belongs to you. If you see things as they appear through its lens, you are taking the measure of the world correctly.

Ven unbuttoned his shirt pocket and took out the jack-rule that had belonged to his great-grandfather, Magnus the Mad. It was a Nain tool used to measure when mining or building, and was the most precious thing he owned. He carefully extended the magnifying lens and looked at the flat piece of stone.

Its edges were smooth, as if someone had carefully polished them. Unlike stones Ven had seen before, which were made up of many different colors, this was solid black, without any variation in hue. And, visible in the jack-rule's magnification, he could see that along the top was a thin slit.

Through which a tiny sliver of gray was peeking.

"Here, Amariel, hold this," Ven said, passing her the jack-rule. "Over the stone so I can see."

"A *please* would be nice. I'm not your sucker fish, having to do whatever you want me to do."

"Sorry. Please."

The merrow took the folding ruler, wincing at the feel of her unwebbed fingers, and held it over the stone. Her green eyes were sparkling. She moved closer so that she could see as well.

Carefully Ven took hold of the thin sliver and pulled it gently from the slit.

A scale-like object slid out of the stone sleeve. It was gray, with a finely tattered edge, and scored across the surface with millions of tiny lines that formed a geometric pattern. It was slightly concave, and etched into its face were symbols in a language he recognized but could not read, and a line drawing of many mountains. When the sunlight hit it, their eyes were dazzled by a million rainbows that ran across its surface and disappeared. Ven gasped.

"This is one of her cards," he whispered.

"I bet it's the Endless Mountains, the one she said was trying to get my attention."

"Whose cards?" Amariel demanded. "What are you talking about?"

Ven looked up to see the forester and the merrow staring at him.

"Madame Sharra," he said reluctantly. "This is one of the dragon scales she uses to read the future."

The Lirin forester's face grew instantly serious.

"Put it away," he ordered. "*Now.*"

Ven pushed the scale back into the Black Ivory sleeve, wishing he had taken the time to look at it more carefully. There was a vibration to it that was pleasant, making him tingle. Once it was back in the sleeve that sensation was gone, leaving him feeling a little bit hollow.

"That thing's in its sleeve for a reason, Ven," said Tuck. "I don't know who this Madame Sharra person is, or what you are talking about. What I do know is that the open road outside of Kingston is *definitely* not the place to be discussing it. Now, let's be on our way. You two settle in back there and I will get us to the crossroads."

His voice grew more gentle as he saw the looks of shock on their faces.

"Remember, stay down, children. It's best that anything passing by thinks you are cargo, nothing more." He got out of the wagon, picked up the vegetables and fruits that had spilled over the sides, tossed them back into the sacks, and mounted again.

"*Het,*" he said to the horses. The team lunged forward, dragging the wagon, then smoothly began the journey east toward the Inn.

"How are you feeling, Amariel?" Ven asked as they slid down below the sides of the wagon, trying to get comfortable.

"Like one of the fish in that cart."

"Oh," Ven said. "I'm sorry it's been a difficult morning. But it will get easier once we're on our way."

"It had better," said the merrow. "For your sake."

Ven couldn't help but smile. "At least you're not going human," he said. "You still sound very merrow to me."

"Thank goodness for that," Amariel said. "Just make certain no one but you touches my cap."

"I will," Ven promised.

The wagon rumbled east into the rising sun. As it climbed higher in the sky the birdsong became louder and the warm wind picked up, rustling the bags and the children's hair. Amariel smoothed the scales that had once formed her tail, looking nervous as they grew drier.

"I hope when I return to the sea this will go back to being the way it was," she said. "I really did have a very beautiful tail."

"Yes, you did, and I'm sure you will again," Ven said. "Try not to worry."

"Don't tell me what to do," said the merrow. "I'll worry if I want to. It's not *your* tail. Hmmph."

In the distance a dog began to bark. A moment later, another joined in, then another. Ven shifted to his side and peered between the slats in the wagon.

Up ahead to the south he saw the gleaming walls of the White Fern Inn.

Mr. Whiting, the owner, was standing in the middle of the lush green front lawn, whitewashing the sign. He put down his brush, then turned and looked in the direction of the wagon.

Ven's stomach sank.

Mr. Whiting is one of the most evil men I have ever met, maybe the most evil. He accused me of theft and murder and had me arrested and locked up in the palace dungeon while the king was away on a state visit. His guard dogs are evil as well. They about tore my friend Nick to shreds on his way home from town one night. Mr. Whiting used them to frighten people away from the Crossroads Inn so that his own place would always be full. He even got Vincent Cadwalder, the steward of Hare Warren, to work with him against Mrs. Snodgrass. I find that strangest of all, since Cadwalder's own parents were murdered at the crossroads when he was a baby, and Mrs. Snodgrass took him in. She has been as much a substitute mother to him as she is to everyone else who lives in Hare Warren or Mouse Lodge.

Mr. Whiting had to pay to repair the damage his dogs did to the Crossroads Inn, and has been warned by the constable to stay away from it, and from me. The fact that Mrs. Snodgrass did not take everything he owned, or, worse yet, have her husband visit him along with the crew of the *Serelinda*, shows what a forgiving and kind woman she is. She even forgave Cadwalder, whom she had taken care of all his life.

I am not as forgiving as Mrs. Snodgrass.

I still don't understand why Mr. Whiting is not in jail.

The muscular dogs barked even louder as the wagon came nearer to the White Fern Inn. They chased each other around in their pen, faster and faster, becoming one great swirl of black and brown fur and snarling teeth. One of them sent up a baying howl, and the others joined in, filling the air with the sound of unnatural screaming.

The horses slowed their pace. Ven could hear Tuck speaking softly to them, encouraging them forward.

Ven reached over and took Amariel's hand. It was shaking.

"Don't worry," he whispered. "They're behind a fence."

"Don't speak, children," Tuck said.

Ven jumped. His words to Amariel had been as soft as he could make them. He was not sure she had even heard him over the hoofbeats, the creaking of the wagon, and the noise of the howling dogs. *Tuck's ears are very sensitive*, he thought. *It must be a Lirin trait, because McLean has it, too.*

The wagon rolled on, even more slowly. Ven lay as low as he could behind the sacks of food and provisions, keeping his eye on the hole between the slats.

As he watched, the neatly pressed sleeves of the innkeeper's shirt came into view.

Ven held his breath.

Then he could see the shoulders of that shirt as Mr. Whiting crouched down, staring at the wagon. His great hooked nose passed by the same hole Ven was watching through.

Then his eyes, dark and menacing, bore into Ven's through the slats.

The dogs screamed louder, their jaws slathering and foaming, as they threw themselves against the fence. Ven could see the wooden gate buckle, nearly opening. He heard Amariel gasp beside him. He rolled over to see her, white and wide-eyed, and clapped his hand quickly over her mouth.

Suddenly the back gate of the wagon rattled. An even higher, more horrifying scream tore through the air as a streak of brown and black fur leapt from the ground.

And hurled itself onto the children.

- 7 -

Leaving Safety Behind

VEN THREW HIMSELF ONTO AMARIEL, LEAVING HIS BACK EXPOSED
to the attack he knew was coming.

He braced himself, keeping his hand over her mouth.

And tried not to yell as he felt his back being gouged and
scratched. He clenched his teeth, waiting for the bite, and closed
his eyes.

As something ran up his shoulders and through his hair, then
disappeared into the sacks.

Ven opened one eye. His face was right next to the merrow's.
Her eyes looked like giant green marbles above his hand.

"Was that a cat?" he whispered. "That felt like a bloody *cat*."

Amariel nodded.

"Not a dog?"

The merrow shook her head. Beneath Ven's hand on her face,
she was trying to keep from sneezing.

Ven let his breath out slowly. His back and neck were throb-
bing.

"Sorry to have bothered you, sir," he heard Tuck say to Mr.
Whiting. "Must have picked up a stray in town."

"Harumph." Mr. Whiting coughed unpleasantly. "Be on your way, man. You're upsetting my dogs, and probably my guests."

"My apologies again," said the forester. He clicked to the horses. The wagon lurched, then began rolling east again.

Ven took his hand off Amariel's mouth. He lay still until he knew they were well out of sight of the White Fern, then sat up and ran a hand over his shoulder. It was bleeding slightly, and the gouges on his back stung.

"Bloody cat," he muttered again.

"Better than one of those dogs," said Tuck from the front of the wagon. Ven jumped again, having forgotten the forester's sensitive ears. "And better than you being noticed."

"Well, that's certainly true," Ven said. "But I'm not looking forward to digging that thing out of the provisions. We certainly don't want it in the wagon."

"Just to let you know, Ven, if you ever jump on me like that again and cover my mouth, I'm going to bite you," Amariel said.

"I wouldn't blame you," Ven admitted. "But I was just trying to keep you safe."

"Hmmph," said the merrow.

The cat did not emerge before the wagon came in sight of the crossroads. Ven rose up on one knee and saw that Char and the others were waiting in front of the Inn, their belongings tied up in small cloth bundles. They were hiding in the shade of an enormous rosebush that Ven did not remember seeing before. He waved to the merrow to come next to him.

"See those people?" he said, pointing. Amariel nodded. "Those are my other friends. See? There's nothing to be worried about. The tiny little girl over by the flowerbed is Saeli. She's a Gwadd, not human at all. Gwadd are an old race of people who love the earth and live in hilly fields, I think. Saeli's very nice, and she's also very shy. She can talk, but she has a very odd voice, so she prefers to speak in flowers."

Amariel looked puzzled. "Flowers?"

"Those anemones you saw in the windowboxes in Kingston, the pretty ones? Those were probably flowers." Ven pointed to wildflowers growing in the fields along the road. "Like those."

"How can somebody *speak* in flowers?" asked the merrow.

"It's hard to explain. Sometimes when she wants to say something, flowers appear at your feet, or a vine gets long and tangly, or a bush grows bigger."

"Never mind," said the merrow. "You're making my head hurt."

"Saeli is so gentle that you can't possibly be afraid of her," Ven went on. "She's—"

"There you go again, telling me what I can and cannot feel," Amariel interrupted. "You should really stop that. Wait 'til you come under the sea with me. We'll see if *you* can keep from being afraid of stuff that doesn't scare *me*. I, for instance, have a good many friends who are sharks. I can't wait for you to meet them."

"You have a point," Ven admitted. "Sorry. Anyway, the tall girl with the dark brown skin—that's Clem. Her real name's Clemency. She's human, but she is the curate-in-training for the Spice Folk who live in the Inn." He stopped at the look of confusion on the merrow's face. "This isn't making any sense to you at all, is it?"

"Not a bit."

"All right, then, I'll stop trying to explain and you can just meet them," Ven said. "I know they're going to be excited to meet you."

The merrow let loose an exasperated shriek. "See, there you

go again, Ven," she said. "You don't know *anything* about how they are going to feel. Who do you think you are, King of the Sea?"

"Definitely not," said Ven.

"I know you are trying to make me less nervous, and that you want to help. Just stop trying to make everything all right and maybe it will be."

"Good enough," said Ven. "We're almost there."

The wagon slowed as it approached the Inn. Ven could see Ida and Clem sorting through a large canvas bag, and Saeli finishing her daily maintenance of the flowerbeds. Char had come out from behind the rosebush and was standing at the edge of the road, his hand shielding his eyes, and was waving excitedly.

Amariel tugged at his sleeve.

"That's the boy who was fishing for birds," she said.

"Yes! His name is Char," Ven said. "He's the one I told you about—my roommate."

"Roommate?"

"We share the same bedroom at the Inn."

"Bedroom?"

"A room where you sleep."

"Well, sleep I know. What's a room?"

"Oh boy," said Ven. "This really is going to be a challenge for both of us to keep anyone from finding out you're a merrow." Amariel looked even more nervous. "Tell you what—if there's something that you don't understand, just grab my elbow, and I'll explain it to you when no one is listening."

"*Great*," said the merrow. "Then they'll all think I'm *stupid*."

"No, they won't," Ven said. "No one who meets you could ever think you're stupid. You're very smart, and that's obvious."

"How diplomatic you are," said Amariel. "Now, quiet down. I

want to hear what everyone is saying." She leaned up over the wagon boards and looked around at the Inn and the wide green fields leading off to woods, her eyes still glowing with wonder.

The wagon came to a halt outside the Inn. Amariel grabbed Ven's elbow and pointed to the golden griffin that was painted on the door. Ven explained quietly what it was.

"Yo! Ven! Hoay!" Char called as he ran alongside the wagon.

"Shhh," Ven said in return. "We're trying to leave without everyone in the world knowing we're gone."

"Well, the Inn is empty of guests. Cadwalder's asleep. And the other kids are takin' stock of supplies and cleanin' the basement, so 'til someone comes along on the road, no one's here to see us."

"Are you sure Cadwalder's asleep? We had a close call with Mr. Whiting when we passed the White Fern."

"Quite sure," Char said. "Or in bed, at least. The Spice Folk are watchin' him."

"Good. Is Nick coming with us?"

Char shook his head. "No. He's got to work. He didn't come inside the Inner Market anyway, so the Thief Queen never saw him. He says he'll be careful, and good luck."

"All right," Ven said. "Char, I'd like you to meet a friend of mine. This is Amariel."

Char blinked. Ven glanced to his right where the merrow had been sitting, looking out over the fields.

She was gone.

Ven turned around. The merrow was crouched behind a large barrel.

The back of the wagon rattled as Char opened the gate.

"Don't worry," Ven whispered.

"Shut up," the merrow whispered back.

Char's thin face and dark, straight hair appeared over the back of the wagon, along with the rest of him a moment later. He looked at the merrow, then his eyebrows drew together in surprise.

"Hi," he said.

Amariel just stared at him.

"Ven, what's goin' on?" Char asked. "What's she doin' here?"

"She's coming with us," Ven said. He stepped over a sack of beans and tried to get to the merrow. Amariel slapped at him.

"You sure?" Char asked doubtfully. "She don't look like she partic'ly wants to. And where did she come from?"

"She's just a little nervous," Ven said as the merrow slapped at him again. "She came from town—and I've known her for a long time."

"What are you *talkin'* about?" Char demanded.

Ven turned around. "Look, Char, I don't have time to explain now. This is all you have to know—her name's Amariel. She's my friend, and she's coming with us. Now go get the others and let's get out of here."

Char shrugged. "You're the boss, I guess. Or at least the biggest target." He whistled for the girls. "Come on, step lively. We need ta get underway."

Saeli wiped her hands on the grass and scurried over to the road. She picked up a tiny gingham bundle and came over to the wagon. Char boosted her up, and Ven helped her aboard. She sat down in the back next to a bushel of apples. Then she caught sight of Amariel.

"Saeli, this is Amariel," Ven said quickly. "She's my friend, and she's coming with us."

Saeli blinked, then nodded. She reached into the apple bushel and pulled out a twig. In her hand it stretched and opened into a stem of pink blossoms. Saeli held it out toward the trembling merrow.

When Amariel didn't move, Ven took the twig and gave it to her.

"Thanks," Amariel mumbled.

Saeli nodded again, then settled down next to the apples. Her head turned, and Ven saw the long, caramel-colored braid of her hair jiggle. Amariel's eyes opened wide as a tiny face peeped out. It looked like it belonged to a puffy brown monkey.

"Dear ocean, she's picked up a *barnacle*," she whispered to Ven.

"No—that's the keekee," Ven whispered back. "It's an odd little animal she rescued from the Gated City. It hides in her hair."

Amariel's hand went quickly over her mouth.

"Ambergris?" Ven inquired.

The merrow nodded.

"It won't hurt you—it's as shy as Saeli. But it can be brave and smart like her, too. They make a good pair."

Over the side of the wagon Clemency's voice could be heard.

"Nope—this is Ciara's. Is this yours? Are you sure? Now, I *know* this is Bridgette's, *this* is Emma's—Ida, for goodness sake, did you pack *anything* that actually belongs to *you*?"

He looked over the side of the wagon as Mrs. Snodgrass came out of the Inn, carrying a huge basket and a small plate. Clem was still rummaging in Ida's bundle, pulling out handkerchiefs and underwear, hair ribbons, combs, and other items that she tucked under her arm as she walked. Ida sauntered after her, a smirk on her face, her colorless hair desperately in need of brushing. The two girls climbed onto the back of the wagon and stopped. They stared at the merrow. Then Clemency looked at Ven.

"Who's that?" she asked.

"Ven's friend," Char said. "Name's Amariel. Get in."

Clemency looked at Ven. "What? What's—"

"Get in, Clem," Ven said tersely. "You too, Ida."

Ida's eyes narrowed but she obeyed. She picked her way around the supplies and sat down right next to Amariel, staring at her. She looked her up and down, and then a grimace of disgust came over her face.

"That's the strangest dress I've ever seen," she said. "Did you just come from the king's ball? And—Ven, she's *wet!* Ugh. She's not even housebroken. Eeeuww—the whole floor of the wagon around her is wet, too. Bleah. I'm moving."

"Shut up, Ida," Ven snapped. He looked at the merrow. Amariel's expression went from nervous to black with anger just as Mrs. Snodgrass's face appeared over the side right next to her.

"You children ready?" the innkeeper asked. She caught sight of the merrow, and her eyes opened wide in surprise. "Oh! Sorry, dearie, didn't know you were there." She looked more carefully, and a gentle look came over her face. "Ven, who's this, now?"

"Amariel," Ven said shortly, glaring at Ida. "My friend."

Mrs. Snodgrass's expression changed again to one of understanding. "Well, good day to you, Amariel. 'Tis a pretty name you have there. You're traveling with Ven and the others?" The merrow nodded timidly. "Very good. Do you have enough clothes for the journey?"

Amariel squeezed Ven's elbow so hard that it hurt. Ven touched the collar of his shirt to indicate what clothes were.

"No," the merrow said. "I don't have anything."

"Ah. Well, not a problem. Come with me, dearie, and I'll see if I can't roust you up some nice things," said Mrs. Snodgrass. "Ven, why don't you help her out of there? She looks like she's been sitting a while, and her legs are probably cramped." She pointed to the corner of the wagon. "You, Ida, move away."

Ven reached down and helped Amariel stand up. The tattered edges of what had once been her tail were still dripping slightly as he walked her through the wagon to the back gate. Mrs. Snodgrass handed the basket and plate to Char, then helped her down. She turned to the children in the wagon.

"We'll be right back," she said. Her words were clipped, spoken in the tone she used in the Inn when she was not pleased. "Once you're underway, there's supper for you all in the basket. Don't you be eating those cookies, however—those are for the trolls at the bridge."

"Yes, ma'am," said Char.

"Make certain you're ready—I assume you've all been to the privy?" A chorus of bored voices answered *yeeessss*. "Good. You need to be on your way. Stay together, now, and behave yourselves."

"How—how did you know about our journey?" Ven stammered.

Mrs. Snodgrass looked surprised.

"Well, Saeli told me she was taking you to see her people past the river," she said. "Is there some reason I *shouldn't* know about that?"

Ven looked down at Saeli, who nodded quickly.

"No, not at all," he said, relieved.

"Just mind your manners while you're there," Mrs. Snodgrass said. "Now, I'm going to get young Amariel here a change of clothes, and we'll be right back."

When the innkeeper and the merrow had gone into the Inn, Ven turned to the others.

"Who told Mrs. Snodgrass?"

Shyly Saeli raised her hand.

"Actually, we all sorta did, Ven," said Char. "You don't think she deserves ta know when a lot of her kitchen staff and residents are just pickin' up and *leavin'*? Don't ya think she's had enough worry about us recently?"

"You're right, I'm sorry. What did you tell her?"

"Saeli offered to take us to visit her family in the Wide Meadows past the river," Clemency said. "She hasn't been home for a long time, and wants to see her aunts, uncles, and cousins. Char said we were headed that way anyway. As I understand it, we're supposed to be hiding from the Raven's Guild, yes?"

"Yes."

"Well, the Gwadd are especially good at hiding. People travel through their lands all the time and never even know the Gwadd are there. Saeli is still very frightened of the Thief Queen. So the Gwadd lands seemed to Char and me like a good place to start hiding, at least for a little while. We figured Saeli could see her family, and we could all hide out for a while. We told Mrs. Snodgrass truthfully that was where we are headed."

Ven scratched his head.

"That's actually a very good idea," he said. "I'm sorry I jumped down all of your throats. It's important to me that all my friends get along—you are very important to me, and so is Amariel. I don't like the way you are treating her, Ida."

Ida shrugged. "I'm being as friendly to her as I am to anyone."

"Well, that may be true, but I would appreciate it if you don't go out of your way to make her feel badly. She's new here, and a little bit nervous, so please try to make her feel welcome."

"It might have been nice to have told us up front that she was coming, Ven," said Clemency in a reproachful tone. "That way it wouldn't have been a surprise. You can't blame us for being rude if you don't give us fair warning."

"I don't get it, Ven," Char said, tucking his small pack inside a coil of rope and sitting down on it. "Here we are, tryin' to sneak away *in secret* before Felonia's spies find us, an' you're bringin' a stranger along with us. Do you really think that's wise, mate?"

Ven's hands grew clammy with sweat. The introduction of Amariel to the group was not going at all as he had expected. His friends were staring at her oddly, which only made the merrow more nervous. "I've told you already, she's not a stranger to me. I've actually known her longer than I've known any of you."

"How's that possible?" Char asked. "Is she from Vaarn?"

Ven swallowed. "Uh—no."

"Then how could you know her longer than *me*? I've been with you every minute since the *Serelinda* found you in the middle of the ocean—well, except when you were in the dungeon and we was in *jail*, right, Ida?" Char turned to the Thief Queen's daughter, and she smirked. "So what is goin' on here, Ven?"

"She's from a place *near* Vaarn," Ven said. "But that doesn't matter. Please just try to be friendly to her. For my sake."

"We've been doin' an awful lot of things for your sake lately, Polywog," said Ida.

"Well, the main thing we're about to do is for your sake as much as mine, Ida," Ven retorted. "It's your bloody *mother* who's looking for us. Especially for *you*."

Just as the words were spoken, a harsh caw was heard overhead. The children looked up.

A score of ravens was circling above them, their black feathers glinting blue in the sun.

– 8 –

The Dash to the River

GREAT," VEN SAID. "JUST WONDERFUL."

"Well, so much for gettin' out of here unnoticed," Char added.

"Get down, children," Tuck said quietly.

Mrs. Snodgrass was returning to the wagon as the children took cover. She had her arm around Amariel's shoulders.

The merrow was now dressed in clean brown trousers and a flowing blue shirt. She was carrying a cloth bundle like those the other children had. Murphy was following her, rubbing at her ankles, and making her look very uncomfortable. Every now and then she would sneeze.

"Look," she said softly to Ven, opening the cloth bundle. "I think Mrs. Snodgrass is worried my tail is going to suddenly grow back—it has no leg holes."

Ven shook his head. "That's a dress. Girls wear those too sometimes."

"Ugh," said the merrow. "Humans are so complicated."

The innkeeper looked up into the sky, shielding her eyes with her hand.

"Shoo!" she called. "Nasty things! Get away from my Inn."

She helped Amariel into the back of the wagon through the gate, then pulled Ven aside.

"Master Polypheme," she said under her breath, "what on earth do you think you're doing, bringing a merrow on land like that?"

Ven blinked in astonishment. "She told you?"

"She didn't have to tell me," Mrs. Snodgrass said in his ear. "I'm a sea captain's wife. You think I don't know a merrow when I see one? I hope you know what you're doing."

Ven could barely speak. "I—I—"

"There's no time to talk about it now. I assume you have her cap?" Ven nodded. "Well, make sure you keep it safe. Don't let anyone else get hold of it. Keep it on you at all times. She should be all right until you get back from the Wide Meadows as long as you keep the cap safe. I've known a few sailors who have married merrows. It's not usually 'til the husband buries the cap, hoping to keep the wife away from the sea, that she starts to lose her merrow nature. It happens very quickly, in about one turn of the moon. Once that happens, I'm not sure she can get it back. At least I've never seen it happen."

"Thank you," Ven said. "And thank you for not telling anyone."

"You're not planning to marry this girl, are you?"

"Of course not," said Ven, horrified. "She's a friend. And I'm only fifty years old."

"Good. Faith, I hope you know what you're doing." Mrs. Snodgrass shook her head. "Remember, Ven, when they get mad, merrows have a tendency to spit." She looked at the children crouching in the wagon. "Goodbye, dearies, and have a good time. Goodbye, Saeli. Give my best your family." The little Gwadd girl smiled.

"Goodbye, Clemency, Ida," the innkeeper continued. "Goodbye, Char."

From the grass at the roadway's edge, the sound of sniffing and sniffling could suddenly be heard.

"What the heck is *that*?" Char asked.

"The Spice Folk," Mrs. Snodgrass replied. "They're very sad to see you go, Char. They're going to miss you."

The sniffs turned into a chorus of wails.

"What is she talkin' about?" Char demanded of Clemency. "They won't miss me. The Spice Folk *hate* me."

"They do not," Clemency insisted. "They love to torture you. That's a sign that they like you. They only pick on you if they do."

"Good thing they don' love me, then," Char muttered. "I'd never survive."

Mrs. Snodgrass waved at the ravens again. "Shoo!" she shouted. The birds ignored her, continuing their dark circle. "Keep your heads covered, loves," the innkeeper said. She blew them all a kiss, then made her way back into the Inn and closed the griffin door.

"Let's get out of here," Ven said to Tuck. The forester nodded and clicked to the horses. The wagon lurched, then began rolling smoothly and quickly eastward toward the Great River.

The ravens above widened their circle and flew after them.

"Bloody spies," Char muttered. "I think we're sunk already, Ven. They're just gonna go right back to Felonia and tell her where we've gone."

So much for making her believe we've left the island on a ship, Ven thought. "I don't know what else we can do," he said.

"Get down," ordered Tuck.

Ven turned to see the forester rise from the seat board and swing a crossbow to a shoulder.

"Duck!" Ven shouted to his friends. He looked up into the sky and watched in shock as the flock of ravens began diving for the wagon, shrieking.

Two *thuds* and two whistling noises came from the front of the wagon. The closest birds fell from the air. A second later, another clicking sound, two more *thuds*, and two more birds fell.

With a whistling scream, four black birds strafed the wagon. Tuck dodged out of the way as they sailed through, low, from front to back, sending the children scrambling for the wagon corners.

Right behind them came four more. These birds did not fly past, but rather aimed for the back left corner, where Saeli had taken cover. They dove at her, their claws extended.

Three flew on as she ducked, swiping at her.

The fourth one snagged her hair.

A high-pitched squeak blurted forth from within Saeli's braid. A tiny face emerged, its wide, glassy eyes darting nervously. Just as the ravens struck at the little Gwadd girl, it dove from her hair, skittering in the opposite direction and into a pile of sacks on the other side of the wagon.

"They're after the bloody *keekee*," Char said, his arm over his head to shield his hair from the white droppings that were raining down from above. "They must be hungry. Ugh. Bloody sky-vermin."

"Here, Saeli, grab my hand!" Clem seized hold of Saeli as the raven dragged the little girl around in a circle by her braid.

Another cry rent the air above, and a large shadow passed over the wagon from the west.

"The albatross!" Amariel shouted in wonder. "What's it doing here, so far from the shore?"

"Looking out for us," Ven shouted back as the giant bird swooped amid the pack of remaining ravens. It flew sideways against their paths, keeping them from flying away as Tuck reloaded and fired again and again. His last shot took down the bird that had hold of Saeli's braid. The little girl let go of Clem and dropped into Ven's arms, knocking him onto the wagon floor. The keekee's head popped out of the pile of bags at the corner of the wagon, its eyes crossed. Then it scrambled quickly onto Saeli's head and disappeared into her hair again.

"Cover your heads," Clemency called to Ida and Char as three remaining ravens circled around, heading low for the wagon. The black birds cawed harshly as they approached, their claws at the ready.

Tuck fired.

Amariel spat.

It was a great, thick wad of sputum that soared like a dart and expertly caught one of the birds square in the eye, causing it to falter.

"Yuck!" shrieked Ida.

One of the birds dropped from flight, impaled on a crossbow bolt. The one the merrow spat at veered off, but the third continued on and dove, slashing Char across the head before Tuck shot it from the sky. It landed in the middle of the road, dead.

"Char!" Ven gasped as bright blood sprayed everywhere. He scrambled over to his friend, whose dark hair was now striped red.

Char put his hand out woozily. "I'm all right, mate," he said, waving Ven away. "Stay down, now."

"No, you're not," Clemency said. She rummaged in her pack

and pulled out a clean handkerchief, then tossed it to Ven. "Here, put pressure on his head." Ven pressed a handkerchief into Char's bloody hair, his hand shaking.

The last raven made a quick circle over the wagon, turned west and flew away as fast as it could.

"Blow me down," Char said, wincing as Ven applied pressure to his bleeding head. "The blighter's getting away! It's headin' straight for Felonia."

"Can't you shoot him, too?" Clemency said desperately to Tuck.

The forester shook his head. "Out of range."

"It'll get back to the Gated City," Ven said. "We're done for."

"Maybe not," Amariel said. She pointed into the sky.

The giant shadow passed over the wagon again, raising a current of air that ruffled the children's clothes as it flew by. The great bird beat its wings several times, gaining speed with each beat, until a moment later it had caught up to the raven. It sailed in front of the black bird, crossing its path in the air. The raven faltered, and flew north, trying to dodge, but the albatross was faster. It crossed the raven's path again, pushing it closer to the ground. The raven beat its wings and flew skyward, but the giant bird crossed it again. The black bird stuttered in flight.

And, cawing harshly, fell from the sky and slammed into the wagon right in the middle of where they were sitting.

"Ow," whispered Char.

"Thank you," Ven called to the albatross.

"That was horrible," said Clemency, grimacing as she moved away from the dead bird. "Eeeuuuwww." She glanced at Amariel, her lips pressed tightly together. "Come here, Saeli." She put out her arms to the Gwadd, but Saeli shook her head.

"What are you talkin' about?" demanded Ida. "That was *great*. Well, at least until Ven's strange friend hocked sludge all over the wagon."

"That was a bit odd," Char admitted.

"Did it work?" Amariel asked. "Then don't complain."

The wagon had never stopped rolling through the attack of the birds. Tuck looked up into the sky and, seeing nothing following them, sat back down on the wagon board, picked up the reins, and continued on as if nothing had happened.

From behind some sacks of grain near Amariel, a polite cough was heard.

"If we're voting, Leo and I think that any time evil birds die it's a good thing," said a feline voice. "And spitting is a cousin to hissing, so I don't have a problem with it."

"Murphy! You're here?"

"Obviously," said the voice, full of disdain.

"Why?" Ven asked.

"Do you have a problem with me being here?"

"No," Ven admitted. "It will be good to have you aboard. But won't Mrs. Snodgrass miss you?"

The orange tabby finally stuck his head out from behind the sacks.

"The Spice Folk will keep the rats under control while I'm gone," he said. "Besides, Trudy wants me to look out for *her*." He nodded in the direction of the merrow, and sighed happily. "And I'm glad to."

"Why?" Ven asked.

"I don't know," Murphy admitted. "There's just something about her that appeals to me, like catnip, or even better, a nice fish head. She smells good."

Ah, Ven thought. *That explains it. Cats think she's a giant fish.*

"I think I'm in love. Leo likes her, too."

"Who's Leo?" Clemency asked.

Murphy's head disappeared for a moment, then reappeared. A second cat's head popped out behind him. It was the brown tabby that had leapt onto Ven's back.

"Meet Leo," Murphy said.

"Great." Ven sighed. "Murphy, you tell Leo if he's going to stay he needs to stop clawing at my back and keep away from me."

"Ven," said Murphy, sounding bored, "you should know better by now than to tell a cat what to do. Just mind your own business and there shouldn't be any trouble."

He and Leo sauntered over to the corner where Amariel was cowering. "I have to admit I've sniffed at the keekee myself," Murphy said. "But there's so little meat under all that fluff that the hairballs I'd be coughing up for *weeks* afterward wouldn't be worth eating it." The orange tabby stretched out his own claws and smiled at the merrow. "Don't worry—if those birds come back, and they come near you, I'll scratch them out of the sky."

The merrow sneezed loudly in reply.

Both cats disappeared back behind the grain sacks.

"You all right, Char?" Ven asked as his best friend sat down, trembling. "You look pale."

"Are you going to throw up ambergris?" Amariel inquired.

Char's bloody forehead wrinkled. "Ambergris?" he demanded. "What do I look like ta you, a *whale*?"

Amariel shrugged. "Just asking."

Char was plumping several sacks of dried peas into a cushion to sit on. "Well, maybe you should keep your weird questions ta yourself. You're making my head hurt."

"I thought the ravens made his head hurt," Amariel whispered in confusion to Ven. "And why would I keep my questions to myself? If I knew the answer, I wouldn't have a question."

"Don't worry about it," Ven whispered back. "Humans."

The merrow nodded.

The children settled down into the wagon and got as comfortable as they could. Clemency helped Ven clean and bandage Char's head, while Ida snagged the dead raven with her pocket knife and tossed it over the side of the wagon. She gathered the feathers that remained.

"These'll make great fletchings for arrows," she said.

"Good thought," said Tuck from the front of the wagon.

This time all the children jumped.

"It's really pretty creepy how he does that," Char whispered to Ven. Ven turned and saw Tuck smile and push his hat back down over his eyes as he clicked to the horses.

The wagon rumbled eastward, toward the Great River. The straight road was largely empty, so Tuck said they could sit up for a while unless he warned them that a cart or other travelers were coming.

At first the children tried to make pleasant conversation, but there was an awkwardness that made words difficult to come up with. Finally they all lapsed into silence, or dozed or looked for pictures in the clouds overhead.

All except for Amariel. The merrow hung over the side of the wagon, watching every squirrel, every patch of meadow flowers, every thicket of berry bushes that they passed. Ven sat beside her, smiling at her excitement, and quietly telling her the names of everything she pointed to when she grabbed his elbow.

Her only source of distress was the attention of the cats, who took every opportunity to sit in her lap, purring happily.

"Why won't you leave Amariel alone?" Ven demanded during a rest stop after she had stood up to get out of the wagon, sneezing and brushing what seemed like several pounds of cat hair from her clothes.

Murphy shrugged as Leo nuzzled the merrow's ankles.

"She smells *so* nice," he said. "Like a lovely rotten fishhead that's been baking in the sun."

"And everyone's always tellin' me *I* have bad hygiene," Ida muttered. "Sheesh."

The merrow glared at her with a look so acid that it made the hairs on Ven's neck stand on end. He could see that she was swishing spit around in her mouth, so he quickly opened the wagon gate for her and pointed to some bushes growing along the roadside. The merrow sulked for a moment, then followed Clem and Saeli. When she returned, she continued to glare at Ida, who met her gaze in return, smirking, a crooked smile on her pale face. Finally the merrow rolled her eyes and went back to watching the scenery.

After a long while, she sat up straight.

"I hear water," she said. "But it doesn't smell right. No salt."

"It's not the sea," Ven said quietly. "That's the sound of the Great River. We're getting almost close enough to see the bridge."

As they rumbled along in the wagon the sound of the river grew louder.

"It sings a totally different song than the sea does," Amariel said to Ven. "It's like another language I can almost understand, but not quite. They are both songs of moving water, but very, very different."

Just as she finished her sentence, the wagon began to slow. Ven sat up straighter and looked over the side as it came to a halt.

"Ven," came Tuck's voice, "come here."

Ven stood up shakily and stretched. He stepped carefully around his friends and the provisions and climbed onto the seat board next to Tuck.

The forester was staring into the east toward the sound of the rushing river. In the distance, Ven could almost make out what he thought was the bridge.

"What's wrong?" he asked.

Tuck shook his head. "There's something not right about the way it looks from here," he said, straining to see. "It's darker than it should be, and the shape looks odd."

Ven stood up and looked as hard as he could, but he could barely see the bridge at all. Then a thought occurred to him.

He unbuttoned the shirt pocket where the merrow's cap lay, carefully folded, and took out his great-grandfather's jack-rule. He extended the telescope lens meant for seeing far away, then looked through it.

At first he couldn't be sure what he was seeing. Then, as he kept looking, all his breath left his body.

"No," he said. "Oh, no."

Char climbed through the wagon and stood behind him. "What's the matter?"

Ven handed him the jack-rule, and the cook's mate had a look for himself. He shook his head, and handed it to the Lirin forester. Tuck looked through it, then gave it back to Ven, who put it to his eye one more time.

From a great distance, he could see that the enormous bridge spanning the Great River was covered, on every stanchion, trestle and beam, with ravens.

Thousands of them.

A low, rumbling cough emerged from the depths of the wagon behind a sack of oats.

"Oh, that's not good."

Everyone turned to see an orange feline head emerge, followed by a brown one.

"This is probably not the best time to be comin' out of hidin'," Char noted.

"Actually, I'm glad you did, Murphy," Ven said. "I need you to do something for me."

"Such as?"

Ven looked over his shoulder at the road they had just traveled down. "I know you'd like to come along with us, but we really have to warn Mrs. Snodgrass about these ravens. She's got guests coming to the Inn who travel this road—and workers and deliverymen."

He thought about the gray stone marker that stood in her

family burying ground marking the grave of her only son, Gregory, who, like Cadwalder's parents, had been killed at the Crossroads by brigands fifteen years before. He also thought about Mr. Whiting's dogs, and how they had almost put the Inn out of business attacking travelers on the road not long before.

"Mrs. Snodgrass needs to know how dangerous it's become around here—but we can't go back to tell her. If she knows about the ravens, maybe she'll want to bring the kids from Hare Warren and Mouse Lodge into the Inn for a while, or get Otis to stay overnight—he travels this road and crosses the bridge every day. Would you and Leo be willing to take the message back to her?"

The old orange tabby stretched lazily, then rubbed up against Amariel, sending her into a fit of sneezing.

"Oh, I *suppose*," he said. "Besides, I can smell those birds from here. *I'm* about to start sneezing myself. Let's go, Leo."

"You can smell the birds?" Char asked.

Murphy sauntered down the wagon bed to the gate, followed by Leo.

"Not as easily as I can smell the rats along the riverbed, but it's clear that there are far more than there should be in any one place. Birds are supposed to be *prey* to us, not predators. If there are that many, Ven's right, and Trudy should know. Besides, if Leo or I die being pecked to death by birds, we'll never live it down."

"Thank you," said Ven. "You should probably keep low in the grass on the way back, so they don't notice and go after you, like they did with the keekee."

"Ven," said Murphy as Leo jumped out of the wagon and onto the road, "don't tell us how to do our job. I think you have enough to worry about. Good luck to you all." He rubbed up against Amariel's legs on the way out of the gate. "Especially you."

"Nice," murmured Clem in disgust as Murphy jumped from the wagon. "I've fed you every morning for the last two years. And you're wishing *her* luck. Thanks a lot."

"You can have that luck if you want it," Amariel said.

"*Now* what are we gonna do?" Char asked as the cats slunk into the highgrass heading west and disappeared.

"It would be suicide to try and cross that bridge now," said the forester. "I don't even want to go a step nearer to it. Right now they don't see us, but ravens have better eyesight than humans do. Fortunately, I'm not human, and Ven owns that tool." He nodded at the jack-rule. "Had either of those things not been the case, we would be covered by them by now. That many ravens can kill a small army."

"So what *do* we do?" Ven asked. "Can we go upriver, to the mill towns? We've been there once before—remember, Char? That's where we saw the windmill."

"Right—it's where we came out of the tunnel after we escaped from the *Gated City*," said Clemency pointedly. "If Felonia is mad enough, and looking hard enough, she might have found that exit—and maybe has someone waiting for us there, too."

"There is another mill town," Tuck said, rubbing his chin. "But it's south on the river, not north. And it's a strange place— a very strange place. I'm not sure which way is safer. If we go north, we may fall into the hands of the Thief Queen. But if we go south, we may end up in the clutches of the King of the River."

"The King of the River?" asked both boys at once.

Tuck nodded. "His name is Regis, and in his own way, he is every bit as much a thief as Felonia. At least the Lirin of the Enchanted Forest think so. It is said that he is no friend to Felonia. But we must decide what we are going to do quickly. The birds are perched there for now, but they won't roost long before sending out a scout."

"So what will it be?" Ven asked. "North or south?"

Saeli coughed, stood up, smoothed her rumpled hair, and pointed south. The keekee poked its head out of the hair at the base of her neck and pointed its tiny finger downriver as well.

"I don't think we want ta be headin' north, no matter what," said Char. "I say we take our chances with the River King. Felonia may want you and Ida back, Ven, but when we were in her cages, she kept tellin' her guards to shoot me first. It might be nice for someone else ta have that honor for a while."

"South it is," Ven said.

Tuck said nothing, but clicked to the horses. The wagon rumbled off, leaving the roadway and heading slowly over the southern fields as the sun began to climb down the sky toward nightfall.

Heading East by Way of the South

In our family, there's an old expression: "He's had one too many turns at the forge." It refers to someone who hears something and takes it in the wrong way, or finds meaning that no one else does in it. This is because the forge is a loud, hot part of the factory where ore is melted and shaped into steel on an anvil, usually by being banged on with hammers. When you've been working the forge for a while, your ears ring so much that you can barely hear what is said to you, and often you just hear pieces of it. So it's easy to misinterpret what people are saying. It also can mean someone who thinks he understands a situation perfectly, but in truth has it totally wrong.

I was never really trusted to work there much, but back at home in Vaarn I was often accused of having had one too many turns at the forge.

I suddenly understood why.

Amariel is the most interesting person I have ever met. Maybe it's because I've never spoken to anyone who has a tail. Maybe it's because she's the first and only merrow I've ever gotten to talk to, or because she saved me from drowning when no one else could. Maybe I was sick with cold and saltwater fever when she told me all her merrow tales and sang me all her songs, because they have taken root in my brain. Each time I see her, I miss her when she goes back into the waves, because I am afraid I may never see her again.

I am so happy she finally agreed to come with me. While my friends and I may be in danger from the Thief Queen's spies, at least we have each other, and Tuck. If I left Westland without taking Amariel with me, she would be waiting around the abandoned pier, wondering what had happened to me. She might feel abandoned herself—or, worse, she might be worried that something had happened to me, like I know my parents did when the Fire Pirates sank my father's ship.

Worst of all, she might have stayed, waiting for me, and gotten caught by the Raven's Guild when the underwater tunnel was unsealed. Without her family, her school of other merrows to protect her, she wouldn't have had a chance. I am so relieved she decided to come along, not just because I miss her when she stays behind, but because I would never stop worrying about her. She is special to me.

So I foolishly expected that my friends would like her as much as I do, or at least enough to welcome her into our group. They are all special to me as well, even Ida, who was being so obnoxious that I was almost tempted to leave her behind. But that turned out to be wrong-headed thinking, because it's not just Ida. Everyone except Saeli had made Amariel feel uncomfortable, frightened, or mad.

Even Char, my best friend.

And they don't mean to.

Just like she has made them feel the same way with her

strange misunderstandings of the dry world, her distrust of humans, and her tendency to spit.

If there was anything I was certain of when I went to town this morning, it was that my friends would like Amariel and she would like them, too. I guess she was right when she told me to stop assuming how anyone else would feel.

Because clearly I've had one too many turns at the forge.

B Y MID-AFTERNOON, THE MOON HAD RISEN. IT FLOATED IN THE pale blue sky, a white shadow of itself, fading in between the clouds passing in front of it.

Tuck had suggested that the children take a nap, because they would arrive at the southern bridge well after nightfall, and it was a good idea to be awake and fresh when crossing the Great River. After a good deal of jostling and shoving, the six of them managed to find places in the wagon to lie down somewhat comfortably in between the bags and barrels. Clemency positioned herself near the wagon's side to keep Saeli from banging into it if the wagon should rock. Ida arranged a small mountain of grain sacks and snuggled down into it. Char curled up in the front of the wagon near Tuck's seat. And Ven lay down in the back end next to Amariel, who had moved as far away from the others as she could.

"Are you feeling better?" he asked the merrow, who was shivering a little as the sun started to go down.

"Not really," Amariel admitted. "I still don't like humans. But the dry world is interesting, I'll say that."

"You aren't getting used to my friends, just a little?" Ven asked hopefully.

"Well, the Gwadd is nice at least."

"Just Saeli? You don't like any of the others?"

Amariel sighed. "In case you hadn't noticed, Ven, they don't like *me*."

"Give them a chance," Ven urged. "Once they get to know you, they will."

"You really don't understand," said the merrow. "This is one of the reasons merrow mothers tell their merrowlings not to trust humans. Even when we look like them, even when we have legs, they can tell we're different. And humans don't like anyone who's different. Surely you must have found that to be true."

Ven thought back to his first day on the Island. Char had flagged down a farmer to give them a ride to the Inn, but when the man discovered that Ven was Nain, he refused to let him into the wagon. Char, in turn, refused to accept the ride, and the man drove off, hurling insults at Ven.

It was no different than what his brothers had experienced many times in Vaarn.

"Yes," he said reluctantly. "I've had a few humans be nasty to me because I'm different. But as you can see, there are more of them who are nice, who don't care whether I'm human or not. Wasn't Mrs. Snodgrass kind to you?"

"She was," said the merrow. "But she knows the sea. So she doesn't count. The rest of your friends aren't happy that I'm here. You wish they were, and maybe some of them will be, but right now it's very uncomfortable. Just leave it alone for a while, Ven. You aren't in charge of whether or not I have a good time in the dry world. I made that decision on my own. You're just in charge of keeping my cap safe and not letting anyone touch it, or even *see* it. As long as you do that, everything will be all right."

Ven smiled. "I will. I promise. I'll try not to even open my pocket unless I have to."

"Good," said the merrow. "Now, stop being such a blabber-mouth and let me get some sleep."

Ven waited until her eyes were closed and she was breathing steadily. Her mouth was open, and he noted that the edges of the lines that had once been her gills fluttered slightly each time she took a breath. When he was sure she was asleep, he rose and moved to the front of the wagon where Char was lying on his back, staring at the passing clouds, and lay down beside him.

"You all right?" Ven asked his roommate.

"Define 'all right'."

"How's your head?"

"Stopped bleedin'," Char said. "Feels like it was bein' used as an anvil all day."

"I'll bet," said Ven. "Sorry."

Char rolled on the side.

"Would you like to tell me what the heck is going on, Ven?" he asked. "When I woke up this mornin', I knew it was gonna be a bad day; Murphy wrote it out for me just in case I wasn't sure." He pulled the leg of his trousers and pointed to the cat-scratch **M**. "But if I'd had any idea just *how* bad, I'd of climbed back inta bed, pulled the pillow over my head, and let the Spice Folk, Cadwalder, and Murphy do their worst to me tryin' to make me get up. I think you owe me an explanation at least."

"I know," Ven said quietly. "Everything happened so quickly that even I don't know exactly what's going on."

"Any little bit o' clarification will help. You came inta the Inn and said we was leavin'—then you went to town, and you came back with a wagon, a driver who's a great shot, and the weirdest girl I've ever met. I liked the way you was actin' like the Cap'n, but I think ya may have a mutiny on your hands soon unless you start explainin' what's goin' on here."

"Do you remember the man who helped us carry the parsnips into the kitchen this morning?"

Char looked perplexed. "I guess so."

"That was the king."

"What king?"

"King Vandemere," Ven said. "I'm not joking. He had to sneak out of his own castle to get an urgent message to me, that ravens were gathering in huge flocks all throughout Westland and were even being seen east of the river. He knows about the Thief Queen, and wanted us to get away as soon as we could—all of us that might be in danger. He left Tuck with us to get us safely out of Westland, because he's a Lirin forester, and knows the lands east of the river better than anyone."

"So where'dya go this mornin', then?" Char asked.

Ven swallowed. He wanted to be honest with his best friend, but he felt that too much was known about the merrow already.

"To town," he said simply. "To get supplies."

"And your friend Amariel," Char said pointedly. "Who I never heard of 'til today."

"Well, given the warm welcome she received from my other friends, perhaps you understand now why I didn't introduce her earlier," Ven said. "Mostly I haven't told you things because the time has been short, Char. But just in case you think I'm not sharing the important stuff, take a look at this."

He held out his hand with the Black Ivory sleeve.

"What's that?" Char asked.

"It's a kind of stone called Black Ivory that's made into boxes and sleeves used for hiding powerful or magical things," Ven said softly. "I saw Madame Sharra in Kingston—"

"*Madame Sharra?*"

Ven clapped his hand over Char's mouth. "Keep your voice down," he cautioned. "She came to find me—I don't know how she got out of the Market when Felonia apparently isn't able to. She said she wanted to know why she was unable to see any future for me. And after she read my palm, she still couldn't see anything."

"Blimey," Char whispered. "Does that mean you're gonna die?"

"I asked the same thing. I don't know. But it doesn't look good."

"Sorry to hear that, mate," Char said. "But I guess at least we'll go down together."

"I hope not," said Ven. "Sharra gave me this stone, but she didn't explain anything about it. When I looked at it with the jack-rule, I could see it was a sleeve, like a wallet or a sheath for a sword—and there's a dragon scale inside it."

"A *dragon scale?*"

"Shhhh—stop repeating what I say," Ven said crossly. He put the stone in his pocket next to the merrow cap and the jack-rule, and buttoned it carefully. "Yes, a dragon scale, like the cards she uses to tell the future. It has that strange writing that we saw in her tent, and a picture of a lot of mountains. I have no idea why she gave it to me. She only told me that she saw the path of my future disappearing soon, and to live as much as I can in the time I have left."

"Oh, man."

"So that's what all the secrecy and hurry is about. We're trying to get away from Westland and Felonia's spies as quickly as possible. And in the meantime, there's a few things the king would like to us to do if we can."

"Uh oh," said Char. "Like what?"

"There's a dragon running amok and burning Nain settlements

somewhere in the fields north of where the Gwadd live," Ven replied. "The king doesn't want us to get in the dragon's way, but he says if we can find out why the dragon is so angry at the Nain, we can trade that information to the Nain for something the Lirin want. And if we get what the Lirin want, we can trade that to them for something the king wants."

"An' what does the king want?"

"I'm not sure," Ven said. "But he gave me a message to deliver to the king of the Lirin, a fairly grumpy man known as Alvarran the Intolerant."

"Great name," Char muttered. "I can tell already *he's* gonna be fun ta deal with."

"Probably," Ven said, smiling slightly. "But he's the least of our worries. In addition to getting over the river, away from Felonia's thugs and spies, the message King Vandemere asked me to deliver to the Lirin king makes me pretty nervous all by itself."

"What was the message?"

"The king made me memorize it exactly as he said it," Ven said. "It went like this: 'King Vandemere states that if you will send him the greatest treasure in your kingdom, he will swear fealty to you and ever after will call you 'sire'."

"Man, oh man," Char whispered. "What the heck does that mean?"

"I don't know," Ven said. "But 'sire' is what someone calls a king when he is that king's *subject*. It sounds almost as if King Vandemere wants whatever the Lirin king has so badly that he is willing to give up *everything*, even his throne, to get it. And if the human king gives up his throne to the Lirin king, imagine the problems that will come about. The Nain and the Lirin don't like each other much in Serendair. King Vandemere is high king over many people that call themselves kings and queens on this island. If he gives up and walks away from that job, I bet there'll be all-out war."

"*Wonderful*," said Char. "So why do you want to help the king do anything? If you're gonna die soon and all?"

"I think that's what Madame Sharra meant when she said I should live as much as I can in the time remaining," Ven said. "And I want to help him in any way I can. The thought of undertaking those missions is like a big puzzle to me, and it makes my curiosity burn like crazy. I want to find out all I can about this place we're living in—and if I can help the king in the meantime, all the better.

"So now I think I've told you about all I can tell you," he finished. "Sorry I didn't have time to do it before we left. But I had the suspicion you would've come anyway."

"O' course."

"Then trust me when I say I don't know exactly where we're heading, or what we'll meet, but it should be an interesting adventure. And it's the only chance the king and I know of for us to escape Felonia and be safe. In the meantime, while we're gone the king is going to have someone he trusts spread the rumor in the Gated City that we've left on a ship. If we can stay away long enough, things should die down there and we can go home to the Inn."

"Hope you're right," Char said.

"Hey, Polywog, can you come and give your friend a poke?" Ida called from near the back of the wagon. "She's snoring like a drunken sailor, and she's keeping me awake."

Clemency groaned. "That's funny, Ida," she retorted sleepily. "You keep all of Mouse Lodge awake sawing wood every night. You're a fine one to complain about someone else snoring. And what do you know about drunken sailors, anyway?"

"More than you think," said Ida. "When they're asleep, it's the best time to take their money off'a them."

"Sorry I asked," Clemency said. "I'll say an extra prayer for you tonight, Ida." She rolled over and went back to sleep.

"Everybody just be quiet," Ven said. He stood up and climbed back through the wagon to where Amariel lay and crouched down beside her. He shook her gently, then, realizing the sound she was making was due to the loss of her gills, he positioned himself between her and the other children to mask the noise and settled down to sleep.

When he woke the sky was dark. The moon was glowing brightly now, casting a silver sheen over the fields, and flooding the wagon with pale light. Char was beside him, shaking him gently.

"Oh, man," he muttered. "You gotta see this, Ven. Now I know why this Regis can call himself the King of the River."

When the king asked me to make note in my journals, it was because he wants someday to have a book of all human knowledge, and a book of all the world's magic. He was hoping I'd be the one to find those things out in the world and make notes and pictures of them, so that one day he could use them in those books.

When I saw what Char was talking about, I decided to start signing every drawing I do in my journals with my initials from now on.

Because I have a really bad feeling I'm not going to be the one who finishes them.

~ 10 ~

The King of the River

VEN SAT UP.

They were at the edge of the river.

The hazy light of the silver moon made it seem almost as if it were morning. The moonlight glittered off the river, making shining pools that spun in the current, then broke apart like silver coins and floated on.

Spanning the river from the near bank to the far shore was a tall arched bridge under which many wide gates could be seen. Water flowed freely through the metal bars, swirling around the stanchions as it passed beneath the bridge. Ven caught his breath. The bridge was easily four times the size of the enormous one to the north where he had crossed the river several times before, the bridge where the ravens had been waiting.

Amazing as the bridge was, it was no match for the marvelous structure atop it.

Rising above the vast bridge was a palace, or at least something that looked like one. It was a huge building made of many interesting angles and towers, all of them filled with glass windows

that looked in every direction. The roofs of each section of the building appeared as if they were shingled with pieces of gleaming metal. Those shingles caught the moonlight and made them shine like the stars reflected in the water of the river.

A passageway that spanned the river crossed west to east through the middle of the building. Ven imagined that the passageway was several times wider than the bridge to the north. At least four wagons could cross the river at the same time side by side. The passageway had a metal grate in front of it, the same as the arches in the water flowing north to south.

The castle was built on massive stilts that would allow even the tallest of barges to pass beneath it easily. On the far bank Ven could see a horse path like the one on the far bank of the river near the northern bridge. Only this path was much wider, with great planks attached to pulleys that seemed as if they were there for the offloading of huge bales of goods.

All along the sides of the castle near where the roofs met the walls was a walkway with stations where guards were walking back and forth, crossbows in their hands, patrolling.

Beyond the walls Ven could hear the sounds of merriment and laughter. Music was playing in the open-air courtyard, and occasionally a firework would shoot off, brightening the sky with colorful sparkles, to thunderous applause and a chorus of *oooos* and *ahhhs* from inside the palace walls.

Char was standing beside him.

"Wouldn't the Spice Folk *love* that," he said. "It makes me almost wish they were here, so they would stop stuffin' their glitter up my nose while I'm sleepin'."

"They only do it because they like you," Ven said absently. "Didn't you hear Clem?"

"Yeah, right. So what now?"

Ven stood and walked toward the front of the wagon, trying to keep from stepping on his friends in the dark. He climbed over the seat board and sat down next to Tuck.

"What do we do now?" he asked the Lirin forester.

"If you want to cross the river at night, you will have to be brought before the River King," Tuck replied. "If you can wait until morning, you can just pay a hefty toll and they will probably leave you alone."

"What time is it?" Ven asked.

"Just barely past nightfall," Tuck said. "We'll be out here without cover for almost nine hours if we wait."

"Sounds like a bad idea to me," Ven said. "I guess we may as well take our chances with Regis."

"As you wish," said Tuck. "Better wake the others." He gave the reins a gentle tap as Ven turned and climbed back into the wagon bed.

Char was already shaking Clemency, who stretched and yawned next to the water barrel. In turn, Clem woke Saeli, who sat up, rubbing her eyes, the keekee yawning and rubbing its eyes from atop her head as well. Ven made his way over to the sacks of grain and carefully poked Ida, who snorted in her sleep and rolled back over. He jabbed her with his finger again.

"Come on, Ida, shake a leg," he said, moving to the back of the wagon. He bent down beside the sleeping merrow and gently touched her shoulder. "Amariel," he whispered. "Wake up."

The merrow stretched and sat up, her long dark hair gleaming silver in the moonlight.

"I was having the most wonderful dream," she murmured. "I was dreaming about a palace—"

"Like that one, maybe?" Ven said, pointing to the bridge.

The merrow's mouth dropped open, and her eyes grew wide.

"Almost exactly," she said. "I wonder if it has a strange twisty-looking thing like it did in my dream."

"What kind of a twisty-looking thing?"

Amariel yawned.

"I don't remember," she said. "It was something you looked through, I think. But it's fading already. You wrecked my dream."

"Sorry about that," Ven said. He started back to the front of the wagon, nudging Ida with his toe as he passed her.

Tuck had maneuvered the wagon to the entrance of the passageway that spanned the river. He stopped at a respectful distance and waited for the guards to come around the corner of the elevated walkway.

"Hail!" he called to them. "Good evening. We seek passage through to the other side."

Two of the guards atop the wall pointed their crossbows at the wagon, while a third one laughed.

"You hardly look as if you can afford the expense of our opening the gates this late," he said cheerfully. "Are you sure you don't want to wait until morning?"

"Alas, we cannot," Tuck answered. "We need to keep to our schedule."

"So be it," said the guard. "You'll have to plead your case to the River King. Be warned, however, he's in the midst of merriment, and he does not take interruption well."

"Thanks for the warning," said Tuck. "Please let us in all the same."

While the two crossbowmen kept their weapons trained on the wagon, the third disappeared around the corner of the wall. A moment later, two massive signal fires sprang to life on either side of the passageway, flooding the riverbank with light.

It looked for a moment as if the sun had come out in the middle of the night. Everyone in the wagon fell back, crying out in pain and shielding their eyes, except for Ida, who was still snoring away.

In the bright light I could see that the palace of the River King was far more beautiful than I had imagined. It was built of many different kinds of wood and stone of all different colors that had been fashioned into a great mural of pictures, some showing scenes of sailing ships, others representing great forests, still others depicting people I did not recognize, probably historical figures. I also saw that to the south where up until now we had seen fields stood a great forest on both sides of the river. From the maps I had seen in the king's castle, I wondered if this was the beginning of the Enchanted Forest that both the king and Tuck had mentioned.

I had heard no tales of the Enchanted Forest, but the name was enough to set my curiosity flaming as brightly as the signal fires.

A great grinding sound could be heard over the noise of merriment beyond the wall. Slowly, the gates of the passageway across the river began to open.

Ven turned around to see the heads of four of his friends peeking above the provisions.

"Somebody kick Ida," he said. "She needs to wake up now."

"Whoa, not me," said Char hastily. "I need both my legs, thank you. I've managed to sail all my life without gettin' a peg leg. Don't wanna change that now. You want her kicked, you kick her."

A slamming sound echoed in the night as the gates opened all the way.

"This way!" shouted a voice from inside the walls. "Hurry—the longer the gates are open, the more it costs you."

Tuck clicked to the horses, and the wagon lurched forward with a jolt. Ida sat upright, slapping at the sacks of grain around her as if she'd been attacked.

"Well, good evenin', Your Majesty," said Char sarcastically.

"We're enterin' the palace now. Ya might wanna freshen up and put your tiara on."

"Whoa," said Ida as the wagon approached the gate. "It *is* a palace."

"River King," Ven said. "Therefore, palace."

Ida looked over at the merrow. "Since we're goin' to meet a king, p'rhaps you should wear your fancy ball gown, Amariel," she said. "Since he's a thief of sorts an' deals in river traffic, he shouldn't have a problem with it bein' so ratty."

Ven felt his temper snap. "Leave her alone!" he shouted. "Stop being a brat. She's done *nothing* to you."

"Stop yelling, Ven," Clemency said. "It doesn't help."

"Yes it does," said Ven. "It keeps me from slapping her."

"You do an' I'll spit in your eye," retorted Ida smugly. "Or I'll get your friend to do it for me."

"Everyone be quiet," commanded Tuck. There was a ring to his voice that sounded like that of the king. The children fell silent.

They passed under the arch of the wall, the wagon wheels clattering on the wooden planks of the bridge. The light from the signal fires was doused, and they found themselves in the darkness of the tunnel leading beneath the palace wall.

A few moments later light returned as the wagon entered an enormous courtyard. Beyond the wall, huge fires burned in roasting pits over which oxen and ducks, turkeys and pigs hung on spits, turned and basted by servants in bright colored clothing. A large band of brass horns and stringed instruments was playing in the center of courtyard, filling it with merry music. And everywhere were people, Lirin and human, talking, laughing, and exchanging money.

Two guards from either side of the tunnel stepped forward and took hold of the horses' bridles.

"Dismount," the one on the left said to Tuck. "And bring your passengers with you. Leave your goods."

"Do you hear that, children?" Tuck said, looking directly at Ven. "Leave all the provisions and supplies in the wagon." His eyes fell on Ven's pocket, and Ven nodded his understanding. He climbed out of the back of the wagon, followed by Char, Clemency, Saeli, and finally Ida. Only Amariel remained in the wagon bed, staring at the sea of humans and Lirin.

Tuck extended his hand to her.

"Don't be afraid," he said. His voice was more gentle than Ven had ever heard it. "Come with us."

"I'm not afraid," Amariel said. "I just don't like the way this place smells."

"Liar," muttered Ida. Clemency snorted softly.

Tuck shot a glance at the girls, who went silent. He turned back to the merrow, who gave him her hand, and Tuck helped her out of the wagon.

Two more guards came forward and signaled for the group to follow them. Tuck led the way, followed by the children, past tables piled high with sweet-smelling pastries reeking of cinnamon and sweet sugar glaze, enormous steaming vats of hot spiced cider spilling clouds of delicious vapor into the air, fruit platters bearing mountains of strawberries and clouds of whipped cream, and wheels of cheese that dwarfed even the largest one that had been delivered to the Crossroads Inn earlier that morning.

Was that really just today? Ven wondered as he passed a fountain of sharp-smelling liquid that bubbled and fizzed as it cascaded in waterfalls over stones made of ice. *It seems like so long ago already.*

They were led halfway across the courtyard and then turned

to the north toward the front of the river palace. There, a giant winding staircase made of polished wood reached up to one of the highest angled sections of the magnificent building.

The guards stopped at the bottom of the stairs. One of them pointed to the top.

"Up you go," he said. The other started up the staircase in front of them.

"Thank you," Tuck replied. "Come along, children."

They climbed the stairs, one by one, making three complete revolutions before reaching the top. When they stepped out onto the platform beyond the staircase, they stopped and gazed in wonder.

The staircase opened to a giant room with soaring ceilings held up by glossy wooden beams. The room was ablaze with light from bright torches on every wall, held by sconces that looked like silver human arms. In a stone fireplace in the eastern wall of the room a mammoth fire glowed, sparking every now and again in bright colors that matched the fireworks in the skies above the palace. Trees grew through the floor, their roots seemingly lodged in the mud of the river below, their branches extending up through the ceiling and into the night sky.

In the middle of the beautiful room stood a polished wooden throne with a glorious tapestry behind it, its arched back set in gleaming coins that ran in channels down the wooden arms of the throne as well. It stood in the middle of an equally glorious carpet atop a platform with two steps leading up to it.

Sitting on the throne was a tall, broad-shouldered man with what appeared to be strong arms and legs, a barrel chest and a rounded belly. His hair was curly and black, his face wide and jolly and rimmed in a thick black beard. In spite of the grandeur of his throne room, he was dressed simply in the clothes of a riverman and he wore no crown on his head. In his hand was a long, curled pipe of polished wood with a beautiful inlay. No smoke came from its bowl.

The expression on the man's face was solemn, but his black eyes twinkled.

"Well, well," he said. "What have we here?"

"This man insisted on nighttime admittance, Regis," said the guard who had escorted them up the stairs. "I explained the penalties, but he insisted."

"Did he, now?" said the River King. "Must be a foolish man. What did he have to ferry across?"

"Only standard provisions, fruits, grains, vegetables, water and the like," said the soldier. "Strangely, it only appears to be enough for personal use. There is certainly not enough for sale. And some streaks of fresh human blood in the wagon."

"Any arms?"

"Only a crossbow and a quiver full of bolts. Looks to be of Lirinved manufacture."

"Interesting," said the River King. "We have Lirinved through here every now and then, but not often, and almost never at night." He looked at Tuck directly, as if sizing him up. Then his gaze turned to Ven.

"But then, he's not the leader of this expedition, is he?" Regis asked, smiling darkly. "This gentleman may be your guide, but *you* are the reason for the summoning of my guards, the entering of my palace at night, the interruption of my revels. Am I wrong?"

"No, sir," Ven said hesitantly.

"Good—honesty is good," said the River King. "It may save you at least some of what you have."

He rose from his seat and came over until he stood directly in front of Ven, looking down at him from the platform.

"What's your name?" he asked flatly.

"Ven Polypheme, sir."

"Polypheme, eh? There's a family of shipwrights by that name that make excellent sailing vessels. Any relation?"

Ven thought about the wisdom of his answer, and about how far away his family was. *If he knows my father, it's probably to my advantage,* he thought. *If he's met one of my brothers, on the other hand, maybe not.* "A distant one," he said finally.

Regis nodded. "Well, then, welcome to my home, Ven Polypheme. You appear to be in good company." He looked around at the group. "Between you and your friends, I imagine you speak many languages."

"A few," Ven said. He wished his voice didn't sound so uncertain.

The River King smiled, showing beautiful white teeth.

"Good," he said. "That might be the only thing that saves your lives."

11

The River King's Riddle

"WHY ARE YOU *THREATENIN'* US?" CHAR EXPLODED. "WE'VE DONE *nothin'* to you!"

"Shhh, Char," Clem whispered.

Ven coughed as the River King turned in the direction of his best friend, the look in his eyes deadly.

"He has a point, sir," he said, hoping to draw the king's attention back to himself. "We are willing to pay the toll for night crossing. Why does that mean our lives are in danger?"

Regis watched Char a moment longer, then turned back to Ven.

"Because you have fresh blood in your wagon," he said. "It's not the juice of meat that you are carting to sell across the river— it's human blood, spilled recently. I am responsible for this region, as well as for this bridge. I mean to see that anyone who crosses through my palace is worthy to do so—and those who are not, well, they don't make it across. It's as simple as that."

"That's *my* blood." Char pointed to the bandage on his head. "Spilled by accident. Surely you're not gonna hold *that* against us."

"How is worthiness determined?" Tuck asked, forestalling Regis's answer.

The River King spread his hands open wide.

"By means of a simple riddle," he said pleasantly. "If you answer it correctly, you will gain my favor and free passage over my bridge. If you answer wrong, or cannot answer it at all, you will be charged whatever I deem appropriate for you to pay. On good days, that may be in coin, and maybe you have enough coin to pay the toll. On bad days, well—let's just hope this is not a bad day."

Ven could hear Clemency, Saeli and Ida all sigh at the same time.

"What's the riddle?" he asked.

The River King's eyes glinted merrily. He stepped down from the platform and walked in front of each of the children, sizing them up carefully. Finally he pointed to Char, Clem, and Ida.

"Step back, please. You three have no chance of answering this riddle." The children looked at each other, then took a step back. Regis turned to Tuck. "Now, you, sir, on the other hand, might be able to do so. Would you like to make your attempt first, or last?"

"First," said Tuck without hesitation.

"Very well," said Regis. He rubbed his hands together with pleasure. *"Fleethe sidriel mux, atonay var. Nidley, hrenx."*

Tuck said nothing.

"Can you answer the riddle?" the River King asked.

"As I do not speak that language, no, I cannot," said Tuck.

"Ah, well," said Regis. "Too bad. Anyone else like to try?"

I had never heard those words, or any like them, before. My command of the Nain language was rusty, but I was certain the words were not in my native tongue. Clearly they were not examples of the Lirin language, either, or Tuck would have known them. For all I knew, they might have been a magical countersign or some sort of religious incantation. I glanced over at Clemency, but her face was blank.

Less than one turn of the sun ago, McLean had said that I had the feel of a big day about me.

I had a sick feeling in the pit of my stomach that we were about to learn whether or not it was a bad day shortly.

The River King turned to Saeli.

"How about you, little one?" he asked, his voice as smooth as honey. "Would you like to take a stab at it? *Fleethe sidriel mux, atonay var. Nidley, hrenx.*"

The tiny Gwadd girl shook her head, then burst into tears. Clemency stepped forward, watching the River King, and put an arm around her shoulders.

"Now, now, buck up, lass," Regis said cheerfully. "Maybe your friends have a better idea." He looked at Ven. "Well, young Polypheme? Do you know the answer?"

"No."

"Tut, tut," Regis clucked, "this isn't going well at *all*. What a shame." He looked at last at the merrow. Amariel was white as a ghost. "One more time," the River King said. "Any guesses? *Fleethe sidriel mux, atonay var. Nidley, hrenx.*"

"Yes, it is," the merrow said.

The smile faded from the River King's face. He regarded Amariel seriously.

"Excuse me?" he said. "What do you mean?"

"Yes, it is," Amariel repeated. "I'm agreeing with you."

"You understand the language?" Regis asked.

"I think so."

The River King leaned closer to her. "And what do the words mean?"

The merrow's brows drew together. "You don't know?"

Regis coughed. "Well, no," he admitted. "If I knew what they meant, it would hardly be a riddle, now, would it?"

Amariel shrugged. "I suppose not," she said. "But it's only a riddle for *you*, then, isn't it?"

Regis cleared his throat. "Your point is well taken," he said. "What do the words mean?"

Amariel glanced at Ven, who nodded quickly. " 'Kindly stop dumping your horse dung in the river,' " she translated. " 'It's disgusting.' "

The River King's jaw dropped. "That's it? Are you certain?"

The merrow shrugged again. "It may be more like 'weird, childless horse dung,' or something like that, but I think I'm close."

Regis continued to stare at her for a long time. Then he turned slowly and went back to his throne, sat down, and began rubbing his beard with his hand.

"Mule—that's the weird, childless horse. Mule dung. All this time," he muttered. "All this time, and that's what she was saying."

Tuck cleared his throat. "May we be on our way, then?"

The River King snapped out of his stupor. "No," he said quickly. "No, not yet. I mean, yes, yes, of course, you can go, and without paying anything." He pointed to Amariel. "She's solved the riddle that no one else has been able to solve. So no toll, and no problems. But I would be grateful if you would all stay a little longer, as my guests." He looked at the merrow. "Especially you, if you're willing. I apologize for my actions earlier."

The children looked at each other, and then at Tuck, who shrugged.

"All right," Ven said. "What else do you want?"

The River King stood up quickly. "I'd like you to meet someone," he said. "And if you, my dear, are willing," he said to Amariel, "I'd appreciate it if you would serve as my interpreter for a few minutes. I promise to pay you handsomely."

"All *right*," said the merrow, sounding annoyed. "Let's get it over with."

"This way," Regis said.

He walked to the other side of the throne room, where an enormous painting of himself hung on the wall. "It's good to be the king," he said loudly. Suddenly, a series of lines appeared in the canvas, splitting into sections and rolling back a moment later like one of King Vandemere's puzzles. A small series of steps rolled down from inside the painting.

"Follow me, please," said the River King.

He led the children and Tuck up the small stairway into a dark and winding tower, with a bright glowing light shining at the top. When he reached the end of the stairway, Regis took a huge ring of keys from his belt, searched quickly until he found the right one, opened a small wooden door at the top of the tower and went into the room.

The children and the forester went inside after him.

Instead of being small and dark like the stairway and the tower, however, the room at the top was bright and full of windows. It was also filled with many beautiful plants, blooming with flowers that filled the air with sweet perfume.

The room was richly furnished, with chairs and a looking glass, and an elegant bed draped with blue, flowing chiffon. Sitting on the bed, looking somewhat surprised, was a beautiful woman with a pale, delicate face and long yellow hair the color of spun flax.

Regis stopped in front of her, waving his hands in excitement.

"Mule dung?" he asked, his voice joyful. "You want us to stop dumping our mule dung in the river? That's all?"

The children looked at each other in confusion. The River King turned to Amariel again.

"Please ask her," he said. "Ask her if that's what she really means."

Amariel stared at the River King, but then she turned to the delicate woman and repeated the question.

"*Fleethe sidriel mux, atonay var. Nidley, brenx.*"

The woman smiled. *"Proste zi limina noduley,"* she said. Her voice was sweet and musical.

"What did she say?" the River King asked. He rubbed his hands together to wipe off the nervous sweat.

"She says my accent is terrible," said Amariel. "Apparently, so is my grammar. Hmmph."

"Oh." Regis looked disappointed. "Well, can you ask her that thing about the mule dung again, please? If that's all she really wants?"

The merrow relayed the message. The delicate woman nodded. Regis sighed in relief.

"Well, tell her that is something we can definitely arrange," he said. "Is there anything else?"

"She would like to go home now," Amariel told him after the woman had spoken some more. "She misses the water more than you can know."

The River King fell silent. Ven and the others stood respectfully for long time. Finally, when no one else spoke, Clemency cleared her throat.

"Uh, Your Majesty," she asked, "what's going on here? If you don't mind my asking?"

Regis looked up. The merriment was gone from his face, and he looked suddenly older.

"One night more than ten years ago, I woke to find her standing over my bed," he said quietly. "I had no idea where she had come from. I only know the moment I saw her I lost my heart to her completely. But all she would say was the same thing over and over again: *Fleethe sidriel mux, atonay var. Nidley, hrenx.*

"I did not know what it meant. I asked anyone who came down the river who spoke a language other than my own. I memorized the words, so I might question people in my travels, but until just now no one had ever understood them. I don't know why she came to me. She's not a prisoner here—she seemed insistent on staying until she got an answer, but of course I couldn't give her one. Now it seems that all she wanted was to ask me to keep the river clean. Oh well."

The children looked at one another. Finally Amariel spoke up.

"That's not a small request," she said. "She's a nixie."

The River King's brows drew together. "A nixie? That's not possible. Nixies are evil. They steal children and drown them."

"Feh," Amariel scoffed. "Those are fishwives' tales, sailors' tales. They're not true. The only time a nixie takes a child is if it finds one alone near a riverbank, where no child should be anyway. Nixies feel sorry for such children. Sometimes they take them to their lands beneath the surface of the water, whether fresh or salt, which are some of the most beautiful places in all the world. They always return them. Humans never believe the stories of the children who have been to the nixie realm, but that's 'cause humans are stupid." Her mouth snapped closed when she saw the looks of astonishment on the faces of the king and the other children.

Clem's face turned red. "Speak for yourself, Amariel."

"She is," said Ida, looking amused.

Ven glanced over at Char, who was staring at the merrow as if she had three heads.

"I—I'm not sure I believe you," said the River King haltingly.

Amariel's eyes rolled in exasperation.

"Oh, for goodness sake." She strode across the floor and lifted the hem of the woman's dress, pointing to a wet spot. "See that?" she asked. "Part of clothes always wet: nixie." She dropped the dress, took the woman's lip and curled it back, much to the horror of the River King. "See? Green teeth: nixie. The language is a little hard to understand, but the accent is unmistakable. She's a river nixie, and she came with a message from her people that dumping mule poop into their water is a vile and repulsive thing to do, and she wants you to stop it. There. Riddle solved."

"How do you know all these things, child?" Regis asked in amazement.

Amariel swallowed. "I pay attention in school."

Ven suppressed a chuckle. He knew what kind of school she

meant. "So can we go, then?" he asked hopefully. "If you don't have any more questions for the nixie?"

The River King sighed. "Yes, of course."

He led them back down the stairs through the painting, which closed behind them as they stepped beyond it. When he got as far as the throne, he turned to them again.

"I really am very sorry about how I've treated you," he said. "If there is a boon you would like to ask of me, please do, and I will try my best to grant it."

Ven rubbed his chin, feeling the two whiskers standing out in excitement.

"What can you tell us about the river and the lands beyond it, sir?"

"That's a question that could take years to answer," said Regis. "Is there anything specific you'd like to know?"

"Have you heard anything about a rampaging dragon, by any chance?"

The River King sat down on the throne. "As a matter of fact, I have," he said. "Most of ferrymen along the river don't believe in such things, even though riverfolk are a superstitious lot. There has been enough talk over the years, however, to make even the most cynical merchant believe it's possible. There has also been enough death and damage in the Nain settlements to cause traders to stay far away from those places.

"Most of the reports of damage have come from the northeast, near the foothills of the High Reaches, as the great white mountains are called. Those tales have been told for years, but lately there seem to be many more of them. If they are true, somewhere across the Wide Meadows must be a dragon's lair. We deal in many kinds of goods here along the river, but we are very careful to make certain none of them were ever stolen from a dragon.

"Legend says a dragon is so possessive of its treasure that if even the smallest, most worthless item is taken from its hoard, the dragon will move the earth and skies themselves to get it back, even if it has to destroy thousands of acres of land and take many lives to do it. We assume that something has been stolen that the dragon wants back, and it will stop at nothing to get it."

"Do you have any suggestions about how to stay out of its way?" Ven asked.

Regis thought for a moment. "Stay clear of forest glens, caves near rivers, or the highest hummock in a hilly field," he said, "for those are the places dragons are rumored to live. Never take anything that doesn't belong to you—that's always good advice, but it will particularly help you with a dragon. Don't travel through lands where a dragon is rumored to have been seen unless you absolutely have to." He watched the faces of the children fall. "Let me guess—you absolutely have to?"

"It seems that way," said Clemency.

"Ah, well. Just try to mind your own business, I guess. And try not smell too much like a cow or a horse. I hear that's their favorite food."

"Good ta know," said Char. "Thanks."

"You might want to take a bath before we leave, then, Ida," said Amariel helpfully. "I've noticed that you and the horses smell almost exactly the same. I wouldn't want to see you get eaten by the dragon."

"Says the girl who cats think is a rotten fish head," retorted Ida.

Amariel started swishing something around in her mouth.

"If you don't mind my asking, sir, how did you get to be called the King of the River?" Ven asked, stepping between them before the merrow could spit. "Was your father king before you?"

Regis shook his head.

"The world is much too big for any one person to be king over everything, lad," he said. "If you travel very far in it, you will meet many kings and queens. I myself have met several. Being a king is about awareness, knowledge, not just control of a spot on a map. If a place becomes powerful enough, sooner or later it needs someone in charge of it, to take care of it, to pay attention to it. I love the river—I have all my life. It needed me, so I tended to it, for many years, with all my time, and all my effort. Eventually, there was no one who knew it better or cared for it more than me. So I became its king.

"The Great River is an amazing, magnificent entity," he continued. "It divides this island in half, north to south, and is spanned by only four bridges in all the miles it travels. The great ships of the world offload their goods and supplies in the north where the Nain live. Those goods travel down the river to all the towns that are built along it, and are sold to people from both sides of its banks.

"Midway down, near the Wide Meadows, grain from the fields is loaded on barges, along with lots of other kinds of food, and taken to the milltowns both north and south of here. The grain is ground into flour, and continues down the river, along with the other goods, into the forests to the south which you can see from the bridge. All along the way people trade for what they need, and whatever passes through the Enchanted Forest and all the way to the river's mouth is picked up by the stalwart ships that brave the Icefields at the bottom of the world, to take it far across the sea to others who need those goods. The mules the nixie mentioned drag the barges back up the river, and the cycle starts all over again. At one time or another, the river feeds and enriches everyone on the Island and many more in the world beyond it. So while you may think a king *rules* a river, in fact the real honor is in *serving* it. It should be that way for any true king. Remember that, lad."

"I will," Ven promised. "Thank you."

"And thank you for your help in solving my riddle," the River King said to Amariel. "What you told me is not what I hoped to hear, but I needed to hear it."

"I suspect if you honor her request, you may hear what you hoped for," said Tuck.

Regis smiled slightly. "Perhaps."

"What are you *talkin'* about?" demanded Ida.

"Never mind," said Clemency. "I'll explain later."

"Any trolls under your bridge?" Char asked. "We brought cookies."

"No trolls here. This is a *toll* bridge, not a *troll* bridge. Well, best of luck to all of you, wherever you're going," the River King said. He stood up from the throne and came down to where Amariel was standing. "Thank you especially, my dear. If you don't mind my asking, are you a nixie yourself?"

Amariel snorted. "Don't be ridiculous," she said. "My teeth aren't green."

"May I see?" Regis asked playfully. "Just for curiosity's sake?"

"*NO,*" said Amariel. She shrank behind Ven.

Amariel is very sensitive about her teeth. She laughed out loud once when I first met her, so I got to see them. They are actually very interesting, shaped a little like the drawings I've seen of whale or porpoise teeth, a little bit pointy, with space between them.

I was very surprised the first time I saw them. I gawked at her, which was unforgivable. I was shipwrecked at the time, and my manners were not up to snuff, but that's no excuse. She *disappeared below the surface of the water and I didn't see her again until she saved me by bringing me an empty lifeboat she had found floating.*

So she did forgive me eventually. But every time she has smiled since then, her mouth has been tightly closed.

I wish I could make her laugh out loud again. But I don't know if it's ever going to happen.

"I think he should check," said Ida to no one in particular. "Her clothes are always wet, but I think that's because she's not housebroken."

"Maybe it's just spit?" Clemency suggested, while Ida snickered.

"Time to go," said Tuck hastily.

"Good fortune in your endeavors," said Regis. He let out a long, low whistle, and in response two of his guards came running into the room. "Give these gentlefolk whatever supplies they ask for, and let the children eat all they want at the festival. Then give them safe passage across the bridge and wish them safety on their way, as I do."

"Thank you, sir," said Ven, "and best of luck to you as well."

"Call me Regis," the River King said. "I never did take well to 'sir.'"

They started toward the stairway when Amariel suddenly froze. She walked away onto a small balcony to the south, then waved for Ven to follow her.

On the balcony was a strange, twisted telescope with a small red stool in front of it.

"Is that the strange, twisty-looking thing in your dream?" Ven asked.

The merrow nodded.

"Would you like to look through it?" Regis asked. "It faces the southern sea."

Amariel said nothing. She climbed up onto the stool and peered through the lens while the River King adjusted it for her. Finally she nodded excitedly, and he stepped away, allowing her to enjoy the view.

"What is it you see?" Ven asked.

"Shhh," whispered the merrow, continuing to stare through the telescope. "I see an underwater city, with a great dome of bubbles to hold in the air."

"The thing must twist until it can see inside her head," said Ida, smirking.

Ven scowled at the Thief Queen's daughter, then when Amariel was done took a turn looking through the odd device. At first all he could see was an endless expanse of sea past the great forest to the south, but after a moment a ring of clouds came into view.

"I—I think I see the Floating Island!" he said excitedly. "Char, come look at this!"

The cook's mate stepped up to the eyepiece. "I dunno what you're talkin' about," he said after a moment. "I see a large field o' grass, like a meadow or sumthin', where a picnic's takin' place. Strange. I could swear I've seen that place before."

The River King smiled. "You have," he said. "The telescope only shows you real places you've been to that you dream about."

"Let's see," said Clemency. She took Char's place, stared for a long time, then shook her head and stepped away.

"What did you see?" Ven asked.

Clem shrugged. "Just the sea. Oh well. I don't dream very much. I sleep the sleep of the Just."

"Just what?" Amariel asked. Clemency shot her a sharp glance.

"The Just—you know, the people who have nothing to be ashamed of."

"They loaned their sleep to *you*? You didn't have any of your own? Hmmm. You must have a *lot* to be ashamed of."

Clemency took a step closer to the merrow, but Ven jumped in between them.

"How about it, Saeli? Do you want to have a look?"

The Gwadd girl nodded. Char boosted her up, and she stared into the lens for a long time. Finally she seemed satisfied and stepped down.

"What did you see, Saeli?" Clemency asked.

"Home." The word came out part growl, part sigh.

"How 'bout you, Ida?" Char offered. "You gonna look?"

Ida shook her head vigorously.

"This way, then," said Regis.

They followed the guards down to the courtyard where the wagon was waiting. While the servants fed and watered their horses and filled the wagon with extra supplies, the children gobbled down sweets and berries, cheese and sausages and biscuits and all the fresh cider they could drink. By the time Tuck summoned them, they were full and happy and chatting excitedly.

They waved goodbye to the River King, who had come to see them off.

"One last boon?" Tuck said as he mounted the wagon board.

"Name it," said Regis.

"Once we've crossed the bridge, forget that we were here. Remember nothing but our good wishes."

The River King smiled. "I do that every day," he said. "Happy travels to you, whoever you were."

The wagon clattered as they drove away over the floorboards of the enormous bridge, leaving the beautiful river palace behind.

They made their way out of the fringe of the forest, heading north toward the Wide Meadows. They stopped to rest that night, and the night that followed, and the night that followed that, sleeping in the fields without a fire, the horses and wagon hidden in whatever copse of trees they could find.

Strangely enough, the farther they traveled from the river, the more they could hear its song in their dreams.

Those three days and nights blended together. They took to sleeping in the daytime and traveling when the sun went down to avoid the dark birds that had followed them across the wide river and that hunted them by day. Though it made them tired and cranky, trading day for night kept them safe.

Until the dark birds began looking for them at night as well.

- 12 -

Dragon's Breath

My mother is not a patient woman.

Or maybe she is. But because her patience is spread across thirteen children and my father, who requires a certain amount of patience himself, it wears thin sometimes. You can tell when it's gone fairly easily, because someone usually ends up with a cauliflower ear.

Whenever my brothers argue, my mother's eyes start to get narrow. This is the first sign of danger. My only sister Matilde and I are pretty good about noticing this change, and we usually make ourselves scarce whenever it occurs. But my brothers are typical Nain. They are pigheaded and love to argue.

My mother is a typical Nain mother. She likes to have peace after a long day of arguing.

So around dinner time, she's had enough Nain nonsense.

When Petar or Osgood or Jaymes or any of the other brothers begin to act pushy or grumpy, my mother gets very quiet. This is the second sign of danger. My mother is a woman of few words in good circumstances, so when she gets quiet, it's like all the air was suddenly sucked out of the room. It's hard to miss this change, but if my brothers or my father are in the mood for a good, rowdy argument, they sometimes overlook it.

To their peril.

The third sign that my mother has had enough is when she rises from her seat. This one is easy to miss, because she usually does it very quietly and quickly. Before you notice, she has sunk her fingertips into the top of your ear. She pinches harder than the vise in my father's factory, which brings any argument to an immediate halt.

Then she slams your head into the head of whoever you're arguing with.

The result is the peace and quiet she expects.

And sore ears.

And occasionally unconsciousness.

This is a tactic I have seen the mothers of all my upworld Nain friends use, too. I even wondered if Mrs. Snodgrass was part Nain, because when I first came to the Crossroads Inn I saw her bash together the heads of two guests who had had too much to drink and were arguing in the tavern.

It made me feel at home right away.

I myself have been the occasional recipient of sore and swollen ears over the course of my short fifty-year lifetime. It's a feeling I don't relish, and one I have never had the urge to visit upon anyone else.

Until I traveled overland with my friends.

I am feeling my eyes beginning to narrow.

THE WIDE MEADOWS PAST THE GREAT RIVER WERE ACCURATELY named. Once they had left the River King's palace behind, the

Enchanted Forest faded from view over the southern horizon. The little towns and settlements along the river grew fewer and fewer as they traveled east, and soon all they could see was waving highgrass dotted with occasional copses of pioneer trees.

As civilization disappeared, boredom began to set in. Day-sleeping was hard on them all, especially Ven, whose Nain eyes saw well in the dark but did not shut out the light of the sun well. His sleep was fitful, with haunting fragments of dreams that left him tired when he woke.

The lack of sleep did not improve the tempers in the wagon, either. Ven felt his fingers itch from time to time, as if they wanted to pinch ears and bang heads together.

Tuck had taken to teaching them how to live as a forester does. He gave them lessons in fire building, tracking, finding water and cooking over a campfire. It kept their hands busy as well as their minds.

Every now and then another wagon would pass by, or a traveling caravan of people on foot. If they were well hidden, Tuck and the children would let them pass without making themselves known, but sometimes it was necessary to smile and wave to keep from looking suspicious.

One day, just such a caravan was approaching from the north when Ven noticed something behind it.

At first he thought the clouds in the summer sky were hanging especially low. He stood up and squinted. After a moment, he could see that the clouds were up where they were supposed to be in the welkin of blue.

What he was seeing, hovering just above the highgrass, was billowing smoke.

"Blimey!" Char said beside him. Ven jumped. "Look a' that! The field's on fire!"

Ven pulled out the jack-rule from his pocket. His hands were trembling so much that he almost dropped it in the tall grass around him. He opened the lens that saw far away and peered through it.

The caravan he had seen coming in the distance was not a slowly moving line of carts with goods bound for market but a scattered group of wildly rocking wagons and people running, mostly children, their faces pale with fear. The white smoke was hovering over blacker clouds that hung above rippling orange waves of fire, some of it burning wide swathes of grass, some of it ripping across what had once been thatched roofs of houses and a barn.

Amariel grabbed his arm, almost making him drop the jack-rule.

"Fire!"

"I know—"

"Is it the king? Is the king trying to set fire to you again?"

"No, no," Ven said quickly. He pulled away from her grasp and stared through the lens again.

Past the billowing smoke he could see dark shadows of men and women beating the grass with what looked like blankets and sticks. A line of figures snaked from what appeared to be a pond to the largest of the blazes, passing buckets of water along to the center of the fire. To the north, another more distant group was shoveling dirt onto the grassfire, their dark shapes blending in with the smoke.

"Ven, get up here and drive the cart," Tuck shouted as he vaulted down from the wagon board. He came around to the wagon bed and dipped a rag in the water barrel. "Keep well ahead of the flames—head east, just out of range." He wrung out the rag and tied it around his nose and mouth.

"Where are you going?" Ven asked.

Tuck nodded in the direction of the bucket line. "To lend a hand."

"I can go, too," Char offered. "I had ta help put out a fire at sea once."

"I can help," added Clem, who had just finished praying for rain.

Tuck nodded. "Get a kerchief and come along."

"Me too," Ven started, but Tuck waved him away.

"No, Ven—you stay here and keep the others safe. You're Nain—it's best if you stay out of it. Clem, Char—stay only at the edges and keep away from the flames. Help beat the sparks out—nothing more." He turned and waded into the smoke.

I felt as if I had been slapped across the face. For a moment I couldn't move, sitting in the back of the wagon as my friends climbed over the edge and ran off to help Tuck.

I wasn't certain why being Nain meant that my assistance was any less valuable, but then I thought back to what the king had said.

First, you must understand that each of the kingdoms over which I am high king has its own ruler, its own set of laws. I may be in charge of all of them, but only loosely. Some of the kingdoms don't get along very well.

Could my being here make the people of this region blame the Nain for this fire? he thought. His stomach turned at the possibility. Especially since the king is hoping that my being here will help end the hostilities, not make them worse.

Next to him Amariel began to choke and cough. Ven turned and saw that she was holding on to her neck where her gills had been, struggling to breathe. His stomach tightened at the grayness of her face. Beside her, Saeli was keeping low, trying to keep the smoke away from herself and the keekee in her braid.

His hands shaking, he jammed the jack-rule back in his pocket, fumbling with the button. His handkerchiefs fell out and onto the floor of the wagon; one blew over the side into the burning grass. He scooped the other two up from the wagon floor and shoved them into his pocket behind the jack-rule, finally getting the button to close.

He crawled over the provisions and onto the wagon board where Tuck had sat, grabbing for the reins. Even though he had never driven a team of horses, he called out nervously in the same way Tuck had done.

"Het!"

The wagon lurched forward. Ven heard a thump in the back as the merrow fell to the floor. *Oh, this isn't going to be pretty*, he thought as he struggled to keep the team heading east. *I hope she doesn't spit at Tuck once we get away from the fire.*

He pulled back on the reins once they got out of the smoke. The horses slowed their pace and came to a halt. Ven sat up on the wagon board and looked around.

Behind them it seemed that the fire had begun to die down. Fewer streaks of orange rippled across the grass. The smoke continued to rise in rolling clouds that caught the wind and began to stretch out toward the northeast. Ven pulled his shirt up around his nose to shield it from bitter stench as it passed over him.

South of the village, the people who had been fleeing had stopped and were standing now, watching the fire die down.

Ven's throat tightened as he saw mothers and fathers being re-united with their children. He thought back to his own parents, and the day they had heard the news that the ship he had been inspecting had been attacked by Fire Pirates. He tried to put the thought out of his head as he watched a soot-stained mother kneel and throw her arms around a little boy standing in the still-green grass.

A cough behind him drew his attention back to the wagon.

"Saeli, Amariel—are you all right?"

The little Gwadd girl emerged from behind the water barrel. Her normally rosy face was pale, her eyes glistening, but she nodded. She opened her handkerchief, and the tiny keekee fell out, wheezing and coughing in a tiny voice.

The merrow pushed herself up from the wagon floor and turned her gaze on Ven. He steeled himself for the glare, wincing in preparation for the spit. But Amariel merely nodded, coughing slightly, and waved the thinning smoke away from her face.

Beyond them he could see the shadows of Tuck, Clemency and Char emerging from the burned village. Behind them was a tall, thin man in soot-stained work clothes holding a shovel. When they got within a few feet of the wagon, the man turned to Tuck and extended his hand. Tuck shook it as Clem and Char climbed unsteadily back into the wagon, reeking of the caustic smell of burned grass.

"Thanks for your help," the man said to Tuck, who nodded.

Saeli passed her handkerchief over the back of her hair, then wrung it out. Ven saw the tail end of the keekee disappear into her braid.

"You all right?" Ven asked Clem and Char. His best friend nodded while the curate-in-training pulled the wet kerchief from her mouth and nose, coughing.

"Any idea how it started?" Tuck asked the farmer.

The man cast a glance into the wagon. His eyes fell on Ven.

"Dunno," he said, staring at him. "Been happening a lot around here of late. Word has it that the Nain settlements to the north of here have been suffering the wrath of a dragon. We've been keeping our distance, but occasionally a spark carries on the wind."

Tuck nodded. "Bad luck in summer, when the grass is dry anyway."

The farmer cleared his throat. "Bad luck to be living south of people without sense," he said, still staring at Ven. "You have to be a natural-born fool not to know it's suicide to anger a dragon—especially that one."

The king's forester glanced Ven's way as well. Ven thought he saw a look of sympathy in his eyes.

"Strange, if it's dragon's breath, why it smells like a normal summer wildfire," he said pleasantly.

The words tumbled out of Ven's mouth before he could stop them.

"Excuse me, sir—*that* one? Do you know this dragon's name, or anything about it?"

"He's not from around here," Tuck said quickly as the man's eyes narrowed.

The man looked at him for a long moment.

"Yes, as a matter of fact, I do," he said finally. "The only dragon I've heard tell of anywhere near these parts is Scarnag."

"Scarnag?" The word scratched Ven's eardrums like a nail. There was something intensely painful about it, almost evil.

The farmer nodded. "They say it means *scourge*, a cause of great suffering, like a plague, an earthquake, a war." He looked over his shoulder, then looked back pointedly. "Or a wildfire."

Ven's curiosity was rising along with the acid in his stomach. "Do you know why he's so angry at the Nain, sir?"

"Couldn't tell you," said the man. "Don't know much about dragons—never seen one. In fact, you're the first *Nain* I've seen. If someone asked me a few years ago, I'd say both dragons and Nain are nothing but made-up creatures in children's stories. But, unfortunately, just as it appears that Nain are real, it seems dragons must be as well."

"A lot of the people *I* know think humans are just legends," said Amariel under her breath. "Hmmph."

Clemency was picking up the fallen sacks of provisions and restoring the wagon bed to order. "Anything else you might be able to tell us, sir?"

The man's expression softened as he looked at her.

"Only that the beast rises from the ground, instead of swooping down from the sky, as dragons are said to do in stories. I'm told that the earth opens unexpectedly, like a terrible yawn. You hear the roar, but by then it's too late."

Ven felt Char shudder beside him.

The farmer turned back to Tuck, then nodded at Char and Clem.

"Thanks again for your help—you too, children. I've got to get back to my family."

"Good luck," said Tuck. "All right, everyone, settle in and we'll be on our way."

"Where are we going?" Ven asked as the forester climbed onto the wagon board beside him.

"I think we should keep heading northeast, away from the fire. The Gwaddlands lie beyond this place. Great open meadows, rolling hills and valleys, with trees here and there. Your friend wishes to visit her family, and I think it is a good idea to get out of sight among those who know how to hide well. We need to move quickly, however. The smoke will only cover us so long."

"Cover us?"

Tuck looked up into the sky. Ven followed his gaze.

Hovering above the thick, billowing clouds, flying in circles, were birds.

Hundreds of them.

Black as the smoke.

- 13 -

Eyes in the Sky

CHAR LET OUT A MISERABLE SIGH.

"Bloody sky-rats," he murmured. "Like sticky black pitch on the deck of a ship. No matter how much you rub it off, it still keeps comin' back."

"Shhhh." Tuck looked into the sky. His voice was quieter than the crackling of the remaining fire. "Hard to say whether they're looking for us or just scavenging—there's a lot of carrion after a fire, mice, moles that didn't make it out." He picked up his crossbow and loaded a bolt, then slowly raised it to his shoulder. "Ven, keep driving. Hold the reins loose, and let the horses walk at their own pace. If I fire, snap the reins."

Ven nodded and took the reins, slippery with sweat, back into his hands.

Behind him he could hear Clemency move closer to Saeli. The small girl was breathing rapidly, and he could almost hear her heart beating.

We can't possibly outrun this flock, he thought. *And Saeli knows it.*

The memory of the ravens pulling her hair made his mouth taste like metal. *If I'm this scared for her, I can't even imagine what she is feeling.*

"Steady," Tuck whispered.

The wagon rolled quietly through the high grass beneath a blanket of smoke that was growing thinner with each moment. Every bump or rock that they hit caused it to shudder, making the children shudder as well. Ven kept his eyes straight ahead, waiting for Tuck to move.

He sat as still as he could, until a drop of rain hit his nose.

Ven started.

Great, he thought. *Now we get rain when the fire's already almost out. Just my luck—it's going to wash away the smoke, and the ravens will find us. I hope all Clem's prayers are answered, because I bet she's praying now.*

"Steady," Tuck repeated. It was almost as if he could hear Ven's thoughts.

The children held their breath, and the forester held his fire, for what seemed like forever. The veil of smoke grew hazier and hazier until at last they could see the sky beyond it.

It was much darker than it had been.

"There's a small thicket of trees and scrub to the north a little ways, Ven," Tuck said quietly. "Can you see it? Just nod, don't speak."

Ven could see the black outline of what looked like several evergreens ahead in the distance. He nodded.

"Steer the wagon in that direction," the forester instructed in a whisper. "Pull back gently on the left rein to turn, then when the horses are heading for the thicket, loose the reins."

"Are the birds still circling?" Ven whispered back.

"Shhhh. Yes."

Ven did as Tuck said. The wagon turned slowly to the north, the horses seeming to know where they were headed. Finally they rolled to a stop inside the thicket. The only sound was the breathing and occasional snorting of the horses.

They remained frozen as the light in the sky above the tree-tops faded into gray, then darkness. Finally, as the stars began to emerge behind the wisps of smoke carried on the breeze, the forester put down his crossbow.

"They're gone," he said. "Let's make camp—Ida, Saeli, you sleep under the wagon, and anyone else who can fit as well. The birds don't appear to be following us, but if they are night-hunters, it's just as well that they see nothing warm-blooded if they fly overhead."

Silently they climbed out of the wagon, Clemency first, followed by Ida, then Char. Ven handed Saeli down to Clem and turned to see Amariel staring above at the stars.

"Amariel?" The merrow didn't seem to hear him, so he moved closer. "Amariel, come on—we need to make camp."

"Oh. All right." She got up slowly and walked to the back of the wagon, her steps unsteady.

"Are you all right?" Ven asked. Amariel nodded and let him help her out of the wagon. "What were you looking at?"

"Nothing. I was looking for the moon—it's set already."

"Oh." Ven scratched his head. "Any particular reason?"

Amariel shrugged. "I think it's waning, but I'm not sure. I like watching the moon. I told you a long time ago—it's kind of like the pilot fish for the earth—leading it through the darkness to wherever it should be going."

Well, at least it's nice to think someone or something knows where we should be going, Ven thought. He smiled at the merrow, and she smiled back, her peg-like teeth glistening in the dark.

Ven tried not to stare. Amariel hadn't shown her teeth in a smile since the first time he met her.

Just then, above his head, a crossbow bolt whistled skyward.

Ven whipped around to see black streaks in the dark diving beneath the wagon. A harsh, horrible cawing that sounded like shattering glass scratched his ears. He covered his eyes with his arms and crouched down as the claws of a squad of ravens flapped in his face.

He could hear the screams and gasps of his friends as they thumped around in terror, banging into the wagon bed above them. He felt around for the merrow, and found her rolled into a ball near the front wagon wheel.

Above them, he could hear the sound of Tuck's crossbow firing.

Just then Saeli's small body was dragged past him and out from under the wagon.

"Saeli!" Ven screamed. He followed her out, scrambling to his feet, with Char right behind him. The black night birds were flapping around the Gwadd girl, who was lying on the ground, slapping helplessly at them. They pecked at her head and hair as Clem crawled out from under the wagon, a look of horror on her face.

The birds seized the little girl by her shoulders and her long, caramel-colored braid. Before anyone could move, they dragged her up all the way out from under the wagon and hovered heavily in the air as Saeli kicked and screamed in her harsh voice.

Ven lunged for the Gwadd girl, followed a second later by Char. They each grabbed one of her legs and held fast as four ravens separated from the flock and circled back, aiming directly for them.

"Steady," Tuck called from somewhere behind them. "Don't move."

"Hurry!" Ven shouted in return.

Tuck got his bearings and fired low, dropping one of the birds carrying Saeli, but the other rank flew to attack Ven, who was pulling as hard as he could to free her from the ravens' clutches. At the last second he let go and ducked, and the birds sailed past the horses. Tuck fired twice, and two more *thumps* rattled the reins.

Ven struggled to his feet and grabbed into the air, trying to regain his hold on Saeli.

"Hurry, mate!" Char yelled. "She's startin' to slip!"

Four more shots whistled past their heads. Four more bodies fell thudding to the ground.

Then, after another round of crossbow fire, the Gwadd tumbled back to earth amid a mess of feathers and bone.

Clemency was there in a heartbeat. She threw her arms around Saeli, who was shaking and sobbing. She pulled Ven's hand off the Gwadd girl and hurried her past him.

"Let go, Ven," she said shortly. "I'll take of her while you go see to Amariel."

Ven felt like he had been slapped. "Wait, Clem—let me see if she's all right—"

"I'll make sure she is. You look after your *friend*—that's all you've been doing since we set out on this miserable journey."

"Whoa, Clem, calm down," Char commanded. "That's not fair."

The curate-in-training paused, then sighed. "I'm sorry. You're right. I guess the sight of Saeli being dragged into the sky has scared everything but the nastiness out of me. I apologize. But once I get her calmed down, we need to decide what we're going to do."

Ven nodded. He waited until Clem and Saeli had disappeared under the wagon, then went over to where the merrow had been lying. He found her straightening up the food sacks that had fallen over during the attack.

"Amariel? What are you doing?"

The merrow turned and looked at him, but he couldn't see anything but her outline in the dark.

"Cleaning up."

"Oh." Ven peeked over the side of the wagon. The provisions had been restored to order. "Why?"

Amariel shrugged. "I don't know. I wasn't sure what else to do."

"Are you hurt?"

"No."

Ven took her by the upper arm and pulled her gently away from the wagon, wondering if she was in shock. "Why don't you come and sit with Ida and Char and me?"

"All right," said the merrow.

Ven's brows knit together in worry as he led her to where the others were. He sank to the ground next to Tuck. "Did you get them all?"

"As far as I can tell. More will come, I imagine."

Ven leaned closer to Char. "Well, I guess that tells us which of us Felonia wants back most," he said, nodding at the wagon beneath which Clem and Saeli were hiding.

"Maybe," said Char. "Or maybe she's the only one they could lift."

"That's true," Ven admitted. "But I'm worried for her anyway. It looked like they came for her intentionally."

"Yep," said Char. "They didn' seem interested in anyone else." He looked over at the merrow, who had gone back to watching the sky. "Amariel seems to be handlin' it pretty well."

"Ven, get over here." Clem's voice came from under the wagon.

Ven let go of Amariel's hand. He patted his pocket nervously, feeling the outline of his jack-rule, the Black Ivory sleeve, and his handkerchiefs, and felt a little better. Then he climbed under the wagon with Ida behind him.

Clem was sitting with her arm around Saeli.

I could see them only because Nain have special eyesight that works well underground and in darkness. If I had been human, I think I would only have been able to see their outlines.

But even if that was all I could see, I would still have been able to tell how terrified Saeli was. Her eyes were open as wide as I'd ever seen them, staring straight ahead. Her breathing was shallow, and she was shaking like a wildflower in the wind.

"We have to get her to a place where she can hide," Clem said in a low voice as she traded places with Char. "We can't take her on with us, Ven, especially if you really want to go north to the foothills where the Nain live. She's not going to survive—either Felonia's ravens are going to find her and drag her back to the Gated City, or she's going to die of fright. But either way, this is crazy."

"Yep," added Char. "No bunch of bloody blackbirds is gonna drag you or me off, Ven—but Saeli doesn't stand a chance, mate. We gotta get her to her family and leave 'er there—at least 'til you think it's safe ta go back."

Ven sighed. "You're right. And Tuck agrees. So we'll go in the morning." He looked around below the wagon bed. "I think we can all fit under here tonight. Let's not take any of those chances Char mentioned—scoot in and let's get as comfortable as we can. It will be a little crowded, but we'll manage."

"Amariel can sleep under the horses," Ida suggested.

"Shut up and move over." Ven glowered at Ida while Char went out to fetch the others. Once everyone had crawled under the wagon, he positioned himself between the merrow and Saeli and settled down to sleep.

In the morning, they rose, grumpy and sore. There was no sign of the birds, so they loaded back into the wagon and made their way north toward where Saeli and Tuck said the Gwaddlands lay.

It took us almost a week to reach those Gwaddlands.

I've had some painful weeks in my life. There was the week that I spent in bed after my brother Jaymes convinced me to try the soup he had been cooking all afternoon. Jaymes's skill with food preparation was what led my father to put him in charge of the section of the factory that made paint. Now he makes some beautiful colors of dye and enamels that decorate our family's ships, but those paints probably taste somewhat better than his soup did. I spent the week with my tongue stuck to roof of my mouth and my stomach trying to exit my body through any escape hatch it could find.

There was also the week when I broke my ankle doing something stupid to impress Maisie Haggerty, the prettiest Nain girl in Vaarn. I was a little kid, no more than 30 years old, and I hadn't gotten my growth spurt yet. I hadn't even reached 45 Knuckles in height, so to make myself look taller I took to standing on pylons along the pier where Maisie couldn't see my feet when she walked by. Most days she ignored me, but one day when she was passing by, Maisie waved to me. I got so excited that I waved back really hard. I slipped on a piece of squid and fell backwards into the water, smacking my leg on a pylon on which I had been balancing. I was so embarrassed that I didn't even tell my mother I'd been injured until my leg swelled up as big as a buoy. The night I spent before they found that it was broken was the most physical pain I ever remember being in.

I'd been thinking about my family a lot as we made our way north in the lands east of the river. Since the king hoped I would be able to help the Nain figure out why the dragon was tormenting them, I expected I would eventually be seeing people of my own race, actual Downworld Nain, something no one in my family had ever done. I thought about my sister Matilde, who was fascinated with our heritage and read as many books about it as she could. For the better part of a week I had been wishing she was here, so that she could get to see what she longed for more than anything. It gave me another kind of pain, the pain that makes your heart hurt even though your body is fine.

But when it comes to heart pain, the kind of pain you feel when someone you know and care about is suffering, I don't think I've ever felt worse than the week it took to get to the Gwaddlands.

Because I think Saeli cried the whole way.

By the time they reached the place where Saeli began looking for her people, the moon was new, and there was no longer any light whatsoever in the sky at night.

The ravens that had been chasing them for so long finally seemed to have lost their trail. Each day the children scanned the sky for the signs of any dark birds following them, but only occasional starlings and crows could be seen circling overhead, cawing harshly, soaring out of the way of the wagon as it clattered by.

The companions breathed a sigh of relief, especially Ven and Ida, every time that happened.

When night came, a blanket of bright stars covered them, allowing them to sleep peacefully. Tuck let them out of the wagon to sleep on the ground whenever he could find a safe spot. The Wide Meadows were aptly named, stretching out for miles without a break. It was not always easy to find shelter, but most of the time the forester was good at locating a small grove of trees or a hollow swale for them to sleep in.

Everyone seemed to be getting more rested and healthier except for Ven and Saeli. The tiny Gwadd girl had trouble falling asleep. Each day she grew quieter and paler.

Ven's nightmares were getting worse as well. Every night his dreams were haunted, even when they started out happy.

He often dreamt of the Great River and its king, in whose palace he and his friends feasted, played, and danced. He could almost smell the roasting meat, taste the sweet pasties, feel the bright silks and linens of the festival booths. But always the scene would turn dark.

One night he dreamt he followed Amariel up the wooden stairs to Regis's throne room where the strange, knobby telescope stood.

"Look through the lens," the River King suggested. In his sleep Ven watched as Amariel put her eye to the glass. "What do you see?"

"The Summer Festival," the merrow answered wistfully. "Everyone is waiting for me—the hippocampus races are about to begin. They have just crowned the Sea King and Queen. All my friends and family are there—and I'm missing it."

The phantom River King then turned the twisted telescope toward Ven.

"And you?" Regis asked. "What do you see?"

Ven looked into the lens. He saw a flock of dark birds circling above the sea to the south, flying over the wreckage of a ship. As he adjusted the instrument, he saw himself floating there below them. He strained to look closer, but as he did, an enormous eye filled the other end of the lens, the beautiful black eye of the Queen of Thieves.

It narrowed as it saw him, staring as if it could see him through the glass.

Then Ven realized the pupil of the eye was thin and vertical, not round like a human's. He pulled back away from the lens. As he did, the pupil on the other end did as well, growing larger.

It was serpentine, set in a lidless eye surrounded by scales, puffs of smoke rising around it.

Still watching him,

He could hear the farmer's voice.

Scarnag. They say it means scourge, *a cause of great suffering.*

From such dreams Ven would wake, sweating and breathing hard. He learned to keep from crying out, and took to staring at the sparkling web of stars above him in an attempt to calm himself enough not to wake his sleeping companions.

How bright they are out here in the Wide Meadows, away from the lights of the city, he thought one night as he waited for the wind to dry the sweat from his forehead. *It's like being back on the sea.* Several nights he wished he *was* on the sea, floating alone on a piece of wreckage, where Felonia and her spies could never find him. He took to looking for constellations the crew of the *Serelinda* had shown him, or making up pictures in the stars himself, until sleep returned.

When daylight came each morning, tempers began growing shorter until sometime during the afternoon they would explode.

"Would you care to share the joke?" Clemency asked tartly one day when Ven and Amariel were laughing quietly in the corner of the wagon.

Ven looked up, surprised.

"It's nothing, really," he said quickly. He didn't want to explain Amariel's confusion about why he and Char would take their rest breaks away from the wagon standing up in the tall grass, while the girls would walk away and disappear by sitting down. *It's something that's only a mystery to an ocean-dweller,* he thought, *and we don't want anyone to know that's what she is.*

"Well, if it's nothing, why are you annoying the rest of us with it?" Clem pressed.

"Why does it annoy you to see other people having a laugh?" Amariel asked, perplexed. "That seems rather crabby. Actually, it's worse. Even crabs aren't *that* resentful when someone else is having a good time as long as they're not getting eaten in the process." She smoothed out the skirt of the dress Mrs. Snodgrass had given her.

I didn't remember ever having seen her wear the dress before. But maybe I just hadn't noticed.

"Where did you *find* this girl, Ven?" Clemency demanded. "She is the rudest person I have ever met."

"Hey—no, she's not," Ida protested as Ven's mouth dropped open and Amariel blinked in surprise. "That's me. She's just the dumbest."

"All right, that's enough," said Ven, expecting that Amariel was preparing to spit. He looked and saw that she wasn't. Instead she was watching the clouds overhead. "What's gotten into you girls lately?"

"They could ask you the same thing, mate," said Char in a low voice. "Ever since you brought your new friend along, everythin's been at odds. We had a great group that worked fine before this. Now, without even askin' us, you bring a total stranger along. And suddenly you're not talkin' to anybody but *her* anymore."

Ven opened his mouth to retort, but as he did, Saeli suddenly stood up in the back of the wagon. She pointed off to the north.

"There!" she said in her strange, growly voice. "Look!"

She did not sound happy.

Something Not Quite Right About This Place

Everyone in the wagon jumped. It had been so long since Saeli had spoken aloud that they had forgotten how odd the sound was, coming from such a tiny person.

"Are these the Gwaddlands, Saeli?" Ven asked. "Where you come from?"

The little girl nodded. The keekee's head appeared atop hers, its large eyes staring in the same direction.

"I advise you again to stay down," said Tuck from the wagon board near the horses. "Remember, you are cargo, nothing more."

The wagon crested a rolling swale, and brought what Saeli was pointing to into view. It was an enormous farming community that stretched as far as the eye could see to the north, east and west. Tall stalks of corn stood in neat rows, with perfect rows of soil between each of them, making for a pretty pattern of pale green and brown stripes on the rolling hills. Between the endless lines of corn were meadows, in the middle of which stood many small white houses, clean and sparkling in the afternoon sun, exactly alike.

The meadows were divided into straight rectangles like a

patchwork quilt in many different colors of green, yellow and brown, sewn together with long seams of corn. Each of the rectangles had a different kind of crop, all as neatly tended as the corn was, each field of which had a leafy tree standing in the very center of it.

"How pretty," Clemency said, sitting up on her knees to get a better look. "This is ever so very much better kept than the farms where I live. You can tell that the Gwadd really know how to take care of the land."

"What *is* this place?" Amariel whispered to Ven.

"A farm," Ven whispered back. "Where food is grown."

The merrow's nose wrinkled. "We have farms where I live, but ours are much nicer," she said. "There are so many colors of fish and anemones in the farmlands beneath the sea—it's like an explosion of rainbows everywhere. Here it's all the same color. It looks like it doesn't feel very well." Ven just smiled.

The closer they got to the enormous farm, the more upset Saeli became.

"What's the matter?" Char asked the small girl.

"Not right," she whispered back in her gravelly voice. "Not right."

"What's not right?" Clem added.

Saeli spread her tiny hands out as far as she could.

"Everything," she said.

Tuck slowed the wagon to a halt while they were still a distance away.

"Look," he said, pointing to the outer edge of the fields. "That might explain how the wildfire south of here got started."

"I don't see anything," Ven said. He unbuttoned his shirt pocket, careful not to let anything fall out, and pulled out his jack-rule. He extended the far-seeing lens and looked through it.

Beneath the rolling gray and white clouds of ash and smoke he could make out many small figures in the distance. They were wearing what appeared to be straw hats like Tuck, the king, and the farmers of Westland wore to keep the sun off their faces. In each of their hands were dry cornstalks, at the tip of which Ven could see a tiny flame burning. They seemed to be setting fire to the grass at the base of the ground.

"What are those Gwadd doing?" he asked Tuck.

"They are clearing the natural brush of the fields by burning it," the Lirin forester replied. "It's a fast, though not always smart, way to turn scrub into plantable soil. But those aren't Gwadd—they're humans."

Ven glanced over at Amariel. She was humming to herself. "Relax," he whispered to her.

The merrow blinked. "Why? Do I seem nervous?"

Ven stared at her. "Actually—no," he admitted. "Did you hear what Tuck said? Those people are humans."

"Yes, I heard him."

The hairs on the back of Ven's neck started to prickle. "And that doesn't worry you?"

Amariel shrugged.

"What's the matter with humans?" Ida demanded crossly.

Saeli held up her hand.

"Don't belong here," she whispered. "Where—where are the Gwadd?"

Silence fell over the wagon, until nothing could be heard but the clopping of the horses' hooves as they danced in place, the squeaking of the wheels and the rattling of the boards.

"What do you mean, Saeli?" Char asked finally. "Are ya sayin' the Gwadd are missin'?"

The little girl peered into the distance, then nodded sadly.

"Maybe they're inside the buildings, eating noon-meal?" Clem offered hopefully.

Saeli shook her head.

"Buildings too big," she said in her strange voice. "Gwadd would never feel comfortable in them."

"Oh dear," Clem whispered to Ven. "Where are the Gwadd? Where's Saeli's family?"

"I have no idea," Ven said. "But whatever is happening here, I'm not liking it."

The Lirin forester clicked to the horses.

"Let's go find out what's going on here," Tuck said. The children settled down in the back in a nervous silence and stared over the side of the wagon as it descended the swale into the valley below.

As the farm grew closer, the buildings seemed to grow larger. The rows of corn went on for miles, standing pale and straight against the sun.

Just as they came to the floor of the valley, the door of one of the houses in the center of the pasturelands opened, and a pleasant-looking human man came out, smiling. He waved to the wagon, then approached it in a friendly manner.

"Hullo, folks!" he said merrily. "The name's Clovis. How can I help you all today?"

"Hello," said Ven. "We're looking for the Gwadd—but we don't see any. Are these not the Gwaddlands?"

Clovis looked surprised.

"Goodness, no," he said. "There haven't been Gwadd here in a *very* long time, years, at least."

"Where did they go?" Char demanded. "What happened to 'em?"

The man's pleasant smile faded a bit.

"I've no idea," he said shortly. "This is a human settlement now. I've never even seen a Gwadd. I don't even know what one looks like."

"It's a lovely place you have here," said Clemency quickly before either boy could speak again. "Perfectly tended—and very pretty."

Clovis's smile returned.

"Thank you so much," he said, sounding pleased. "We work very hard to keep it shining. Would you like a tour?"

"Absolutely," said Clem quickly. "But I think I'm going to stay here and nap a bit, if nobody minds." She stretched lazily and then pulled the horse blanket up over her shoulders, hiding Saeli beneath it as well.

Char and Ven immediately understood.

"Thank you very much," Ven added. "We'd love to see this pretty place. Come on, mates, let's take the tour."

Char and Ida got out of the wagon, followed a moment later by Ven and Amariel. They fell in line behind Clovis, who took them proudly around the pastures that were each perfectly planted in the vegetable assigned to them, without so much as a wildflower growing out of place. He walked them along the long rows of spectacular corn, each stalk the same size as all the others around it. He let them stop and offered them a drink at a sparkling stream, which they politely declined, took them around to the Fairy Forts, the tall, leafy trees that upon closer inspection seemed to be braided with razor wire through their branches.

"Why are they called Fairy Forts?" Char wondered aloud.

"Oh, when we cleared each field we left a single tree to serve as home to the fairies that live in that field," Clovis said, running his hand proudly across the tops of the stalks and smoothing out the cornsilk in each of them. "The presence of the fairies brings luck and good fortune to the field."

"That's interesting," said Ven.

"It's really just an old superstition," said Clovis. "Of course there are no such things as fairies."

"How I wish *that* was true," Char whispered to Ven.

"They use razor wire to keep the nonexistent fairies in," Ven whispered back. "This place scares me."

"Would you like to see the cows?" Clovis asked Amariel sweetly. Amariel looked at Ven in confusion. Ven nodded quickly, so Amariel did as well. "Good," Clovis said. "The cow houses are back here."

"Cow *houses*?" Ida muttered under her breath.

"Wire in trees," said Char. "Don't think too hard about it— you'll hurt your head."

They followed Clovis into a stand of long white buildings with small, rectangular windows. Inside each of the buildings

were many black and white spotted cows side by side in pens, quietly chewing their cud or chomping hay. Ida wrinkled up her nose at the smell and hurried to the other end of the building past Clovis and out the door.

"Are you thirsty?" Clovis asked as they came outside near a large shelf on which many bright metal milk cans were standing.

"A little," Ven admitted.

"Ah! Well, I have just the thing for you, then," said Clovis. He took five gleaming mugs off the shelf, unscrewed the top of a milk can and poured the silky white contents into each of them.

"Drink up," he said, taking one and doing so.

The children looked at each other, then each took a drink.

It's hard to explain how it tasted. It wasn't bad, really, but there was something just not right about it. It was not too sour, or too sweet, it was just, well, wrong.

They placed their empty mugs on the shelf next to Clovis's.

"Sun's going down," Clovis said, shielding his eyes. "We'll be having supper soon and turning in for the night. Where are you young folks heading?"

"We're never sure," said Char.

Clovis nodded. "Well, if you're looking for a place to stay for the night, you are more than welcome in the bunkhouse here. Supper's good and filling, and the price is right—you just have to help with the washing afterward. You kids aren't allergic to good, honest work, are you?"

"Not at all, sir," said Ven.

"Define 'honest,' " said Ida.

"Thank you for the invitation," said Char quickly. "We'd love ta stay." He shot Ida a vicious glance.

"Why don't you go get your friends in the wagon?" Clovis suggested. "I'll show you the dining hall and the bunkhouse. You can get something to eat and make yourselves comfortable."

"Did you notice the spots on those cows?" Char asked Ven under his breath as they headed back to the wagon. "They were all *exactly* the same," Char said. "Not a little bit, but exactly, as if it were the same cow, over and over."

"What do you think about this place, Tuck?" they asked the forester when they returned to the wagon.

"Do you think it's evil?" Ven added.

The forester exhaled. He looked around the farm from west to east, then shook his head.

"Can't say for sure, but I don't think so," he said. "There's something wrong here, as Saeli said, but I have no idea what it is. It's not the sort of place Lirinved would stay—but that doesn't make it evil."

"What do you think happened to the Gwadd?" Clemency asked.

The forester shook his head. "I don't know, but we can keep looking. It won't hurt if we are heading north to the Nain lands anyway."

They had their fill of a generous supper, once again noting the while the corn was beautiful, it was paler and duller tasting than they were used to. Clemency even took some out to Saeli, who was still hiding in the wagon, but the little girl shook her head violently and refused all food.

After they had finished washing up they snuck Saeli and the keekee into the bunkhouse with them, hiding them in Clemency's pack, and settled down for the night. The bunks were comfortable and clean, and Ven fell into a deep sleep almost immediately.

His dreams were grand and warm. He was on the deck of the *Angelia*, the ship that his father had built and he had accidentally sunk trying to fend off a Fire Pirate attack. But now the ship was whole again, and all the crew alive and well. He sat on a barrel with them amidships and ate delicious apple fritters and sang thrilling sea chanteys until morning crept in at the window, spilling a beam of dusty light onto the floor.

He had finally gotten a good night's sleep.

It was the last he would have for a while.

‑ 15 ‑

The Hidden Valley

THE NEXT MORNING THE CHILDREN AND TUCK SAID A PLEASANT IF nervous farewell to Clovis, got back in the wagon, ready to continue northward toward the lands of the Nain.

"Are you certain you wouldn't like to stay and work?" Clovis asked, disappointed. "We have all the land west to the Great River, and a good deal of the Wide Meadows to the east. It's a pleasant life, it really is."

"Thank you, but no," said Clemency. "We really must be on our way, but we do appreciate your hospitality."

"Come back anytime," Clovis said as they got into the wagon.

"Excuse me—by any chance, have you heard anything about a dragon in these parts?" Ven asked as Tuck took his seat on the wagon board.

"Don't be ridiculous." Clovis said. "There are no dragons—it's just superstition."

"Well, thank you anyway."

Once they had departed, they slowed and consulted Saeli, who was pale and wan.

"Where to now?" Tuck asked Ven. "Shall we head for the foothills of the High Reaches?"

The companions nodded except for Saeli, who shook her head violently.

"What do you want to do instead, Saeli?" Ven asked gently. "I know you must be very upset, but Clovis didn't think there had been Gwadd around here for *years*. Are you certain this is the place your family came from?"

Saeli nodded grimly.

"The Wide Meadows might be an easy place to mistake," Char added. "How many miles of highgrass did we plow through that all looked the same? Maybe our compass is off, maybe we are just missin' it by a few miles."

The little girl shook her head.

"You might not know this, having lived your whole life on the sea, Char, but when you grow up in a place where your family farms, you never forget that land," Clemency said. "Especially the Gwadd. I came from a town near the source of the Great River, but my family got to know a lot of Gwadd as they portaged their grain, their fruits and vegetables downriver. They're the ones who taught me to speak to and see the Spice Folk, by the way. There is no mistaking it when they live in a place—they are a gentle people who love the land, and it shows. If Saeli says this is where her family once lived, I'm sure she's right."

"Then what should we do?" Ven asked sadly.

Saeli thought for a moment, then pointed to the ground. Tuck slowed the horses to a halt. The Gwadd girl got out of the back of the wagon, followed by the others. She stared at the highgrass, concentrating.

After a few moments, it seemed to Ven that the grass was

beginning to wither, or at least to shrink back into the earth. As Saeli continued to concentrate, he was certain of it.

A large, kidney-shaped area of the grass all but disappeared, leaving nothing but a barely green stain on the ground. Then, before their eyes, it began to reappear, but in various heights, showing hills and swales, hummocks and pits.

In the far west of the grass-map a wide swath of forget-me-nots swelled forth from the ground and burst into vibrant blue, painting a ribbon that ran north-south in tiny blossoms.

"What is that, Saeli?" Clemency asked.

Saeli continued to concentrate. "Great River," she whispered.

Ven looked to the west, then to the north, calibrating the boundaries.

"She's drawing a map," he said aloud, mostly to Amariel, Char and Ida. Tuck was already watching intently.

The areas that had appeared to be pits a moment before swelled with blue myrtle, taking on the resemblance of ponds. Ven looked east and saw one large one in the middle of a nearby meadow that closely matched its counterpart on the map. He kept watching, fascinated, as Saeli continued to call forth flowers and grasses in shades of blue, yellow, silver and green indicating copses of trees, wagon paths, and streams.

Finally, some tiny sprigs of heather emerged, tucked away beneath taller green grass that appeared to be a hillside. It looked like a soft purple shadow dotted here and there with tiny dabs of brightly colored wildflowers that Ven could not place a meaning to. He looked to the north, where a hill crested toward the morning sky, and saw that the topography looked exactly the same.

"Is that this hill?" he asked Saeli.

The Gwadd girl nodded excitedly.

Ven pointed to the purple shadow. "And what's this?"

Saeli stared north at the hillside.

"Hidden Valley," she whispered.

"There's a hidden valley in the lee of that hillside?" Tuck asked.

Saeli nodded again.

"Do you want to look for your family there?"

Yet another nod.

"It's on the way north to the foothills where the Nain settlements are," said Tuck. "We can head in that direction and see if we can find it."

The children piled back in the wagon as the highgrass grew rapidly again, blotting out any sign that the map had ever been there.

The journey now was less quiet, less reserved. Saeli seemed hopeful, almost happy, but Amariel was strangely silent. She sat in the back of the wagon and stared out behind her at the wake they were making in the highgrass.

By noon-meal they were in the shadow of the hillside, so they did not stop to eat, but passed apples and carrots around the wagon, sharing them with Tuck and the horses.

"So Ven, what's the chance that Clovis is right?" Char asked as they cleaned up the apple cores and carrot tops. "Maybe it *is* just superstition. Is it possible that the fires didn't come from a dragon at all, but from these bloody idiots burnin' the brush to clear out the farmland?"

"That's possible," Ven admitted. "I hope you're right. That might make the Nain problem a lot easier to solve for the king— too easy, I bet."

"Yeah, prolly," Char agreed.

Tuck cleared his throat. "I think we're at the edge of the purple shadow, are we not, Saeli?"

Ven turned to look at the Gwadd girl. Her tiny, heart-shaped face was shining, and the long, caramel-colored braid that hung down her back bobbed excitedly in agreement.

"Can we get there by wagon?"

Saeli shook her head.

Tuck sighed and let the horses bring the cart to a slow stop.

"All right, then," he said. "Anyone staying behind, or shall I shelter them?"

Ven looked around. The other children were shaking their heads, indicating they wanted to come, all except the merrow. She was staring placidly at the sky, as if she were thinking.

"Amariel? Are you coming?" he asked.

"I'd be happy to."

"Well, that's a change," sneered Ida. "You ain't been happy to do *anything* the entire time we've been away."

"Leave her alone," Ven said. He stood up and made his way to the back of the wagon, opened the gate, and held out his hand to the merrow. She allowed him to help her down from the wagon.

"Thank you," she said as she stepped into the grass.

"Whoa," said Char. "Are you sure she's all right, Ven?" Char had stopped trying to help her down even before they crossed the Great River, because Amariel had threatened to bite him.

Without thinking, Ven's hand went to his shirt pocket. He felt for and found the outlines of the Black Ivory sleeve and the jack-rule, heard the slight rustle of a handkerchief, then nodded, relieved.

"She's fine," he said, helping Saeli out of the wagon next. "Who else is coming?"

Clem, Char, and Ida climbed down. They followed Tuck and Saeli on an almost invisible path down the windward face of the hillside into its lee, the place where the wind did not touch.

The path Saeli was following switched back and forth in both east and west directions, crossing with other grassy paths that had Ven completely confused by the time they got to a fork in the pathway. He glanced down at Saeli and saw that the green-gold high grass had subtly changed color to a soft purple, due to the heather that was now mixed into it. *This must be the purple shadow she drew for us in flowers,* he realized.

Finally, Saeli stopped directly at a place in the hillside that was overgrown completely with ivy. She knocked in the air as if she were knocking on a door.

The ivy shriveled before their eyes, looking now like a hanging curtain.

Saeli drew the curtain back, smiling, and held it open for her friends to enter.

One by one, they stepped through. As he did, Ven caught his breath.

Below them stretched a beautiful, lush valley dotted with bright patches of wildflowers in every possible color. The air beyond the ivy curtain was sweet, as if it had rained recently, and the perfume of flowers hung heavy in it. Trees, both great and small, grew randomly throughout the rich green grasslands. A silver-blue river trickled through the valley, sparkling and laughing as it went.

A shaft of afternoon sunlight filtered down from above, giving the little valley a drowsy feel.

Ven's mouth was open. He shut it as soon as he realized it, but still the sense of awe he felt was overwhelming.

"What an amazing place," he murmured. "No wonder you were sad when you were afraid it had been taken over by the humans."

Saeli nodded, looking relieved.

"Where does your family live, Saeli?" Clemency asked. "Can we meet them?"

The Gwadd girl giggled, then nodded. She pointed at the clusters of bright wildflowers dotting the valley.

"There," she said huskily. She pulled the curtain of ivy closed behind them, and immediately it swelled with moisture again, taking on its former appearance.

She led them down a winding path lined with pink primroses to the valley floor where the bright patches grew. As they got closer, Ven could see they were little shelters made of willow boughs woven through with many different kinds of flowers and plants, with arched doorways and windows. Each window had a flower box beneath it filled with growing flowers or plants of the same varieties.

Beside many of the houses were smaller patches of the same kind of flowers. Once Saeli came into view, those patches peeled back, and small, heart-shaped faces appeared, smiling broadly.

"Look at all the *Gwadd*," Clem whispered excitedly to Ven, who nodded in agreement. "I've seen Saeli bring flowers around herself a few times when she's nervous—the others must have seen us coming and hidden in plain sight."

The way magic does, thought Ven. *I must draw this as best as I can for the king. He would love this place.*

He turned to the merrow, who was standing beside him.

"Sometimes when you talk about all the bright colors under the sea, the anemones and the coral reefs, I imagine something like this," he said. "Do those things look anything like this?"

"Not really," said the merrow placidly. "But this is pretty."

Ven's brows drew together. He patted his pocket again, but the rustle was still there.

"Are you feeling all right?" he asked, concerned.

"Of course," said the merrow. "Just fine."

Beyond the valley were rich green fields. Cows of all colors and sizes mooed pleasantly in the pastures as they grazed on the grass, the bells around their necks emitting a soft tinkling sound. Jagged rows of corn of every height swirled in random patterns, choking with what appeared to be weeds. Unlike the neatly manicured rows of pale yellow and brown back in the human farming settlement, however, the kernels that peeked through the silk at the top of the dark green leaves were golden and warm like the sun.

With a harsh cry, Saeli leapt forward and began running in the direction of a tiny shelter made of white dwarf birch twigs. From the fresh mound of white blossoms outside the shelter a tiny old woman emerged, bent over at the waist with age, but still rosy-cheeked and bright-eyed. Loose curls from her silver hair had escaped the bun in the back of her head, and she hurried toward Saeli, her arms open and her skirts flying. They embraced in joy, then Saeli waved the others to come over.

As they approached, she spoke in her odd, deep voice.

"Betula Nana!" she said happily, pointing to the old woman.

"That's her grandmother," Clem whispered.

"Does she have parents?" Ven asked.

Clemency shook her head. "But she does have a little brother."

She scanned the flower patches, then pointed to a towheaded youth with chubby cheeks and little waterfalls of hair hanging from every place on his head. "I think that's Cecil."

"Cecil?" Ida asked.

"Cecil Bean," Clem said.

"Poor kid," Ida said.

"Hey, at least he knows his real name," Char muttered. "Better than you or I could say, Ida."

"I've been told my real name's pretty at least," said the colorless girl, watching the Gwadd swarm around Saeli. "You're named after burned food. That's swell."

The little white-haired boy ran over to introduce himself.

"Hi," he said in his own version of Saeli's strange voice which was vaguely squeaky. "We're glad to meet you. Thank you for bringing Saeli home."

"It's our pleasure," Ven replied.

"Auntie Hepatica is going to make tea at her house," Cecil continued, pointing to a shelter decorated with gorgeous purple flowers unlike any others in the valley. "You are all invited to come."

Ven looked at Amariel, who generally disliked being around a lot of people.

"Is that all right?"

"Of course," the merrow replied.

Ven patted his pocket again.

"Then, yes," he said uncertainly to Cecil, who giggled and ran off after all the small people scurrying toward the purple shelter. He waited until Char, Clem, Ida, and Tuck had followed Cecil, then went over to Amariel and took her by the elbow.

"You're making me nervous," he said quietly. "Are you feeling all right?"

"Yes, fine," said the merrow.

Ven sighed. He wasn't certain what was going on, but he took Amariel by the arm to lead her toward Auntie Hepatica's house. When she didn't pull away, he grew even more worried, but had no idea what to make of it.

The tea in the house of the Gwadd was charming. The little people were hospitable even if they were shy, and offered plates piled high with ripe strawberries, sweet whipped cream, raspberry tarts and other summer fruits and vegetables that the companions agreed were the best things they had had to eat since leaving the Crossroads Inn.

"This is how milk should taste," Clem said, sipping a frothy glass. "I don't know how to explain the difference between this and what we had last night, but that just tasted wrong somehow."

"So did everything else," said Ida. "The corn, the cheese—it wasn't spoiled, I don't think. I dunno. It was weird."

Saeli was deep in conversation with her grandmother. The joy had left her eyes, and her face was sad again. When they paused, Ven interrupted gently.

"What is going on, Saeli?" he asked. "Why are the Gwadd all hidden away here, rather than in the lands where the humans live now?"

Saeli posed the question in the Gwadd language to her grandmother, who turned to Ven and smiled sadly.

"Once all of these lands were ours," she said. Her voice was rough and aged, but she sounded very much like Ven's own grandmother. *I guess everyone ends up sounding like a Gwadd eventually, he thought.* "We lived and farmed this part of the Wide Meadows from the First Age, when we came to this island, fleeing the floods that had destroyed our home across the sea. But lately the humans have come. I'm not sure they even knew we were here, because they do not tend the land as we do. They just moved in, and took over the place we had loved for centuries."

"Why didn't you fight for it?" asked Ida, amazed.

Betula Nana chuckled. "Spoken like a Big person," she said. "Look at us—with what would we fight, even if we knew how? No, we had no choice but to retreat here, to this secret place which has been our haven all our lives. The Big Ones have burned the high grass, have undone everything we have done, have only planted the Oldest Sister, not the other two—"

"Oldest sister?" Ven asked. His head was itching.

Betula Nana nodded. "The corn is planted first, followed by beans, then squash between the rows," she said, pointing at the fields beyond the valley. "They are called the Three Sisters. They sustain each other, the earth, and us. But the Big Ones do not know that. They do not care for the earth, and its children, properly."

"Is that why their food tastes strange?" Clemency asked.

Betula Nana shrugged. "I would imagine," she said in her croaking voice. "When we farmed that same land, it gave to us in the same way it now gives to us here. The Gwadd love the earth beyond measure."

In the corner of the little house, a tattoo on a tiny drum began to sound, followed a moment later by the sweet, high sound of a flute. One by one, the Gwadd gleefully gathered their strange-looking instruments and joined in, filling Auntie Hepatica's house with so much music that the party had to move outside. Soon the entire hidden valley was dancing, even the humans, Tuck, Ven, and the keekee.

All except the merrow. She had found herself a quiet spot under a magnolia tree and was sitting there, watching the merriment, her face serene.

The party grew larger and louder, past sunset and into the dusk hours, when stars began to appear in the darkening sky. A sliver of the waxing moon could be seen, hanging over the beautiful valley.

Truly this is what the king means when he says that magic hides in plain sight, Ven thought, watching the revels. The happier and merrier the crowd grew, the more the flowers and trees blossomed, bursting with color and succulent nectar.

Finally, as the evening wore into night, Tuck coughed politely between songs.

"I'm sorry, but we really do need to be moving on," he said. "The horses need to be watered, and we should be on our way."

The crowd of Gwadd made no sound, but the disappointment was so thick that Ven could feel it in the air. Beneath his feet, the wildflowers of the valley closed their petals and shrank back into the grass for the night.

He went over to Auntie Hepatica, Betula Nana, and Cecil to say goodbye.

"I hope we will get to see you again one day soon," he said sincerely. "This has been a lovely place to stop and rest on what has otherwise been a pretty trying journey."

"Come back anytime," said Betula Nana. "Any friend of Saeli's is welcome here, as long as the Gwadd live in the valley. Thank you for bringing her home."

"I hope the humans never find this place," said Ida.

"Thank you," said Auntie Hepatica. "So do we."

The companions each took a turn hugging Saeli goodbye, all except Ida, who coughed nervously.

"We'll miss you," Ven said, taking his turn last. "If it's ever safe again, we will come back for you."

Saeli smiled as Ven patted the keekee sitting on top of her head.

"Don't hurry," she said in her rough voice.

The children followed Tuck back up the switchback path, through the ivy curtain, and into the dull, dry fields again. The land beyond the curtain that had once seemed so lush and beautiful now was almost ugly to their sight.

Ven waited until the others had climbed into the wagon, then helped boost Amariel in without protest. He sat down beside her and put his hand on her forehead, as his mother had done to him when he felt sick as a child. It was cool and dry, without a hint of a fever.

"All right, what's going on?" he said quietly as the wagon began to rumble north toward the foothills of the High Reaches again. "You've not been yourself all day."

Amariel blinked. "Who have I been?"

"I don't know," Ven whispered, "but not a merrow, that's for certain." The second the words were out of his mouth, he regretted it. He looked over at the wagon board where Tuck was sitting, under his straw hat, driving the team, but the Lirin forester said nothing except for occasional clicks and encouragements to the horses.

He put his hand on his pocket and felt around. Everything seemed normal, but Amariel was acting so strangely that he decided to see if the cap had been damaged. When everyone else was asleep or not looking, he unbuttoned the pocket and took out the jack-rule first, then the Black Ivory sleeve, and finally the handkerchief that had contained the merrow's cap.

Which, to his horror, had mysteriously vanished, leaving in its place nothing but two empty handkerchiefs.

~ 16 ~

Things Get Uglier Still

WHEN HE RECOVERED HIS VOICE, VEN REACHED OVER TO WHERE Ida was snoring and shook her violently.

"All right, Ida," he said, trying to keep his voice under control. "Not funny. Where is it?"

Ida yawned, opening her mouth as wide as a horse's.

"What are you blathering about, Polywog?" she demanded sleepily.

"Where is Amariel's cap?"

"Hmmm?" Clem said, stirring. "Cap? What cap? What are you talking about?"

Ida stared at Ven. "I dunno." A crooked smile played at the corners of her mouth.

Ven's anger was rising faster than the smoke from the human settlement's fires. He had to struggle to keep from slapping her.

"Where is it?" he demanded again.

"I dunno," the Thief Queen's daughter repeated. "Not my turn to watch it. In fact, I don' think I've ever seen it."

Ven grabbed her knapsack and began to rifle through it, spilling its contents all over the floor of the wagon. Ida scrambled to her feet and grabbed for it back.

"Hey! What the heck do you think you're *doin'*?" she snarled. "Gimme my stuff!"

Ven's anger boiled over. He turned the pack upside down and dumped everything left in the bag onto the wagon floor. He was too livid to notice that Tuck had clicked at the horses to slow to a halt. Instead he was rooting through Ida's collection of knives and juggling balls, dirty underwear, and snacks stolen from the provisions. He kicked aside a small wooden-headed doll, sending it spinning into the side of the wagon.

Ida's shock melted into fury. With a howl of rage she threw herself at him and grabbed him around the neck. He was not prepared for her frontal assault, and she had both reach and leverage on him, so he fell over onto his back, helpless, while Ida banged his head repeatedly onto the wagon floor.

"Whoa! All right, now, stop that." Tuck vaulted off the wagon board and into the back of the wagon. He pushed aside Char and Clem, who were frozen in shock, dragged Ida off Ven and interposed himself between them, ignoring her struggle to resume her pounding of Ven's head. Tuck, however, had both reach and leverage on *her,* so she remained in the front corner of the wagon, spitting and scratching like a cat until she changed her mind and began brutally kicking a sack of rutabagas.

"What's all *this* about?" Tuck asked Ven, pulling him to his feet.

"She stole something *very* important," Ven puffed. "I need it back, and I need it back *now.*"

The Lirin forester turned to Ida. "Did you?"

The Thief Queen's daughter shrugged.

"See? I told you. Give it back, you rotten, no-good, miserable—"

"Stop that!" Char shouted. "You have no idea whether she stole the stupid cap, so stop insultin' her. What's the matter with you, Ven? It's like you're a different person these days. And whoever that guy is, he's someone I don' especially like."

There was something in Char's words, in the tone of his voice, that stopped me in my tracks. Char had absolutely never yelled at me before in anger, and it was so strange to hear him do it that all my fury melted and ran off me like sweat.

I stared at him in shock. Char was panting. Enraged as I had been, it was Char's voice that broke through the brick wall in my head and made me calm down.

At least a little.

Ven glanced over at Amariel. Throughout the ruckus she had remained calm, even when Ida was pounding his head into the floor. She had taken all the clothes out of her bundle, refolded them neatly, and was now packing them back up again.

"Did you take the cap?" Ven asked Ida, his voice calmer.

"Stuff it up your nose."

Ven turned to Char, who looked away, then Tuck, who was watching him intently. "She took Amariel's cap—or someone else did."

"Why don't we search the wagon?" Clemency suggested as Ida began picking up her undergarments and other possessions. "Maybe it fell off her head and got lost. What does it look like? I don't remember ever seeing her wearing a cap." She began helping Ida gather her belongings. When she came across the doll in the corner of the wagon, Ida snatched it away stuffed it back in her knapsack, glaring at Ven.

"Give it back," Ven said to Ida.

"Leave her alone," Clem commanded.

"Stay out of this, Clem, unless *you're* the one who stole it."

The curate-in-training's mouth dropped open.

"Out," said Char, pointing to the ground. "Now, Ven."

Ven stared at him, but upon seeing the determination in Char's eyes, he sighed, climbed out of the wagon and stepped away into the night.

The cook's mate was behind him a moment later. He pushed Ven ahead of him until they were out of earshot of the wagon.

"What in *blazes* do you think you're doin'?" he demanded. "I'm your best friend, and I barely recognize you, Ven. Somethin' about that girl is turnin' you into a complete *idiot*! What is it? Tell me, right now, or I'm gonna choke it out of you."

"I can't," Ven said, wishing he could keep silent.

"Like heck." Char ran a hand through his straight dark hair, now soaking with angry sweat. "You tell me what's she's doin' to you, or I'm gonna ask her. An' I'm not gonna be nice about it."

"No. Back off, Char, you—"

"Stow it, Polypheme." The cook's mate's voice rang with an authority that sounded like the Captain's. "We came out here, in the middle of utterly *nowhere*, for *you*—to help *you*. The bloody Thief Queen is looking for all of us, because of *you*. And don't go gettin' all guilty about it—that's what friends do for other friends. So the least you can do is tell us what's goin' on. What is it? Tell me. That's an order."

In spite of himself, Ven felt a small smile twitch the corners of his mouth. He looked back at the wagon, where everyone had sat back down again, then looked Char in the eye.

"All right," he said finally. "You're my best friend, and I owe you that much."

"Darn right," said Char flatly. "Tell me."

Ven breathed out all the breath from his lungs. The new air he took in was sharp with smoke.

"Amariel is not human," he said. "She's a merrow."

Char looked blank. "A what?"

Ven rolled his eyes. "Do you remember when we first met, after I was brought on board the *Serelinda*, half drowned?" Char nodded. "Think back. Do you remember how you told me you thought you saw a seal over the side?"

"Oh, *yeah*," Char said, scratching his chin. "An' you said you thought it wasn't a seal, it was a mermaid."

"A merrow," Ven corrected. "I told you I thought it was a merrow, because I had *seen* one. Remember?"

"Yeah, I guess so."

"Well, that was Amariel." Ven's face grew hot, telling the tale he had promised never to tell. "She's a merrow—you know, fish tail, scales up to her armpits—and she is the one who saved me from drowning when my father's ship and the Fire Pirates' vessel blew up."

"Man," Char whistled.

"That's why I told you she's the friend I've known the longest here, even longer than you," Ven went on. "Her father's a merrow, but her mother's a selkie, which is almost the same, but they have cloaks that make them look—"

"Like seals!" Char finished. "Blimey, I have heard about 'em from the sailors. But I thought it was just a lot o' superstitious hogwash."

Ven sighed. "Magic hides in plain sight, remember, Char? I learned that on my fiftieth birthday, and I've been seeing it ever since. She and I kept promising each other—well, inviting each other, I guess—to see each other's worlds since we met.

Finally she decided to take me up on my invitation and come with me."

"So how'd she grow legs?"

"A merrow can do that if she gives her red pearl cap to a human man," Ven said sadly. "It was probably a bad idea, but she wanted to come, and I wanted her to see our world—plus the Raven's Guild was searching the harbor, underwater, for us, so I was worried about what would happen to her if she didn't come with us when we left. The transformation from merrow to—well, whatever she is now—was really scary, and I almost put her cap on her head and tossed her back in the harbor right then. But she wanted to see the dry world, so I let her."

He began to pace back and forth in the dark. "And she made me swear I wouldn't tell anyone about her—she's desperately afraid of humans, because her mother has warned her all about you. Human men have a tendency to take advantage of a merrow's curiosity. Normally they're pretty spunky, but if the man takes and hides a merrow's cap, she becomes a perfect wife and kitchen slave, quiet, patient, obedient—it's sickening that anyone would do that to such an independent creature."

"So you're going to marry her, then?" Char asked.

Ven looked horrified. "Don't be ridiculous," he said. "I don't even know how old she is—neither does she, by our reckoning. And I'm only fifty years old, for goodness sake. Get back on target, Char. That's the story, and why I have to find that bloody cap."

"I'll help you," Char promised. "But Ven, you sure just made a horrible mess. This whole time you've been ignorin' everybody, favorin' Amariel—and all you had ta do was trust us with the secret. We would have understood."

"She wouldn't let me."

"I understand that. But we're your friends, too. Not just

everyday, ordinary friends, but the kind that risked *dyin'* for you. Several times over. You owe us, Ven. You owe us your trust, if nothin' else. And, in a way, by makin' you keep her secret, Amariel's stolen that from *us*. That might be why nobody likes her."

"And that's such a shame, because she's amazing," Ven said. "Just like all my friends are. Especially my best friend."

"Well, right now your best friend is pretty mad at you, mate," Char said. "An' I imagine it's gonna be a while before the others are gonna forgive you. So you should set about making amends pretty darn quick, before we run into the dragon and the girls toss you to him to give them time to get away."

"I would deserve it," Ven said. "Thanks for setting me straight."

"So you gonna explain about Amariel to Clem an' Ida?"

Ven shuddered. "Not yet." He withered at the look on Char's face. "I told you—give me some time with the others, please? It's not my secret to tell—or yours."

"Well, if you want their help in findin' her cap, you may have to do some things you don't wanna do."

"I know," Ven said. "Let's go back.

Inside the wagon, the silence was deafening. Ven cleared his throat and apologized, but no one responded. He asked again if anyone had seen the red pearl cap. but the girls were sitting with their backs to the middle of the wagon, looking out over the sides.

Away from him.

Ven sighed and sat down in the corner. "I'm sorry I accused you, Ida—" he began.

"Shut up, Polywog."

"Drop it, Ven," Clem said. "I'll try to talk to her later. Leave it alone for now."

"I'll search the wagon," Char said.

"Are you ready to go back there?" Tuck asked from the wagon board.

A quiet chorus of *yes, sure, yeah*, answered him.

Tuck picked up the reins and nickered to the horses.

"Good," he said. "Because the ravens are back, just beyond the horizon, and the fire I'm smelling is growing stronger. *And* it lies directly in the path of where we are going."

"*Fire?*" the companions asked in unison.

Tuck said nothing, but continued to drive. The team clopped along until the wagon reached the top of a high swale. The forester dragged the horses to a stop.

"Ven, you might want to look at this," he said.

Ven rose from the corner of the wagon bed and made his way past the others to the front. He looked over Tuck's shoulder and gasped.

The field below the top of the swale was scorched, smoldering still. A great rip in the earth lay open like a gaping wound.

And just beyond it, great letters as tall as the roof of the Crossroads Inn, were burned into the hillside.

SCARNAG.

"I guess he knows you're coming, Ven," said Tuck.

- 17 -

From Bad to Worse

VEN WAS DREAMING OF FIRE PIRATES CHASING HIM THROUGH THE hold of a dark ship when he felt his shoulder being shaken.

He opened his eyes. He could see nothing but inky blackness all around him.

They were sleeping in the open because the glade in which Tuck had sheltered the horses was too small for the rest of them. The crescent moon had set, taking any light with it. The stars that had been so bright the evening before had disappeared behind racing clouds. All he could feel was the breath of the wind, rustling the grass around his head.

It smelled like the burned porridge in the bottom of Char's cooking pot.

"Get up," Tuck said quietly. "It's time to go."

Ven sat straight up and looked around. He could see the shapes of his friends beginning to move as they, too, shook off sleep. He knew they could see even less than he could.

"What's burning?" he asked nervously.

Tuck's voice came from behind where he sat. Ven had not seen him move.

"Fields," the Lirin forester said. "The grasslands to the north of here, I'd wager. I'm surprised you're not used to the smell by now."

"Is it the dragon?"

Tuck came around in front of him and crouched down. "Maybe. If it is, this fire has caught and spread from a spark. But this itself is not from the beast. Can't miss the smell of dragon's breath."

"Wh—why?" Char stammered from the darkness next to Ven. "What does it smell like?"

The forester was helping Amariel to her feet. He turned and looked at Char for a moment, thinking.

"There's a dirt smell to it, like wet firecoals," he said at last. "But sharper, like acid or pitch has been poured into the smoke. Once you've smelled it, you never forget it. It haunts your dreams."

"Great," Ven muttered. "My dreams aren't haunted enough."

"Let's move out," Tuck said, hoisting his enormous pack onto his shoulder. "The night-hunting ravens sleep when the moon goes down. Those that hunt by day will be up with the sun again. We have to travel fast."

Ven slung his own pack onto his back, as did the others. They followed Tuck's dark outline over the fields, stepping through the highgrass that billowed like waves on the sea.

After what seemed like an eternity of wading through endless scrub, they came to the thicket where the horses stood, the wagon hidden among the trees. Tuck tossed his pack into the back of the wagon and helped the children in, then climbed up onto the seat board and took the reins.

"Go back to sleep," he said over his shoulder.

"Yeah, *that's* gonna happen," Char said under his breath.

"May as well rest while you can," Tuck replied. Char jumped. He had forgotten how sensitive the forester's ears were. "Not a good idea to deal with a dragon when you're tired. We're not far from some of the Nain settlements now."

"I, for one, don't think it will be hard to fall asleep at all," said Clem, shoving aside a sack of cornmeal and moving away from the water barrel, which had leaked a little and dampened the floor of the wagon. "I feel like I could sleep for days."

Not me, Ven thought. His scalp was on fire, his fingers tingling. It was all he could do to keep from peering over the edge of the wagon, but Tuck's warning was still ringing in his ears, drowning out his curiosity for the moment. *Stay down, children. It's best that anything passing by thinks you are cargo, nothing more.*

Surrounded by blackness, his mind was racing. He tried to think of home, of his family, of boring lessons in school, anything to get his thoughts to settle down and allow him to fall asleep again.

Inside his shirt pocket, the thin sleeve of Black Ivory vibrated slightly. Ven put his hand on top of it and was surprised that he could feel warmth, even through the fabric. There was a pleasant buzz in his skin, even through the smooth stone. Without thinking, he slid the tip of the dragon scale out of the protective sleeve and ran his finger over the edge.

The rim of the scale was so finely tattered that it felt as soft as flax, but I knew that if I pressed too hard it would slice through my skin to the bone. There was a hum that tickled my fingertip, a feeling of old magic that shot through me, all the way to the roots of my hair, to my toenails as well. Even the two whiskers on my chin vibrated.

In that magical buzz there was a sense of joy. That's really the only word I can think of to describe it. Just touching something so ancient, so magical, made me feel good all over.

Even in the scary darkness, even running from those who sought us by night and those that would return with day's light, I was excited.

At least I was until someone grabbed my throat.

All the breath choked out of Ven. His head spun woozily and he felt sick as he was hauled out of the wagon and up onto the board behind the horses.

Tuck's voice spoke quietly in his ear, its tone deadly.

"Put that bloody thing away, Ven. Do you *want* the dragon to find us?"

"N—no," Ven whispered.

Tuck's grip on his collar tightened. "Well, *I* can feel it when you pull it out of the Black Ivory—it vibrates so strongly that my teeth sting. So if *I* can feel it, don't you think a *dragon* can? Perhaps from miles away?"

"Sorry," Ven said. He pushed the scale back into its envelope, and the envelope back into his pocket. The vibration vanished, taking with it the joy that had been coursing through him a moment before.

Tuck shook his head in disgust and released his grip on Ven, who slid off the board and clattered back into the wagon. The eyes of the other children were wide, staring at him in the darkness, even Amariel, who smiled at him after a moment. Ven's face flushed hot in embarrassment, so he turned around and settled back down between two sacks of carrots, pretending to sleep.

Great, he thought. *I've just annoyed the king's forester, frightened my friends, and possibly alerted the dragon to our presence. I wonder if carrying around this dragon scale is making me more stupid than usual.*

He sighed miserably. Not since he had been floating on the wreckage of his father's ship after the Fire Pirate attack had he felt so vulnerable. The edges of the night seemed to be endless, especially when the moon was down. It was a little like being lost at sea, without the safety of the Crossroads Inn to return to. *What have I done, bringing my friends out here, with no settlements around for miles?* he thought. *If something happens to Tuck, how will we ever get home?*

He raised himself up a little and glanced back over his shoulder. The wind was growing stronger, battering the wagon and blowing the children's hair and the manes of the horses wildly about. Behind him Clem was shivering, even though the night was hot. The Mouse Lodge steward pulled her woolen cloak closer around her shoulders.

Just as she did, Ven caught sight of a tiny flicker of light in the fields behind her.

He sat up and peered over the side of the wagon behind the girls. The tiny light had vanished, but suddenly several more winked in the moving sea of highgrass.

Ven spun and looked out the side of the wagon next to him. At first he saw nothing but blackness, but after a moment the little lights appeared within the meadow grass there as well, a few at first, then several more, and finally dozens of them, only to disappear as quickly as they had come.

He reached over the sacks of carrots and grabbed Char by the sleeve.

"Look out there," he said, trying to keep his voice low. "What *is* that?"

The cook's mate scooted closer to the edge and peered through the slats in the wagon.

"What's what?"

"Those flickering lights—can't you see them?"

"Blimey, I dunno," Char whispered. "Hey, Clem, come 'ere, quick!"

The house steward raised her head sleepily. "Huumm?"

"Come an' look at this," Char insisted.

An annoyed snorting sound came up from the depths of the wagon. "All *right*, just a minute." The sacks of carrots wiggled as Clemency crawled over them, looking less than pleased. "What do you want *now*?"

"There's about a bajillion tiny flickering lights out there," Char whispered.

Clem looked over the side of the wagon and stared into the dark.

"Fireflies," she said. "Lightning bugs. You've never seen them before?"

"Never *heard* of 'em," Char replied as Ven shook his head. "*Lightning* bugs?"

"It certainly is obvious that you grew up on the sea, Char, and you in a city, Ven," Clem said. "Anyone who's ever been in the countryside knows about lightning bugs. You can see them all over the fields where I live, mostly in the summer."

A soft cough came from the board of the wagon.

"Those are not lightning bugs," Tuck said quietly. The children looked at each other. Again the king's forester had heard them over the rattling of the wagon, the clopping of the horses, and the howl of the wind, even though they had been whispering.

Ven raised himself onto his knees. "What are they, then, Tuck?"

The forester clicked reassuringly to the horses, who had begun to nicker nervously.

"They're the points of tracer arrows," he said.

Ven looked out over the side of the wagon again. For as far as he could see around him in the highgrass were thousands of twinkling lights, glittering like the stars above the sea at night. They winked in and out, not moving, hovering in the scrub. He turned to Clem and Char, whose faces were as white as the moon had been.

"Tracer arrows?" he repeated.

The Lirin forester nodded, urging the horses forward, though the wagon had slowed.

"Arrows whose points have been dipped in a kind of concoction that glows in the dark. They only glow when they are just about to be fired, sparked by being drawn across a bow string. Their radiance lasts long enough to leave a path of light for others to see, so that the target is easier to hit.

"And behind each one is an archer."

~ 18 ~

The Lirindarc

"Don't move," Tuck said quietly. "Or speak."

Slowly the Lirin forester stood up on the wagon board, allowing the wagon to roll to a smooth stop in the darkness.

He didn't have to remind us. I kept my head steady, but I could feel my eyes darting around in it like birds that had just taken flight. My companions were frozen as well. Char and Clem, who were sitting next to me, had backs as straight as broom handles.

The only one I couldn't see was Amariel, because she was asleep.

Tuck waited until the wagon had stopped completely, then spoke aloud in a language Ven didn't recognize. It was musical and pretty, but had a sharp edge to it, not the harsh sound of the language his family spoke in their home, but crisp and biting, like the sound of the wind. *The Lirin tongue*, he thought.

For a long moment there was nothing but silence.

Then, from somewhere amid the grassy sea of twinkling lights, a voice called back in the same language. It sounded like a question, but a threatening one.

"I am carrying children and foodstuffs, nothing more," Tuck replied in the common tongue. "The children are not Lirin, they do not understand our words."

A harsh command was shouted in reply. Then another, which seemed to be directed at the fields of grass around them. The sparkling lights winked out. *Whoever is in command must have told them to hold their fire*, Ven thought.

The dark sea of grass swayed, then parted. Shadows of human-like figures, tall and slender, appeared around the wagon. Ven could not make out their features in the moonless night. One of them stopped next to where the horses were hitched to the wagon.

He grasped the side of the wagon and shook it. The merrow sat upright and looked around, rubbing the sleep from her eyes.

"Stand up, all of you," came the voice from the figure, spoken in the common language with a thin accent. "I advise you to keep your hands still."

At first the children remained frozen in place. Then, slowly, Ven stood and nodded to the others.

"If these are Lirin, why are they bein' unfriendly to *Tuck*?" Char whispered in Ven's ear as he rose beside him. The king's forester turned quickly and shot the boys a stern warning glance. Even though they could not see his face in the absolute dark, there was no mistaking the meaning.

The dark figure slowly began to circle the wagon. As it came closer to him, Ven could see it was a man with what appeared to be dark hair bound neatly back, carrying a long slender bow.

He could see the whites of the man's eyes as they searched the front of the wagon. They came to rest on Amariel, who was still sitting, crouched behind some sacks of potatoes. The man stopped.

"Get up," he ordered.

The merrow looked at Ven. He nodded encouragingly. Slowly she obeyed, and rose unsteadily to her feet.

"Come here," the man said, indicating the side of the wagon.

The merrow shrank away.

"Come to the edge of the wagon," the man repeated.

Ven watched her nervously. He tried to smile to give her confidence, but the merrow did not seem comforted. Finally, she picked her way over the provisions and came to the side of the wagon.

The man stood and stared at her for a few moments. Then he turned away and continued making his rounds. Ven sighed in relief.

Until the man came to a sudden halt directly in front of him.

Ven shuddered. He wasn't certain why, but it seemed that the eyes were staring at him as if he were a monster in the dark.

"Nain!" the man shouted to the others in the wide, waving sea of highgrass.

Instantly the sparks of light flickered into life again.

"He is in my charge," Tuck began, but his words were drowned by the sound of dozens of arrows singing through the air and thudding into the wagon board on which the forester was standing.

"Silence!" commanded the shadowy figure, looking at Tuck. He turned again to Ven. "Come over here, Nain, and keep your hands where I can see them."

It never occurred to me that being Nain would put me, or my friends, in danger. Even when Tuck had left me out of the firefighting, no one else suffered because of what I was.

I had experienced a few times when people did not treat me well because of my race. And my older brothers and sister, Matilde, occasionally told me stories of what it was like before I was born, when the humans in Vaarn teased them or even avoided them because they were Nain. Most of that ended the day Luther, my third oldest brother, bit off the thumb of Jimbly Toddsworth and spat it into the bay. Toddsworth was an obnoxious human boy who was bothering Matilde every day on her way home from school, and Luther is big and not all that bright. So when Jimbly wouldn't stop, after repeated warnings from Petar and Osgood, Brothers One and Two, Brother Number Three reacted the only way he knew how.

I guess they are right when they say Number Three is the charm.

Anyway, after that, no one really bothered my family very much. By the time that I, Brother Number Twelve, the thirteenth child, came along, we had been treated normally for many years, so I never knew what racial prejudice felt like until I came to Serendair.

Now it seemed I was about to discover how bad it can really be.

The king had warned me that the Lirin and the Nain didn't get along too well. I guess I assumed that wouldn't apply to me. But now that I was standing in the dark in a wagon, surrounded by Lirin who seemed a little less than pleased to see me, I knew how foolish I was to assume anything like that.

If I survive, I will have to make a note to avoid that assumption in the future.

"Ven," Tuck said quietly, "don't you have something to say to these men?"

Ven swallowed hard. "I-I'm Nain, yes, but a peaceful one," he stammered. "I mean you no harm—"

His sentence was choked off as the dark shadow seized him and dragged him out of the wagon.

The world swam before his eyes as his head hit the side of the wagon. Ven could hear the gasping of his friends as he thudded to the ground. All the air was knocked from his lungs. He found himself momentarily staring at the dark clouds racing along the black sky above him, knowing that his head was about to ring with pain as the shock wore off. Just as it started to, he was flipped onto his face in the grassy earth, his hands tied quickly behind his back.

From what seemed like far away, he heard Tuck's voice calling urgently.

"Please! Let him speak! Ven, can you hear me?"

Ven's ears were barely working as he was dragged to his feet. He could tell that he was in the clutches of many men now, roughly tying him and beginning to stuff a gag into his mouth.

"Ven! What were you told to say?"

Over the pounding of his head, Ven struggled to make sense of the forester's words. He tried to concentrate, but his brain felt loose and wobbly. He tried to think back to the moment he had met Tuck, the beginning of what was turning out to be a nightmarish journey. *What was the king thinking, sending us out like this into the eastern lands?* he wondered, trying to hold onto consciousness. *Surely this is even worse than being chased by the spies of the Thief Queen.*

At the thought of the king, the memory came to him. He turned his head quickly away to avoid the gag.

"I-I am the herald—" he began.

His words disappeared as a heavy cloth was shoved roughly into his mouth.

"Let him speak!" he could hear Tuck insist as he began to black out again. He struggled to breathe as Tuck's words returned to the Lirin tongue.

A moment later, the gag was pulled from his mouth.

"Speak," growled the dark man.

Ven spat out a wad of spit, coughing, and drew a deep, ragged breath. His heart was beating hard in his chest.

"I am the herald of—His Majesty," he began, "Vandemere, high king of Serendair." The air in his lungs ran out, and he took another painful breath.

"Keep going," the forester said.

"And as such I—claim his—*protection*." Ven pushed out the last word before everything went dark around him. He was vaguely aware of the highgrass around his forehead as he fell forward on his knees.

He remained there, breathing shallowly and trying to regain full consciousness as the Lirin voices began talking again in their strange, musical language. It was the last thing he remembered before the darkness took over, and he fell into a dreamless sleep.

The next thing he knew, Tuck was shaking him gently by the shoulder. It seemed as if almost no time had passed.

"Is there more?" the Lirin forester asked quietly.

"Hmmm? What?"

"Did the king give you any instruction past claiming his protection?"

"Yes. Why? What's happening?"

"Don't try to move," Tuck said. "Lie still and listen." His

voice was soft. "We have come across a large patrol of Lirindarc soldiers, forest dwellers who do not often leave the woods. They are guarding the fields above the northernmost edge of the Enchanted Forest, a place they normally do not roam."

"Is that why they are so unfriendly? Because they are a different kind of Lirin than you are?"

"They are Lirindarc, but generally they get along well with Lirinved. I am not sure why they are so hostile. But I actually think they are more angry about your presence than mine. When the Lirin feel threatened, they are suspicious of all Nain, as the Nain are of Lirin."

Ven thought back to his father's shipbuilding shop in Vaarn, where he had occasionally waited on Lirin. *Best type of customers to have*, his father had once said of them. *Respectful, courteous, don't talk much, honest, always pay on time, and expect high-quality work. Welcome in our shop anytime*. He rubbed his eyes. *How different things are here from my home.*

"Why are they so angry and suspicious?" he asked.

"It's a question of broken trust. I can't speak for the Nain, obviously, but the Lirin dislike and distrust the Nain for breaking faith, for shattering the trust that was between them long ago. It means that Lirin born long after that breaking of faith still resent it, even though it occurred in another lifetime, and hate the Nain for it.

"Your claim of the king's protection is being checked out while we wait," Tuck continued. "A group of messengers have been sent out. I don't know to whom they have gone—probably a local commander or perhaps the forest warden inside the tree line. But whoever it is, I hope he or she believes you, because if not, we may be parting company here. It's their intent to imprison you as a Nain spy. If that happens, what do you want me to do with your friends?"

Ven shook his head, trying not to vomit.

"I don't have any idea," he said. "If they let you go, I guess you should take them back to the castle, all except Amariel. You've got to get her—well, if you take her to the Inn, Mrs. Snodgrass will know what to do with her." He fell silent, realizing that without the cap, Amariel would never be able to return to the sea.

Tuck nodded.

"I hope King Vandemere will be kind to the others," Ven whispered. "Maybe he can get Clem back home, and find Char a spot on a ship—"

"Do not get ahead of yourself," Tuck said. "Wait and see what the puzzle is before you try to solve it."

"Are the others all right?"

Tuck nodded again. "They are very nervous, but at least they're not fighting."

"That's good," Ven said, trying to remain calm. "All that fighting was my fault—Nain are good at causing conflict. Back in Vaarn, my brothers say good morning by kicking each other off the wharf."

Tuck smiled. "Try and stay quiet. We are still surrounded by as many archers as you have hairs on your head. There is nothing else to do but wait."

"Can I go back to the wagon?" Ven asked. "I want to make certain my friends are all right."

Tuck put the question to the all-but-invisible guards in their strange language, and received a reply a few moments later. The highgrass parted, and another shadowy guard appeared next to Ven.

"Keep your hands high in the air," Tuck advised. "Do not give them any reason to use their tracer arrows."

They don't seem to need much of a reason, Ven thought as he made his way through the grass and back to the wagon. *They shot the wagon board just because they heard a Nain was inside. I'd hate to think what they'd do if we gave them a* real *reason.*

He opened the gate in the back and climbed in.

"Shhh," he said as his companions flinched nervously. "It's just me."

"Is anybody aiming at you?" Ida asked. "If so, sit as far away from me as you can."

"Not that I know of," he replied. "But it's always possible."

"It's always possible with *you*, Ven," Clem said pointedly. "I'm trained to be a curate, for goodness sake. I'm supposed to be respectable. If my pastor knew how many times I've been under arrest or at the point of an arrow since I've known you, he would call me home in a heartbeat—or fire me."

"People certainly do seem to get set on fire a lot around here," Amariel said.

"Shut up," said Ida. "You should talk, with your ugly neckscars and your jagged teeth. You look like you barely survived a fire yourself."

"I didn't mean to be disrespectful," said the merrow. "I apologize." Ven shuddered at the softness of her voice, the lack of spirit in it.

From the darkness of his corner of the wagon, Char sighed.

"Stow it, all of you," he said. "What's goin' on *now*, Ven?"

"We're waiting to see whether they are going to arrest me as a spy or not."

"Oh joy," said Clemency. "And if they do, what's going to happen to *us*?"

Before Ven could answer, a shout went up from the wide grassy fields. The wagon lurched forward, causing the children to fall over like clothespins popping off a line that is snapped.

"I guess we're about to find out," said Char.

The wagon rumbled over the bumpy ground, slowly following the moving waves of highgrass. Ven could sense that the Lirindarc soldiers were closer around them now, even though he still could not see them in the moonless night.

The merrow looked over the side of the wagon, then up into the sky and shuddered.

"In the sea, we never travel when the moon is gone," she whispered to Ven. "It's like a shark traveling without a pilot fish—not a good idea. It's so easy to get lost when the world is so big, and so dark."

"Why are you two always whispering?" Clem demanded. "If you have something important to say, it might be nice to share it. And if it's not important, it's probably not worth risking us getting shot."

As if to punctuate this point, the fields to both sides of the wagon lit up with streamers of fiery light. A volley of arrows thudded into the long sides of the wagon, causing the children to jump, then settle into anxious silence.

The anxious silence became anxious sleep as the wagon traveled on. Ven rested his aching head on one of the horse blankets, trying to blot out the nightmares of what was waiting for him at the end of the ride. He woke and fell asleep again time after time, each new dream bringing even worse horror with it. By the time the wagon rolled to a stop, he was totally frightened and not at all rested.

He sat up as the wagon stopped.

The night was gone. He knew that even before he looked into

the gray sky from the sound of the birdsong in the moist feel of morning dew in the air. The grass smelled sweeter than it had the night before. His friends were stretching and waking nervously.

Clemency was the first to look over the side of the wagon.

"Oh dear," she whispered. "Well, Ven, it's been good to know you."

~ 19 ~

Alvarran the Intolerant

Ven RAISED HIMSELF UP ON ONE KNEE SO HE COULD SEE OVER Amariel's head.

Now that dawn had broken, he could see the vast expanse of the Wide Meadows all the way to the horizon. Rolling hills of green-gold highgrass stretched until they met the lightening sky, fringed with occasional stands of trees to the north. To the south he could see the northernmost tip of the Enchanted Forest in the distance, its immense trees dark green and vibrant, like living mountains.

Between the wagon and the forest stood a massive army. Now that the sun had risen, the Lirindarc were visible. They stood in loose rows by the thousands, many more than Ven could count, fanning out in an ever-widening triangle that reached as far as he could see. The Lirindarc were tall, slender people, men and women alike, with broad shoulders and lean, muscular arms and legs. Their skin was brown from the sun, and their hair, eyes and clothing all blended in with the color of the grass.

And every one of them was armed.

"Criminey," Char whispered behind him.

Standing at the point of the triangle was an honor guard of soldiers. A semicircle of eight archers had their arrows trained on the wagon, while two more with wicked-looking spears stood on either side of a solitary man.

He was unarmed.

He wore on his head a wooden crown in the middle of which a golden leaf was carved.

The man stood straight as an arrow himself. His dark hair was long and striped with gray, framing a face that did not have even a hint of a smile. His eyes were also dark, and he stared directly at the children as if he were looking into their souls. His clothing, while regal, was also simple, made for wearing in all kinds of weather. In his hand was a long, twisted staff made of polished wood, on top of which was a golden leaf like that in his crown.

"Any idea who that might be?" Clemency asked.

"If I had to guess, I would say that's Alvarran the Intolerant," said Ven.

"Who?" demanded Ida.

"The king of the forest Lirin."

Tuck nodded. "Aye."

"We're in trouble," said Char.

As if to prove his point, the Lirin king banged his staff on the ground.

In response, the front rows of archers pointed their arrows at the wagon as well.

Alvarran cleared his throat. Even from the long distance away, the children could hear the rumble.

"You are wasting my time," he

said in a voice that sounded like thunder. As if in reply, the wind picked up, making the highgrass bow down respectfully before him. "Get out of that wagon and get over here."

Ven hurried to the back of the wagon and opened the gate. He vaulted down onto the grass, as the arrow sights followed him, and held out his hand to Amariel.

"Come on," he urged the others. "No point in making him grumpy."

"I'm guessing we're a little late for that," Clem said in a low voice. She waited until Ven had helped Amariel out of the wagon, then climbed down and offered her own hand to Ida, who refused it. Char jumped down after her. Tuck climbed down from the wagon board and followed them.

They hurried through the billowing grass until they were in easy sight of the Lirin king. They continued approaching until Alvarran banged his staff on the ground again. The vibration brought them to a halt.

The Lirin king stared at them for a long time. The only sound in their ears was the gusting of the wind around them.

"King Vandemere must have lost his mind," Alvarran said finally, disdain dripping in his voice. "What would possess him to send a Nain messenger to me—a Nain brat, no less? It is a sure sign of his youth and inexperience. How regrettable. Does he not know what a grave insult this is?"

I opened my mouth to speak, but no words came out.

When King Vandemere mentioned the task he wanted to accomplish—the puzzle of figuring out why a dragon was attacking Nain settlements, discovering what would make it stop and telling the Nain in return to give back what the Lirin wanted, which in turn would make the Lirin give him what he wanted—I was certain that he was only trying to help the kingdoms over which he was the high ruler get past their grudges. Now, however, it seemed as if his attempt to make peace by sending me there was something that could in fact lead to an even more unpleasant situation.

I wanted to explain that. I wanted to try to fix the situation, to be a good ambassador for the king.

But the look on the face of the man who had the words "the Intolerant" as part of his name was so terrifying that all I could do was stare at him.

That probably wasn't helping the situation very much at all.

"I'm sure he didn't mean it that way, sire," Ven said when he could finally speak.

"Is that so?" demanded Alvarran. "Then perhaps I should explain this to you, Nain child. Had you been an adult, coming to the borders of my lands at a time when your people are preparing to invade, you surely would have been put to death before you could deliver *any* sort of message. But rather than that happening as it should, because of your age it is necessary for me to hear you out before I kill you, rather than be seen as unfair. I have a long enough name as it has. I have no desire to be called 'Alvarran the Intolerant *and* the Unfair.'

"So what do you want? Or, more correctly, what does King Vandemere want? Speak, so that my archers can do their job, and I can return to my breakfast."

"Er—" Ven began. Suddenly his stomach flipped as beads of sweat popped out on his forehead. He could hear the sound of thousands of bowstrings being drawn just a little tighter. Whatever he was about to say disappeared from his brain as the curiosity that had been brewing there turned to terror.

Tuck cleared his throat.

Ven glanced over at the Lirin forester. His face with solemn, but his green eyes were twinkling. He nodded slightly, a gesture of encouragement. And as he did, Ven remembered what the king had told him to say.

He cleared his own throat and took in a deep breath through his nose.

"King Vandemere states that if you will send him the greatest treasure in your kingdom, he will swear fealty to you and ever after will call you 'sire'—er, sire."

The king of the Lirin stared at him even more intensely.

"Really?" His voice was low and deadly. "I cannot imagine what would possibly entice me to grant such a request."

"Perhaps if I can return to you whatever the Nain have that you want back, you would be willing to consider it."

Alvarran's eyes opened wide and his nostrils flared.

"You know of the Theft, then?"

Ven could feel his friends behind him beginning to twitch nervously.

"I know nothing of a theft, Your Majesty," he said quickly. "I'm not from this land—I came to Serendair only recently. But I'm on my way north to see if I can discover why a dragon is burning the Nain settlements in the foothills of the High Reaches. If I can discover that answer, perhaps I can persuade the Nain to give you back what you want returned. And if I can arrange that, it is my hope that you will give to King Vandemere what he asks for."

The Lirin king put a hand to his chin and rubbed thoughtfully. "Hmmm," he said. "That's an interesting proposition, Nain child. There is but one problem I see with it."

"What's that, Your Majesty?" Ven asked.

The king's eyes went black with anger.

"There *is* no dragon burning the Nain settlements," he spat. "It's all a lie, to mask their planned attack on my kingdom. I have seen the flames, I have smelt the smoke—it's not dragon's breath, but rather plain, ordinary fire, a tool they've used before to conquer Lirin lands. The Nain are liars, thieves. They hide behind such tales to spread panic, particularly west of here, where innocent folk like the Gwadd make their homes. By the time the deception is discovered, it is too late. But unlike the Nain, the Lirin remember their history. I will not be fooled by such a tactic twice. So Vandemere has sent you on a fool's errand, Nain child."

Tuck bowed. "If that be so, then, Your Majesty, what harm is there in agreeing to allow him to try?"

For the first time the Lirin king looked at the forester. His eyes narrowed. When he spoke, his voice was low and calm, but with an undertone of threat.

"Tell me, what would cause a Lirinved forester to throw in his lot with a Nain child, risking the ire of his brothers, and their king?"

"The forester's loyalty to those brothers, and their king," Tuck replied, "but mostly to the High King over us all. King Vandemere asked me to serve as guide to these children. It was my honor to agree, and to obey. If you do not wish to accept the Nain child's offer, then I ask you and your soldiers to stand aside and let us pass in peace, so that we may fulfill our quest. If, however, you wish him to try and return to you what you have lost—"

"What the Nain *took*," Alvarran interrupted angrily. "It was a *Theft*. The Nain broke trust long ago. Once we were allies, now we are enemies."

"Even so, your grudge is not against *this* Nain, *this* child," said Tuck. "Perhaps he will be able to make amends for *his* brothers. Now, sire, what say you?"

Alvarran glared at Tuck, then turned his gaze on Ven. He glanced at the other children, then returned to the young messenger standing before him.

"Very well," he said at last. "Leave this place immediately. My soldiers will escort you north to the borderlands, even though you will not see them do so. Take heed, and pass carefully. If you do indeed return to me that which the Nain stole from our lands long ago, I will consider King Vandemere's request."

Ven coughed. "Only consider it, Your Majesty? Not just, uh, grant it?"

Alvarran the Intolerant's nostrils flared.

"It is not a request I have the power to grant on my own," he said. "But I will *consider* it. That offer alone is worth far more than you know, far more than you can even understand. Now get out of my lands and away from my forest before I change my mind."

"Thank you," Ven said quickly. He turned and nodded to his companions, who darted for the wagon as fast as they could before the grumpy king could change his mind.

They ran all the way to the back gate. Char leapt in first, followed by Clem. Ida vaulted into the wagon bed, and scooted away quickly to keep from having to help Amariel up. Ven gave the merrow a boost, then climbed aboard himself. He settled down with the others among the remaining provisions as Tuck clicked to the horses and the wagon began to roll northward.

When he was sure they were on their way, and no fiery arrows were screaming toward the wagon, Ven glanced back over his shoulder.

The king and his army were gone.

All he could see was the beautiful green forest in the distance to the south.

And an ocean of billowing highgrass that stretched all the way to the horizon.

Nothing more.

I could not imagine it was possible that an army of thousands of soldiers could disappear on the wind in the twinkling of an eye. They were too far from the forest to have taken shelter there so quickly, so I assumed they had returned to hiding in the grass, something they did as easily as we breathed the air.

I glanced over at Amariel. My eyes fell on the scars on her neck, where her gills had once been. As if she could read my thoughts, she immediately covered them with her hands in embarrassment. I looked away, but thought about how breathing the air is something we dry-worlders take for granted. It was good to remember that there are others who live among us that find it harder to do.

Seeing Amariel begin to fade into human-dom was beginning to eat my soul.

I only had one option if we could not find her cap.

It was an option I had been warned to only use if I was willing to accept terrible consequences.

Ven turned to the others in the wagon.

"Look," he said, "I know I've been a fool and a bad friend to you. I know you are suffering because of things I've done, and I'm sorry. But I really, really need to find Amariel's cap. Would you please look through your knapsacks, and help me search the wagon again? Because if it doesn't turn up—well, things might get even worse."

He looked down at the picture of the hourglass and the scissors in his palm.

A lot *worse*, he thought. *Because you never know what might happen when you alter Time to try and undo something you've done in the past.*

- 20 -

Smoke in the Foothills

O NCE AWAY FROM THE FOREST'S EDGE AND BACK INTO THE WIDE Meadows heading north, Ven settled down to sleep.

At first he slept dreamlessly and badly, rocking back and forth in the wagon as it made it way out of the smooth, grassy land of the Wide Meadows and into the more stony ground of the foothills of the High Reaches. What had once been a pleasant rocking motion was now threatening to make him more sick than he had ever been on the sea, so Ven took to counting stars on his back again, the only position in which he did not feel like he was going to throw up.

When finally he slept deeply, his haunted dreams returned. In each one of them, Amariel's cap had been stolen, but each time it was by someone else. His mind flipped through hazy images of it being taken by the River King, by Mrs. Snodgrass, by Cadwalder and Nick back home in the Inn. He dreamt it had been stolen by Tuck, by Alvarran, by a dragon he had never met. By the time each dream ended, he was more exhausted than he had been when he went to sleep.

I wish I had never looked through that stupid telescope in the River

King's palace, he thought. *It's made my dreams worse than they ever were.*

Each time he woke, he checked on Amariel. Each time he checked, she seemed more distant, more unlike herself. Her eyes had taken on a dull, lifeless sheen, just like the eyes of the fish in the monger's cart, staring up glassily into the sun. Char and Clem had looked in every knapsack, every food sack and water barrel, had scoured the floor of the wagon, had even checked the wagon bed from underneath, but there was no sign of Amariel's cap. She was slipping away before his eyes, and Ven despaired, knowing that his chances of ever finding her cap again were smaller than one of Saeli's fingernails.

I only have until the moon wanes, Ven thought. *I can't let a whole turn of it go by, or she will be human forever.*

Eventually he became so upset he could barely speak. Char and Clem tried at first to keep up pleasant conversation, but with Amariel becoming more reserved and Ven more depressed, they eventually fell silent. Ida, who had never been much for conversation anyway, just watched as she always did. Often they passed an entire day without speaking much more than a few words to each other.

When morning came each day, Tuck put them through their tasks and chores, but still the silence remained. Each day the smell of acidic smoke that the forester had smelled in the distance before their capture grew stronger, until it filled Ven's nostrils, making his stomach turn even more. He thought back to Tuck's words, and his own in reply.

Can't miss the smell of dragon's breath. There's a dirt smell to it, like wet firecoals, but sharper, like acid or pitch has been poured into the smoke. Once you've smelled it, you never forget it. It haunts your dreams.

Though no giant letters were burned into the earth, he was now certain of what he was smelling.

Finally, when the moon was waxing fat again on its way to being full, they came to the smoldering wreckage of what had once apparently been a settlement of Nain. Ven could tell immediately by the height of the blackened doorways, the width of the broken chairs lying about, and the style of wall with bolt-nocks for crossbow bolts that it had at one time served Nain soldiers. The excitement he had felt about meeting others of his race when they first crossed the Great River was gone, replaced by dread.

And, still, curiosity.

He was not eager to see new instances of hidden magic, however. Now his mind burned to solve the puzzle the human king had posed for him, in which every kingdom and every beast got what it wanted, restoring the trust that Tuck said had long ago been broken. It was a challenge that kept his mind buzzing, even on the edge of sleep. But as each day came and went he did not grow any closer to an answer.

They were still almost a league away from the smoldering settlement when a shout went up from the foothills, followed by a volley of crossbow bolts.

"Oh goody, *this* again," said Clemency sourly as she settled down on the wagon floor. "I am so sick of being used for target practice."

Ven's reply was cut short by a terrible jerk of the wagon, followed by a horrible gasp, as Tuck lurched backwards, grabbed his shoulder, and fell off the wagon board. The horses barely missed running over his head with their hooves and the wagon's wheels.

Ven was on his feet in an instant. He looked around in the dark, something as a Nain he had always been good at.

In a line all along the front of the burned-out settlement, as well as in the boulders and rocky ledge above it, were Nain of every shape and size. All of them had beards of Thicket length or longer, meaning they were men, not boys.

And all of them were armed with crossbows pointed at the wagon.

He reached into his memory for the words in the Nain tongue that was spoken in his parents' home.

"Friends!" he shouted. "We are friends, not foes! Hold your fire!"

The wide, bearded figures on the battlements froze, then looked at each other.

Then they broke out in raucous laughter.

"Playmates?" a voice shouted back in the common tongue. "We are playmates, not warts! Hang on to your burning butt!"

Ven felt sheepish. "Is that what I said?" he asked, also in the common language.

"Yep, that's about it."

I was worried that might happen, Ven thought miserably. *Oh well. Maybe the laughter will keep them from shooting again.*

"The man on the ground is not an enemy," he called into the darkness at the figures around the smoldering wreckage.

The voice that called back was harsh and threatening.

"We disagree. He is Lirin, and the Lirin are most definitely our enemies. As are those who travel with them."

The sound of crossbows reloading echoed through the night.

"I am Nain," Ven called back quickly. "My name is Ven Polypheme, son of Pepin Polypheme of Vaarn. I am here on the orders of His Majesty, King Vandemere, as his herald." He thought about the rest of the quote the king had made him memorize. "And as such I claim his protection."

The broad-shouldered men looked at each other again in the

dark. Finally one very large, very long-bearded Nain stepped off the battlement above the outpost and walked forward until he was about a hundred forearm's lengths in front of the wagon.

"If anyone fires at me, my men will shoot the driver again," he said. "And then each of you until the wagon is empty."

"We wouldn't dream of it," Ven replied nervously.

"Not the horses, however."

"Good," Ven said.

"So what do you want, Ven Polypheme, if that's really your name?" the Nain leader asked. "These are bad times to be wandering around the foothills of our kingdom with a Lirin driver. You're lucky you know a little of the tongue—very little, and very bad grammar, of course—or you would have been shot next after the Lirin spy."

"I've come to try to figure out what is burning your settlements, and why," Ven replied.

An explosion of bitter laughter rose up behind the leader.

"Toss me a torch," the leader called to the men behind him. One of them ran closer and handed him a burning stalk of wheygrass, which he held aloft to light his way.

The man stepped closer. Ven could see he was dark of beard and eye, with a pleasant face by Nain standards. His eyes glittered in the torchlight.

"I am Garson," he said, bowing slightly. "I could have saved you a very long journey, Ven Polypheme, if you really did come all the way from King Vandemere. What is attacking our settlements is a dragon. We know this. Thank you for your interest. Now we will take your Lirin spy and attend to him before he bleeds to death."

"He is no spy," Ven insisted as soldiers from the burned outpost came forward to where Tuck was lying, prone, on the rocky ground. "He is a forester, a good friend of the king—and you shot him without reason."

Behind Garson, a multitude of crossbows were cocked. The sound echoed off the foothills and into the mountains.

Garson smiled.

"What you consider 'without reason' and what I consider 'without reason' are two different things, apparently, Ven Polypheme," he said. "Why would the king send such a youthful lad to me? Faith, boy, your Bramble hasn't even begun to grow in yet. How old are you? Twenty-five? Thirty?"

"Fifty," Ven replied, stung. "But let's get back to the case at hand. You say your settlements are being attacked by a dragon."

"Yes."

"And the attacks are becoming worse, and more frequent?"

"That is also true."

Ven felt a surge of bravery rush through him. "Then I have come to you with good reason, at least," he said. "I will seek out the dragon, and try to discover what it wants, and why it is attacking you."

"Why?"

Ven blinked. "So we can get it to stop,"

The Nain behind Garson laughed again.

"Nothing can make a dragon stop once it gets the idea in its head, lad," said the Nain leader almost kindly. "It has developed a grudge against us, just as the Lirin did, and similarly for no reason. No, this dragon will continue to attack us until we are all dead, or driven back completely within our mountain home. There is no other recourse."

"What if there were?"

"There is *not*," said Garson. "We know this dragon better than you, boy. We know its name, and what it is capable of. It's a vicious killer named Scarnag—does your limited vocabulary in your native tongue allow you to translate that?"

"Yes," Ven said. "It means 'scourge.' It has already told me its name—it burned the word into a hillside south of here."

"And do you know what a scourge is?"

"A cause of terrible tragedy and suffering?"

"That would be right. And I can assure you that the beast is aptly named. This monster has been around for centuries, and committed horrible, unspeakable acts of terror and destruction. It stole our history. Worst of all, lad, proof that the beast has no soul, no heart, is that he violated the unbreakable rule of his own kind."

"Which is?"

"He killed another dragon," Garson said. Behind him the archers shifted from foot to foot, their breathing labored with sadness. "No true dragon will kill another of its kind, not even the most selfish, evil one ever spawned. There are so very few of them in the world, Ven Polypheme, and they swear a sacred oath at birth to guard the very world itself. Each time that a dragon dies, the world is more vulnerable to the evil that dwells deep within it. Dragons are the shield between us and that evil—and each loss leaves a hole. Dragons, no matter how petty or vicious their argument, would never ever consider taking the life of another of its kind—all dragons, that is, but one."

"Scarnag?"

"That would be the one."

From behind Garson, Ven could hear the sound of agony as the soldiers dropped Tuck on the ground.

"Will you tell me the story?" Ven asked. "Of the dragon he killed? And why?"

"No one knows why," said Garson bitterly.

"Well, Scarnag does," said Ven.

Garson was shaking with anger. "There could never be a reason—at least a good reason—why. The dragon he killed was only a wyrmling—a *child*, boy—young and innocent and brilliant. The wyrmling's name was Ganrax—a word that means *wisdom*—and he was not only a wise, gentle, intelligent child, he was the hope for our future, and our past. That dragonling would never have hurt a fly—all he ever wanted to do was to read, to play hide and seek, and eat kiran berries, his favorite treat. Scarnag killed him, as best as we can tell, for his *cave*—a cave, nothing more, something that there are thousands of in every range of mountains on this island.

"So now you know our situation. Whatever it was that caused us to earn the dragon's anger, we will not be able to stand against it. We are pulling our outposts now, preparing to go back within our mountains, cutting off ties with all other nations beneath King Vandemere's scepter. We will retreat into our own world, boy—and one day soon, you should probably decide to come with us. For if it's Nain the dragon is after, he will hunt you down until some cold and moonless night he will find you. Your youth will not save you as he tears you limb from limb and swallows your head whole. Your smartest choices are to come within the mountain with us—or run. Catch a ship, if you have the stomach for it. Polyphemes are shipbuilders, if I remember correctly, so you may be able to handle the voyage. But they are also descended of a madman, if I also remember correctly, so if my advice falls on deaf ears, at least it is a tradition in your family. For whatever that's worth. Now, be on your way."

"Not without my friend," Ven said. "He's of no use to you."

"He is if he is a spy," Garson retorted. "Keeping him here as a hostage prevents the Lirin from finding the routes into our mountains, should they desire to attack us. Save your breath. You're not getting him back—even if he does live."

"Oh, for goodness' sake!" Ven shouted, exasperated. "The Lirin blame all their problems on you. You blame all your problems on the Lirin. You both think the other is going to attack, when neither of you have any interest in doing so. Let me propose a deal."

Garson folded his hands patiently, but his eyes were dark and piercing.

"Propose."

"If I can discover why the dragon is really attacking your settlements, you will give me back my friend," Ven said. "And if I can determine how to keep the dragon from attacking you ever again, you will return to the Lirin what you have of theirs. Is it a deal?"

Garson wheeled back as if struck across the face.

"You disrespectful whelp," he said through his teeth. "What we have does not belong to the Lirin in any way—it belongs to *us*. Or, more correctly, to itself. It is a dragon's egg—and we *found* it, we did not steal it, in spite of their accusations of theft. We have it in the warmest, safest place on this island—the proof being that we have had it for centuries, and neither Scarnag nor the Lirin have ever found it. It is our hope to hatch it, and rear it with great love and gentleness, but to also train it to defend our kingdom. In this way, we hope to ease a small bit of the agony we feel for the loss of Ganrax, who was so young and special.

"So, no—I will promise you nothing about the egg, as if I would even believe such a prevention was possible. But I am a fair man. If you can discover the reason the dragon has a vendetta against the Nain, I will allow you to ransom back your friend. Agreed?"

"Agreed," said Ven. Unlike Alvarran, who was of an unfamiliar culture, he knew Garson would expect a handshake, as any Nain would. So he held his hands up in the air and climbed down from the wagon, then offered his hand.

"You are very grown up for a beardless Nain," Garson said as he shook it. "It's unfortunate that you are choosing to throw your life away and die young, much the way Ganrax did. In his case, however, it wasn't his fault. In yours, it is. Make certain you write to your family before you approach the dragon's lair. They should get to hear from you one last time—unless your letter burns when you do."

"Do you know how to get to the lair, and where it is?"

Garson smiled. "I do—we all do, because the beast now occupies the magnificent fortress that was built for the little wyrmling Ganrax by Nain long ago. I will draw a map for you, but the easiest way to find it is to follow the sun west and follow the wind south. If you do that, you will come upon a lake so clear that you can see all the way to the bottom. At Crystal Lake, follow the stream that flows southwest, and you will eventually find a large, circular mound coiled like a great serpent. That is the dragon's lair. It's a magnificent structure, which is nice, as it is the last thing you will ever see."

"Thank you for the directions," Ven said. "Take good care of my friend. I will be back for him shortly. And then, depending on what I find, I will propose my offer to you again."

Garson laughed aloud. "Well, if I had to waste a bolt on a Lirin spy, at least it was worth it to have gotten to spar with you, Ven Polypheme. I wish you were going to live longer—you would be fun to talk to. Good luck—I hope it's as painless a death as possible. But I doubt it will be."

Ven bowed and returned to the wagon.

"Clem," he said, "you drive. You're the tallest."

Clem nodded silently and climbed onto Tuck's seat on the wagon board.

Ven climbed into the back.

"All right," he said to Char. "On to the last piece of the puzzle—and the only one from which we may not recover."

- 21 -

A Decision for the Ages

THEY TRAVELED IN SILENCE, JUST AS THEY HAD SINCE THE BIG fight over the cap.

Ven tried hard not to think about the merrow. She had become pleasant, never spitting, glaring or even disagreeing with anyone anymore. The picture in his hand itched, reminding him that unless by some miracle her cap could be found, he only had one option left for her.

One night he ran his hand through his pocket again, as he had done a million times before, just in case he had missed it. It was not there, of course, but instead his hand brushed the jack-rule. Having nothing better to do, and being afraid of the dreams that would come with sleep, Ven took the tool out of his pocket and examined it idly.

The fact that this tool had been the pride and joy of both his father, Pepin, and his great-grandfather, Magnus the Mad, had made it a favorite of Ven's, too. He had received it from Pepin on his fiftieth birthday, the last time he had seen anyone in his family. He was only about twelve in human years, but he felt much older.

He ran his fingers over the beautiful folding ruler, admiring its tiny hinges and the tools hidden within it. There was something soothing about it, a vibration that reminded him of his family, and of home.

Homesickness started to overwhelm him, so he quickly put the jack-rule back in his pocket.

As he did, his fingers brushed the smooth envelope of Black Ivory that had been next to it.

Carefully Ven withdrew the envelope and ran his fingertip over the sharp edge of the dragon scale card that stuck out of the top. He had not taken it out or even looked at it since the night Tuck had become so angry at him.

Put that bloody thing away, Ven. Do you want the dragon to find us?
N—no.

Well, I can feel it when you pull it out of the Black Ivory—it vibrates so strongly that my teeth sting. So if I can feel it, don't you think a dragon can? Perhaps from miles away.

Interesting, Ven thought now as he examined the Black Ivory sleeve. *Here we are, so close to the dragon's lair—maybe this will come in useful after all.*

He shook Char awake, then the others. The girls rubbed their eyes in confusion, wondering why the sky was still dark.

"I have a thought," he said to them.

Ida rolled over, preparing to go back to sleep. "Don't worry— it will die of loneliness in a minute or two. Good night."

Ven nudged her with his toe.

"Wake up, Ida," he said quietly. "I have something important to tell you—all of you."

"What is it?" Char asked drowsily.

Ven held up the sleeve.

"This is a wallet of sorts, given to me by Madame Sharra just before we left on this journey," he said. The other children blinked, and Ven felt a sudden rush of pleasure and relief at finally being able to spill the secrets he had carried so long. "It's made of a substance called Black Ivory, which is basically stone that is completely dead. Anything housed within Black Ivory is almost impossible to detect, even by someone who is very good at reading vibrations on the wind."

"Like a dragon?" Clem asked, staring at the sleeve.

"Yes. As interesting as that is, what's inside the sleeve is even more interesting—it's one of the cards she uses to tell fortunes in the Thieves' Market."

"You're kidding," said Clem, now fully awake.

"I'm not. She appeared to me in Kingston and tried to read my fortune, because she said she was unable to see a path for me beyond the next hill. In other words, she doesn't think I have much of a future."

"What does that mean?" asked Ida from the corner of the wagon.

"I don't know," said Ven. "Maybe I'm about to die." He held up his hand as Clem gasped. "Who knows? It could mean anything. But one thing I am determined to have it mean is that I make a good decision about what to do with this gift.

"When we were in the Market, before the Queen of Thieves got hold of us, Madame Sharra told me in my first reading that most of the cards in her deck were really dragon scales that were given freely by the dragons long ago, when the world was pretty new. Those dragons gave these scales to do something very noble, something that saved the world. Each scale came from a different dragon. A little bit of each dragon's magical lore, the power it could use that came from the earth itself, is still in the scales.

"Each time a new dragon is born in the world, the scales grow in power. That has always been a rare event, but it is even more so now. That power dwindles as each dragon dies as well. One day, as man or Time finally destroys the dragon race, the scales will be nothing more than cards with images on them no one can see any longer. At least that's what Madame Sharra said."

"What's your point?" Ida asked impatiently.

Ven sighed. "Inside this sleeve is one of those cards. I have no idea why she gave it to me—when I looked back to ask her, she was gone. It's called the Endless Mountains, and that's what the picture on it looks like. I would show it to you, but if the dragon's in his lair, he will immediately know that it, and we, are here.

"I've decided the scale would be a good offering to this dragon, Scarnag," he went on. "I have to get him to trust me, and I think this might be the thing to do it."

"You're a funny one to talk about trust, Ven," Clemency said quietly.

"I know. I know, and I'm sorry. I haven't been very trusting, or trustworthy, and if we all live through this, I am hoping you will all let me make amends to you. Learning to make amends is what everyone the king sent me to needs—the Lirin, the Nain, maybe even this dragon. He killed a baby dragon named Ganrax—at least the Nain think he did. Maybe he just *told* them that he did. Who knows? But we never will find out unless we try. Since I don't seem to have that much time left to me, I guess I'm the one to do it."

"How?" asked Clemency.

"I think I just need to give this scale to him. Maybe it was his in the first place—I bet he was one of those old dragons who do-nated a scale to that noble undertaking that saved the world. I need to get him to trust me. If I give it back without asking for anything in return, in a gesture of trust, perhaps the dragon will tell me what I need to know to save Tuck, and maybe the Nain in the process."

"Even if you do, you're never gonna get those Nain to give the Lirin back that dragon's egg," Char pointed out. "Never in a million years."

"Maybe not," said Ven. "But one thing at a time. First I have to survive the scourge of the Island." He stood up and stretched. "And even before that, I need to tell you all that I'm sorry for not trusting you as I should have, and for making you feel you are less important to me than you are. After my family, you are the most important people in the world to me. If I live, I will make amends to each of you by telling you the truth about Amariel, as well as any other secret I still have left. If I don't, please believe that I love each of you very much—and get safely home."

He looked down at the sleeve with the scale in his hand.

"Now, while I still have feet, I'm going to leave some footprints in the sands of time."

- 22 -

Into the Jaws of the Beast

After he had hugged all his friends goodbye, even the passive merrow, Ven followed the stream that flowed southwest, as Garson had said.

The stream wound into what must have been, centuries before, part of the basin of the Great River. The ground was damp and marshy, perfect to surround a dragon's lair, Ven realized, because anything fleeing the cave would become bogged down in the mire.

I'm not worried, he thought. Death was in the back of his mind, but it did not hover like a threat, but rather lingered, a little bit like someone holding the door open for him.

Finally he came to a circular mound, part of a giant hillside carved to resemble a coiled serpent. Ven held his breath. The structure was magnificent and terrifying at the same time, with battlements that seemed impenetrable surrounding it.

He traveled all the way around the hill to the far side to find the entrance. It was an enormous portal, shaped like the open mouth of a massive serpent, stalactite fangs hanging from the roof both inside and outside. Even as calm as he was, those pointed stone spikes made the hair on the back of his head stand up.

He was but a few steps from that frightening entrance when a voice, deep in tone and hissing in vibration, blasted his ears.

"Ah, how long it has been since a young fool has come calling at my door," the terrifying voice said. In spite of its depth and hiss, it was also smooth and sweet like honey. "And a Nain, at that. What are you doing here, boy? Can youth no longer find less painful ways to die these days?"

"I did not come to die, unless you insist—"

"Yes, if I do, you will."

"—but rather with a gift instead," Ven said into the large opening.

There was a moment of silence, then a deep and nasty chuckle.

"A gift? How nice. Actually, they used to call that *tribute*. Today they call it a bribe."

"Not at all," Ven objected. "A bribe is a payment of a sort to get something in return. There is nothing I want from you except to return what I have with me, if it belongs to you."

"And if it does not, but I still want it, you know that I will take it, yes? Out of your dead hand, if necessary?"

"Yes," Ven agreed. "I know you can do that if you want. I'm hoping you won't, of course."

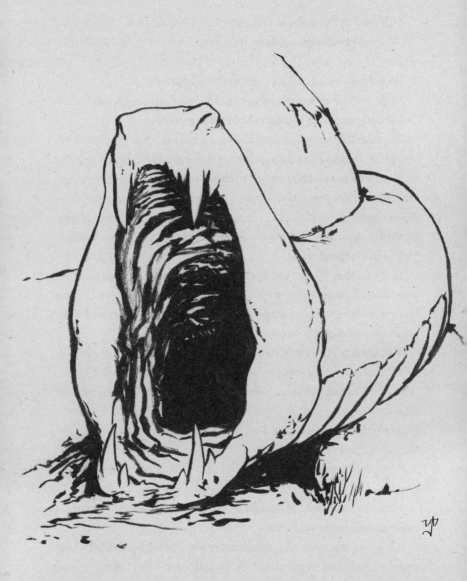

"Of course. So what is this gift?"

"I would be happy to show it to you," Ven said. "May I come in?"

The dragon laughed an extremely ugly laugh.

"Oh, yes, by all means, come in. I loved delivered food."

Ven stepped over the threshold and into the cave.

Beyond the serpent's mouth was a tunnel that glowed with red light, twisting in a spiral down to the ground below the hillside. Ven followed the tunnel, turning round and round in ever-smaller spirals, going deeper and deeper below the surface. His Nain eyes adjusted quickly, and he stared, fascinated, at the beautiful drawings and maps of the world that had been painted long ago on those walls.

"I hear that Nain are rather tasty roasted and dipped in chocolate," came the rumbling voice as he traveled deeper into the cave. "Do you have any objection to being devoured that way, if it satisfies my curiosity?"

Ven shrugged. "If you're going to devour me, chocolate seems fitting, as it's one of my favorite dipping sauces," he said as he walked. "But, being Nain, you should probably roll me in nuts as well before you eat me—Nain are very fond of nuts. Of course, you could also soak me in rum before you roast me—Nain are also very fond of rum."

"Oh, you are going to be delicious, I can just tell," said the dragon's voice.

"Good," said Ven. "I would hate to leave a bad taste in anyone's mouth, even a dragon's."

All along the way, the dragon taunted him. Sometimes the voice threatened, sometimes it hissed, but every word it uttered was a threat of ugliness that grew the closer he got to the bottom.

As he descended, the light from the lair at the bottom of the tunnel grew almost dazzlingly bright. Ven had to shield his eyes to be able to even see where the tunnel walls were.

Finally, just as he was about to turn the corner, the voice spoke more loudly than it had up until that point.

"Wait!" it said sternly. "This is your last chance to leave, boy. I've toyed with you long enough. If you round that corner, there will be no turning back."

Ven paused, still calm.

"I know," he said.

He came around the corner.

At first his eyes were almost blinded by the radiance of the inside of the dragon's lair. It was filled from the floor to the top of the ceiling with treasure that sparkled as if all the stars in the sky had been swept up and left in there.

But what was most amazing was the kind of treasure it was.

The center of the cave was an enormous vault of books of every sort. Maps and globes and scrolls hung on the walls, were piled on tables or even in stacks on the carpeted floor, rising all the way to the ceiling.

In the center of the room sat the dragon, the beast known as Scarnag. At first the sight of him took Ven's breath away. He was so big that his body almost filled the enormous chamber. He seemed to be formed from living earth itself, his brown, clay-like hide striped in colors of purple and vermillion, red and green and aquamarine. His head was roughly shaped, with cruel spines descending all the way down his back to a tail that had softly rounded spikes on it. In the stone-like claws of one hand he was playing idly with some ruby-red gems. Puffs of acid smoke emerged like clouds from his nostrils.

On his broad, blunt nose rested a pair of eyeglasses.

Ven blinked in surprise.

"Do I have the pleasure of addressing, er, Scarnag?" he asked politely.

The dragon let loose a growl that rocked the walls like thunder.

"Yessss, you do," he hissed. "And do not let my appearance fool you. Just because you caught me reading doesn't mean I'm unwilling to spill your blood. I'm just unwilling to spill it on my books. Where's this gift you mentioned?"

Ven pulled the Black Ivory sleeve from his pocket.

"Here," he said.

The dragon snorted, unimpressed.

"I have plenty of Black Ivory. This whole cave is made of

Black Ivory. How do you think I spare myself from stupid knights and Nain dragon hunters seeking revenge?"

"The sleeve is not the gift," Ven said. "It's what's inside."

"I see," said the dragon. "Well, what would that be?"

Carefully Ven pulled the scale from the sleeve and held it out to the dragon.

"This," he said simply.

The dragon reared back in surprise. His eyes glinted angrily, and acid smoke poured from his nostrils. For a long moment, he was speechless. When he could finally form words, they came out in an angry hiss.

"You have brought this to me, to ransom it—for what price?"

"Not at all," said Ven. "As I told you, it's a gift."

"NO!" the dragon screamed. "I will not have that! If it is a gift, then part of it still belongs to *you*, Nain. It must be free and clear—I will buy it from you. Name your price."

"There is nothing that I want," Ven said.

Slowly the dragon crept closer until its giant nostrils were pressed up against Ven's face.

"Name—your—price," he repeated.

Ven struggled to breathe amid the acid smoke and his fear.

"All right, then," he said. "I want the story of what happened to Ganrax."

The dragon stared at him.

"It is simple," he said finally. "He is dead. Give me the scale."

"A poor excuse for a story," Ven said. The words came out of his mouth, unbidden, as if disconnected from his brain. "Tell me what happened."

"I told you," said the dragon. "He is dead."

"All right, then," Ven said. "If you don't want to tell me what happened to him, then tell me what happened to *you*—Ganrax."

- 23 -

The Librarian

THE DRAGON'S MASSIVE JAW DROPPED SO SUDDENLY THAT HIS eyeglasses fell from his nose and shattered on the stone floor.

"How—how did you know my name?" he stammered.

Ven shrugged. "You wrote it out for me," he said. "In very tall letters—*SCARNAG*, burned into a hillside."

"I do like to sign my work whenever possible," the dragon admitted.

"Me too."

The great earthen beast shook its head. "For centuries, no one has made the connection between Ganrax and Scarnag," the beast said, wiping his brow with his strange, nubby tail. "How did you figure it out?"

"First, tell me your story," Ven said. "After all, I still haven't been paid for the scale." His stomach did a sudden flip as he realized how easily his life could end if he offended the dragon.

Scarnag stared at him, then looked at his shattered glasses on the floor and sighed. A blast of steam rolled out of his nostrils, making him look like he was rising out of a cloud. He rose from the floor at the center of the room and went over to a cabinet, where he rooted around in one of the drawers. His claw emerged with another pair of spectacles, which he promptly set on his nose again.

"I go through *so* many of these," he said. "Stone cave floors and eyeglasses don't like each other very much. Sit. It's a long tale—you may as well be comfortable. Especially if you are going to back out of the transaction, since it's nicer to die sitting than standing."

"I would *never* renege on a deal," said Ven, horrified. "To the Nain, a man's word sealed with a firm handshake is the most important thing he has." He sat down on the carpet in front of the dragon.

The dragon chuckled. "Well, you're hardly a *man*," he said. "You only have two whiskers to your name—that's not even a Bramble, is it?"

"No, it isn't," Ven said. He pulled out the journal the king had given him. "Whenever you're ready, I'm ready. I hope you don't mind me taking notes?"

"And if I do?"

"Well, I suppose you could always eat me, but I don't see any chocolate around here."

The dragon's craggy teeth formed a terrifying smile.

"This cave has quite a few rooms," he said. "One never keeps chocolate near important papers—didn't *anyone* ever teach you *anything*?"

"Nothing as important as the tale I'm about to hear," Ven said. He dipped the albatross feather he used as a quill into his small inkpot and waited patiently, the tip of the pen above a new page.

Then he told me his story, a tale of terrible betrayal, of trust broken. It took a long time. But when he was finished, the vibration of it rang in the cave like a bell that cannot be unrung. Before I left, he told me that it would be there forever, if anyone wanted badly enough to hear it.

When the dragon finished his tale, he settled into a pile of gold pieces and gemstones on the carpet that covered the floor of his enormous library, his scales damp, his muscles strained, and began running his claws through the jewels he was sitting on.

"Thank you," Ven said. "That must have been a difficult story to tell."

"It was," the beast said, wiping his brow with his strange, nubby tail. "So the least you could do is tell me how you figured out that I was born Ganrax."

"In the course of my last journey, I've seen—and made— some rather embarrassing mistakes with language," Ven admitted. "I told the Nain that we were playmates, not warts, and to hang on to their burning butts when I was trying to sound strong and impressive. They laughed at me, of course. A mysterious message that a king had been trying to decode for years turned out to be nothing more than a request to keep mule dung out of the river. A friend of mine from a very different place than I live is always misunderstanding the meaning of common phrases. So lately I'm more aware of words, I think.

"When the Nain were speaking sadly about Ganrax, I was trying to imagine how that word was spelled in their language— and then I realized with the X sound it was the backwards form of the word 'scarnag.' Of course, seeing it written in letters across a hill didn't hurt, especially after the Nain told me the story of your—er, death."

"And did you tell them of the connection?" the dragon asked, idly running the red jewels between the talons of his claws again.

Ven thought about whether it was wise to admit the truth about something that the dragon probably didn't want known. "No," he said finally. "I wasn't certain until you told me the story."

"Good," said the dragon. "I don't really want them to know. If you can keep the secret, I won't have to eat you."

Ven sighed. "You know, much as I would like not to be eaten, keeping other people's secrets has cost me a great deal lately. I suppose there are times when it is necessary, but most of the time it just puts a strain on trust. I was hoping you might tell me why you are attacking the Nain settlements—assuming that's you—"

"Yes. I do nice work, don't you think?"

"Well, as destruction goes, you *are* very talented," Ven said. "But considering that you are more librarian than monster, I can't believe that's really what you want to be doing. Isn't there something the Nain can do to make amends for the wrongs that have been committed against you?"

A puff of angry smoke issued forth from Scarnag's nostrils. "Are you joking?"

"Not at all. The Nain who betrayed you are long dead. The people you are attacking had nothing to do with Ganrax. They don't know the story of what happened—and they never will, because *you* have all the history books. The knowledge of why you are angry with them died with those who betrayed you. They don't regret the actions of their ancestors—they only blame *you* for *your* actions. If they could apologize—"

"Which would mean *nothing*," said the dragon. "How can they be sorry for something they had no hand in?"

"Exactly. So that gets back to what I just asked you—isn't

there something they can do begin to make amends? To bring them understanding of what you suffered? To perhaps forge a friendship again between the Nain and the dragon who holds all of their history?" He pointed to the massive trove of books and maps. "It's very sad to me to see people who don't know their own story and a dragon who clearly still has a lot of 'ganrax' in him acting like a scourge."

The dragon idly ran the red stones under his massive jaw.

"I suppose there is something they could do," he said finally.

Ven leaned closer to hear.

"The egg that the Nain have secreted away within their mountains—I want it returned to the Lirin of the Enchanted Forest," the dragon said.

Ven was thunderstruck. "All right," he said when he recovered his voice. "I can tell them that—but can you tell me, just out of curiosity, why you are taking the side of the Lirin over that of the Nain? Are you so angry with the Nain that you just want to humiliate them with their enemies?"

Scarnag chuckled. It was a low sound like the rumble of thunder in his massive earthen throat.

"Not at all. The Lirin do not want the egg for themselves—they want to return it to its mother."

Curiosity shot through Ven so strongly that the hair on his head almost stood straight up.

"Its mother? Who is its mother?"

The dragon rose and went over to a massive pile of old encyclopedias. He grabbed one with his tail and placed it nimbly on the floor before Ven. With the nubby end of his tail he easily opened the book and flipped the corners of the pages until he found the one he wanted. Then he tapped the page.

Ven peered into the ancient tome. On the page the dragon had pointed to with his tail was a color engraving of a beautiful dragon, very different from any picture he had seen before, with wings that seemed to be made of starlight and a body that was green as forest leaves. It was twined around the base of an immense oak tree that towered over all the other trees in the picture.

The dragon adjusted his glasses and looked at the text.

"At the beginning of the world, there were five places it is said that Time began," he said. "Each of those places is the birthplace of one of the five elements—fire, water, air, earth, and the substance known as ether, the element of magic, made by the light of the stars. At each of those places, an immense and beautiful tree grows, each one different. They are known as World Trees, because their roots run deeply throughout the earth and are all connected. Each of those trees is guarded by an ancient dragon, one of the Five Daughters of the first dragon ever to be born in this world. They are sometimes also called the Five Guardians.

"The oldest of all these trees is Sagia, the great oak that grows in the Enchanted Forest. Sagia's magic is what protects the forest, and keeps the magic of this part of the world alive. The tree is protected by the Guardian known as Marisynos. It is her egg that the Nain found one day. They took it back to their mountainous realm, not realizing the anguish that action would cause its mother—mostly because they are stupid and selfish."

"They think they are protecting it," Ven said. "They have it somewhere safe and warm—"

"And hidden away from the only one who can bring it to life," Scarnag said dryly. "You cannot imagine the mother's agony— having to give up searching for her child because to do so would mean abandoning her guardianship of Sagia. The Nain have no idea how much pain they have caused her, and are causing her still. It's an unforgivable offense."

"Unless the mother chooses to forgive it," said Ven. "Nothing is unforgivable, really. The Nain don't want to harm the baby dragon—they miss the one they lost more than they know how to express. That's what they are trying to do—make up for that loss the only way they know how."

Scarnag continued to play with the gemstones, but said nothing. Finally he sighed.

"You know, I really don't have time to be torching the Nain, although I have to admit it has been fun. There is a lot of work to be done in a library—cataloging of books, maintaining materials— I'm really very busy keeping up with it. I'll make you an offer: tell the Nain who I am. If they want to make amends to me, they will immediately return that unborn dragon child to the Lirin, who will give it back to its mother. You should deliver it—the Lirin may attack the Nain if they come themselves, thinking it's an invasion."

Ven sighed. "Yes, that's exactly what would happen."

"If they do this, and do it immediately, I may one day consider giving them back their history, a little at a time. It's going to take me a while before I want to meet any of them—old wounds take a long time to heal. But you have taught me something about forgiveness and making amends, boy. It feels a lot better than carrying the acid of hatred and anger around all the time."

"Yes, I believe it does," Ven said. "I'm counting on that in my own situation."

"Tell them my terms," the dragon continued, "and also tell them they have until the next turn of the moon to accomplish them. Otherwise, I'm going to continue to burn their settlements—and one day I will come after that egg myself. One thing

THE DRAGON'S LAIR {279}

I learned from the Nain as a child, even if I haven't believed it of them for centuries—family is everything. There are all forms of family, and dragons are a very big one. I feel responsible to Marisynos to make sure her child is returned to her. There are few enough dragons in the world as it is."

"I'll pass along your terms," said Ven. He rose from the carpet. "Thank you for hearing me out and not eating me."

"My pleasure," said the dragon. "Would you like to sign my guestbook on your way out? You'll be the first." He pointed with his tail to a large stand on which an even larger book, dusty and leatherbound, sat open, an inkwell next to it. "No one ever came by to visit who wasn't trying to vanquish me. It would be nice to finally have the signature of someone who just came by to talk."

"I'd be honored," Ven said. He walked over to the guest book and brushed the dust off the first blank page, then took the quill from the inkwell.

Black powder fell from its tip.

"I guess it's a little dry from age," said the dragon. The red streaks in his hide glowed brighter with embarrassment.

"Not a problem," Ven said. "I have a waterskin."

He mixed a few drops of water with the ancient powder to re-form the ink, then carefully wrote at the top of the page:

I am honored to have been your first guest.
Thank you for your hospitality, and especially for not
eating me.

Cordially, and with warm affection,
Charles Magnus Ven Polypheme

"There," he said, laying the quill beside the inkwell.

"Thank you," said the dragon, sounding pleased.

"Might I ask two more questions of you?"

"Certainly," said Scarnag. "Librarians love to answer questions."

"First—are you the one starting the fires near the Enchanted Forest, or in the Wide Meadows?"

The dragon snorted in disgust.

"No, that's the work of those human idiots who think it's a good idea to burn off brush for farmland. I wouldn't even eat one of their stupid identical cows for fear it would give me diarrhea. You might want to suggest to the Lirin *and* the Nain that they get together and put a stop to *that*—before they burn down the Enchanted Forest. What's the other question?"

"The scale I gave you—did you donate that long ago in a noble cause that saved the world?"

The dragon smiled slightly.

"No," he said. "I was not yet hatched when that occurred. But my mother was alive—and this is the scale she gave." He took the scale from its case, held it up to his hide, and tilted it to catch the light. The color was exactly the same. "When you first showed it to me, I thought you were going to bargain for everything I had, and I would have given it to you to get this back, because it's all I have of her. I never knew her, you know."

"Yes," Ven said. "I'm sorry."

"Where did you get this, by the way? I didn't even know it existed, but the moment you showed it to me I knew what it was, and from whom it had come."

Ven took a deep breath, then told the dragon the story of the Gated City, how he had met Madame Sharra, and about the reading she had done for him. He told Scarnag about how she had appeared to him again, before he left Kingston, and what she had said.

The dragon listened intently.

"So what she said to you, about not seeing your footprints— did that make you believe you are going to die soon, then?"

Ven shrugged. "I don't know if it did. But I guess it's a possibility I never thought about until she said it."

The dragon nodded. "The young don't think about death much, I suppose. It's a little like you're wrapped in Black Ivory yourself—protected from life, and from the dangers it poses. You should keep that envelope with you all the time, just to remind you what awaits you, good and bad, in the world.

"Black Ivory is an interesting thing. In some ways, it's the best example of something that is totally and completely dead. And yet that is one of the things in all the world that can mask the vibrations that something, or someone, gives off in the process of being alive. It can hide something's true name, making it invisible even to those beings who can see things that are hidden. So it knows more about life than almost anything. It is, in a way, the ultimate librarian."

"What are some of the others?" Ven asked. "Is there anything else that can hide a person besides Black Ivory? I have a lot of bad people looking for me, but I don't want to live in a cave forever."

The dragon thought for a moment. "The only one I can think of, the only one mentioned in the books, is the sea. But there may be others. I can research it for you, if you want to come back."

"I'd love to," Ven said. "Thank you for the invitation—and for telling me your story. I should be going now—I have an egg to bargain for and deliver, and a friend that really needs to get home."

"Before you go, take these," said Scarnag. He patted the colorful book with the engraving of the World Tree, and another box, with his tail. "The first one you may keep—I have another copy of it. But the book in the box is one of a kind, so it's on loan *only*." He pulled off the top.

Ven peered inside.

"You can open it, if you're careful," said the dragon.

Ven unwrapped the book from its packing of silk and picked it up. The box it was in was lined with gold, and smelled of ancient magic.

The leather cover was imprinted with the raised picture of a dragon. Inside, each page bore a picture of a dragon as well, beautifully detailed and colored, but with no words.

"Thank you," Ven said, his voice filled with awe.

"Remember, on loan only," said the dragon. "And dragon late fees are *dreadful*."

Then he extended his claw and held out the red gems he had

been playing with. Ven took them; they were hard and shiny and deep ruby red. "Take these as well. I've been playing with them for centuries, squeezing them in anger, remembering the great wrong that was done to me. I guess I don't need them anymore. I hope you will keep them to remember what you've taught me—and what it sounds like you've learned yourself."

Ven stared at the little gems.

"Thank you. What are they?"

The dragon smiled broadly, showing rows of pointed teeth.

"Kiran berries," he said.

– 24 –

A Promise Fulfilled

So I hurried back to my friends.

And we hurried back to where we had met the Nain.

Along the way I told them everything that had happened. It felt wonderful to be able to share the story, even the parts that the dragon had originally wanted kept secret, without having to hold anything back. Clemency seemed to have forgiven me, and Ida—well, Ida is Ida. She sat in the corner of the wagon and stared at me, smirking occasionally and making rude comments.

But that's nothing new. I hope she has forgiven me as well.

With Char, it's like nothing ever happened.

All the way to the Nain outpost, Clemency handled the driving, which was good, because the ground between the dragon's lair and the rocky foothills was hard to navigate. Char, Ida and I were occasionally sick. Amariel slept most of the way.

WHEN AT LAST THEY GOT TO THE BURNED OUTPOST, THE NAIN were waiting for them. Garson had seen them coming from a lookout in one of the higher peaks of the foothills. As a result, Tuck was lying on a stretcher, waiting for them.

The Lirin forester was doing much better. True to their word, the Nain had patched him up and bandaged him, though he had been kept in their prison, which had seemed to have no visible impact on him. By the time the children saw him, he only had a sling on his arm and a bandage on his chest.

When Ven told the Nain the story of the dragon's lair, that Scarnag actually was Ganrax, and what his demand for amends was, the Nain were silent for hours. Tuck, Char, Clem, Ida, and Ven sat in the wagon and played cards or mumblety-peg while the Nain discussed what to do. Finally, they returned in the middle of the mumblety-peg championship, announcing they had made a decision. Everyone was happy except Ida, who always won mumblety-peg games and hadn't gotten to her turn yet.

A procession was set up, with Nain guards led by Garson escorting them with great solemnity inside the foothills through a tunnel hidden by many layers of rock slabs. Even Tuck was allowed to come inside, an honor few Lirin had ever experienced.

The tunnels within the hills did not appeal to the Lirin forester and the human children, but to Ven it was like returning home, even though he had never been inside one in his life. Something about the way the stone sang inside the earth, the way it smelled, the colors of the different layers of rock was just beautiful to him. It made him feel happy deep inside, probably back in his blood to a time when Polyphemes still lived underground, before Magnus the Mad decided to go upworld, move to the seashore, and open a factory building ships. It made him giggly, the way his father and brothers got when they were drinking rum.

"Criminey, mate, get *over* it," Char whispered as they passed a waterfall inside the mountain, running in silver sheets down the rock walls. "You're embarrassin' yourself."

"Sorry," Ven said. "This is just so exciting to me. I wish I could stay longer. I hope I get to come back."

"If you say so," said Char doubtfully.

"Ick," said Ida. "Get me outta here fast—I'm startin' to get hives."

The air inside the mountains got warmer the farther in they went. They saw many more Nain, guards and soldiers mostly, as the network of tunnels grew and expanded to many crossing paths. Garson had to check in with each guard to allow them through every checkpoint. It was starting to look a little like an anthill when suddenly Garson stopped and pointed to an opening on the left.

The children and their forester guide followed him down an immense winding staircase made of stone that led deeper into the dark. Ida was starting to get nervous, so Char took her hand, something that made her go from nervous to agitated. Tempers were getting pretty grim until they finally saw a light at the base of the stairs.

They descended the staircase one at a time. Once they got to the bottom they were led along a final tunnel, where the light grew brighter and brighter, and the air got warmer and warmer. They could hear the sound of rushing water in the distance, and it grew louder as they approached.

Finally, when the light and the heat and the sound were at their most intense, Garson led them through one last opening.

There, in an elevated chamber, was a huge nest of Black Ivory.

In it was an oval gemstone that looked like an opal, pearly and colorful and smooth. It glowed in many colors, casting a glorious light around its hidden nursery, causing the walls to shine softly. The moment he laid eyes on it, Ven knew why the Nain had taken it.

Anybody would have.

Or any Nain at least.

There was just something about it that made you want to protect it, to keep it warm, to help it be born. I can't explain it any better than that.

Rushing below the elevated chamber was a river of molten gold. All the light and the heat and the sound they'd been hearing

and feeling was coming from the river. Ven's skin pricked at the sight of it.

The liquid gold danced like water. It looked just the way iron looked in the forges of the Polypheme factory. It made Ven laugh, knowing if he had described it to his brothers, they would have thought that he had had one too many turns at the forge.

Solemnly and with great awe, the Nain wrapped the egg carefully, leaving it in the Black Ivory nest, and carried it all the way back through the tunnels to the wagon, where they secured it and wrapped it with pots of molten gold to keep it warm on the journey. While the companions had been gone, a crew of Nain craftsmen had been refitting the wagon and its wheels so that it was no longer rickety or unstable but as smooth and solid a machine as anyone could have asked for.

Nain are good at this kind of thing—it's our specialty.

Ven and the others thanked the Nain and said goodbye. Before they left, Garson asked Ven if he could come back someday and take him, and perhaps a few other Nain, to meet the dragon, to see his library, and start learning their history again.

Ven thought about Madame Sharra's reading. "I'd be happy to, if the sands of Time don't run out on me first," he said. The older Nain laughed, not having any idea how serious he was.

The ride back to the Enchanted Forest was vastly easier than our first journey had been. The wagon rode beautifully, I had made amends with my friends, and we were in the presence of this magical egg that just felt good to be around. We didn't talk much, because it was a little like having a sleeping baby in the wagon with us. I was grateful for the silence, because it gave me time to think.

And because we didn't have to discuss Amariel yet, even though I knew that was coming.

Because the moon was almost full.

And soon it would be waning again.

One Delivery Down,
Two More to Go

BY THE TIME THEY WERE IN SIGHT OF THE ENCHANTED FOREST, word of their arrival had undoubtedly reached the king, because an entire contingent of Lirin soldiers, an honor guard, and Alvarran himself were awaiting them.

The face of the Lirindarc king was still solemn, his expression still intimidating, but there was surprise in his expression that even he could not hide. He stood with the same group of soldiers who had originally accompanied him with one added, a beautiful young woman with light eyes, fair skin and long dark hair. She wore trousers and a doublet, like the soldiers, but with different insignia, and she stood behind the king, smiling, holding a square wooden box with an intricate inlay on the top and around the edges.

The Lirindarc king was clearly struggling to contain his amazement when the wagon rolled up in front of him. Ven hopped down and walked up to him. He stopped, then bowed politely.

"Good morning, Your Majesty," he said cheerfully.

"Stop being so smiley," Alvarran replied. "It's disturbing on a Nain."

"I'm sorry—I can't help it," Ven said. "I've brought the egg—"

"So I see. How did you get it?"

Ven shrugged. "The Nain wish to make amends," he said. "They don't feel they stole it—they found it, and have been taking excellent care of it all this time, as you can see. They wish you, and the dragon's mother, peace."

Alvarran stood in stony silence for a moment. Then, abruptly, he turned to the young woman and waved her forward. She came, moving quickly and gracefully, stopping by his side.

"Here is my end of the bargain," the Lirindarc king said. The young woman handed him the box, which he in turn handed to Ven. "Give this to King Vandemere—with my, er—blessing."

"I will," said Ven. "Thank you very much, sire." He winced at the word, remembering Vandemere's promise as well. "By the way, you're right—the burning on the border of your realm was not done by a dragon, but it wasn't the Nain preparing for an attack, either."

"No?" said the king. "Then what was it?"

"Human farmers have taken possession of the lands formerly tended by the Gwadd," Ven said. "They are burning the scrub and the grass to expand their plantings. The sparks from their grass fires carry a long way on the wind."

"Idiots," muttered the king. "Agrarians, dirt pushers. Even I, a hunter-gatherer, know better than that. I guess I shall have to pay them a visit to discuss appropriate land management techniques and neighborly courtesy."

Ven smiled at the thought. "So if you didn't know it was farmers, how did you know it *wasn't* a dragon?"

Alvarran's mouth tightened.

"She told me," he said, nodding to the egg in the cart.

"Who?"

"The dragon."

At first Ven had no idea what he meant. Then he remembered the story Scarnag had told him of the Five World Trees, and the dragon Marisynos, who protected the one in the Enchanted Forest. He thought about how sad she must have been, and what a terrible choice it must have been to give up searching for her egg because to do so would mean abandoning the Tree.

"Well, I am glad everything is working out for the best," he said finally. "And now, if you will excuse us, sire, we will be on our way."

Alvarran exhaled. "Would you—would you like to see her, before you go?" The words came out with so much effort that Ven almost expected to see blood dripping from the Lirindarc king's mouth.

"Her, sire?"

"Sagia—the World Tree. Would you like to see her? She is the great wonder of the world. And you can meet—Marisynos— if you wish. I'm sure she'd like to—thank you." The words now looked like they were causing him pain.

Ven considered. "How far away is it?"

"A week's journey into the Enchanted Forest," said the Lirindarc king. "For us, at least. Perhaps two for you, since you are not used to forest travel."

"Thank you," Ven said. His disappointment was fighting with his ability to get the words out, so he used the same ones that he and Amariel had exchanged a million times. "I want to, but I can't today. One day, maybe. Goodbye."

Alvarran looked thunderstruck. "Are you certain?"

"Yes, Your Majesty. Thank you again."

Ven bowed and walked away as quickly as he could, leaving the Lirindarc monarch shocked into speechlessness.

- 26 -

Making Amends

"I CAN'T BELIEVE MY EARS," CHAR SAID AS VEN CLIMBED INTO the wagon beside him. "Did I just hear you turn down an invitation from the bloody Lirin king to see what is prolly the greatest wonder of the world, and meet a dragon that owes you for returnin' her long-lost egg?"

Ven nodded to Tuck. The Lirin forester just smiled and clicked to the horses.

"That's right," he said to Char as the wagon began to roll.

"You're *daft*!"

"That's right also."

"I can't believe it, either, Ven," Clemency said. "Your curiosity must be driving you mad right now."

"It is," Ven admitted. "I want to scratch my skin off with my jack-rule, it's itching so much."

"Then why did you pass up the chance?" demanded Char.

"Well, that's something else I have to tell you all. Now that we're underway, I have plenty of time to tell you, and the girls, the whole story."

So as the wagon rolled westward toward the southern bridge

across the Great River, Ven told them the story of Amariel from the very beginning.

He explained his shipwreck, how he had been responsible for the explosion that had sunk both the Fire Pirate ship that had attacked them and his father's ship as well. He told them how the merrow had stayed with him, singing him songs and telling stories that kept him awake and alive through that lonely, terrifying time. He told them that she had left her family to follow him to Serendair, and that she had stayed, probably because she was as curious about him as he was about her. He told them that it had been she that towed their boat out of the harbor when they had to find the Floating Island in order to save Ida. He told them everything he could think of about her, how she was easily excited and easily hurt, easily offended and easily willing to help in any situation.

Then he told them how she had finally trusted him enough to give him her cap, how she had grown human legs and her gills had sealed shut. He described the transformation, which made everyone but Ida wince, and how the loss of her cap had made her begin to lose herself.

"So that's why I gave up going to see the Tree and the dragon, something that I would have loved to do," he said, watching the countryside roll by. "I have to get her back to the sea—it's more important than anything right now, even though I don't have her cap. The moon is full, and in a few days it will be waning. I don't know what will happen to her, but I think I should at least start by taking her home." *And making a choice about whether or not to use a power that may do more harm than good,* he thought, looking at the image on his palm.

"I think you're gettin' really brave, mate," Char said admiringly. "I mean it—you can just walk into a dragon's lair or out of a king's presence. When did *that* happen?"

"I think when Madame Sharra told me she didn't see my foot-prints going much farther," Ven answered. "When you stop worrying about dying, you start living more bravely. I've seen so much on this last journey, both good and bad. Mostly I now understand what King Vandemere said when he first told me about *his* journeys as a kid. The king saw a lot of magic hiding in plain sight, but he said the magic was mostly in the people. Now I understand what he meant. After meeting the Gwadd, and the Lirin, and even the Nain, I know what he means." He smiled at his friends. "But then, I've been seeing it all along, because I've known you."

Clemency sniffed out loud. Ven and Ida turned at the same time to see sentimental tears form in her eyes and spill onto her cheeks.

"Oh, *please*," groaned Ida as Clemency reached into her pocket for her handkerchief. She unfolded it neatly and raised it to her nose, then suddenly pulled away, a look of surprise on her face.

"What's this?" she asked, her brow furrowed.

She opened the handkerchief wider.

Within its folds was a fragile circle of what looked like red lace, encrusted with tiny white pearls.

Ven's face went slack with delight.

"Her cap! Amariel's cap! You found it!"

"This is it? *This* is what you were looking for?"

Ven held out his hand, and Clemency put the handkerchief carefully into it.

"This is it!" he said, his voice shaking with joy. "I can't believe you found it!"

Clemency's face was as red as the cap, and she was about to cry. "I can't believe I had it in the first place. I only have one handkerchief, and I haven't had reason to cry or blow my nose, so I didn't even think to look in it. I didn't think a cap would look like this, anyway. I probably wouldn't even have recognized it if I *did* look."

"Actually, that's my handkerchief," Ven said. "I thought it might have fallen out of the wagon during the fire in the fields. But how did you get it?"

"No," Clem insisted, "it's mine. I picked it up on the wagon floor just after I used it to bandage Char's head when the ravens attacked. I thought the red cap was a blood stain."

"Bleah," said Ida.

"Nope," said Char, pulling a stained handkerchief out of his pocket. "I didn't think you wanted this one back. Sorry, Ven. When we were searching our knapsacks and the wagon, I guess we never thought to look on *ourselves*."

"I feel terrible," Clem whispered, fighting back tears as Ven put the handkerchief back in his pocket with great care and buttoned it. "I don't really have a good reason why I didn't look harder, Ven. I guess—I suppose I was just jealous of all the attention you were paying to Amariel. If I'd known what she was, it never would have bothered me—I'm sure I would have tried to help her feel comfortable in the dry world, too. But I didn't know she was a *merrow*, I thought she was just a snotty rich girl with a tattered ballgown and a bad attitude. I feel terrible, I really do—and I'm so, so sorry." The tears won the battle and began rolling down her cheeks.

Ven passed her his clean handkerchief, smiling.

"I hope—you—can forgive—me, Ven," Clem went on, hiccupping in between words. "But I understand if you won't."

Ven laughed. "Of course I will, Clem. It was an honest mistake."

He looked at Amariel, who was quietly humming to herself. "Once she gets back to her old form, *she* probably won't, but we'll work on that."

"First we gotta work on gettin' her back," said Char.

"I'm driving straight to the pier once we get to Westland," Tuck said casually from the wagon board. Once again, all the children in the back jumped.

True to his word, the Lirin forester kept the horses in steady canter, choosing the easiest and fastest paths and roadways back to the Great River. Ven used the jack-rule from a distance and saw that the ravens were gone from the northern bridge closest to the Inn, so they crossed there. They stopped long enough to leave the cookies Mrs. Snodgrass had given them for the trolls on the rocky bank, still in their parchment wrapper, and then traveled relentlessly west toward Kingston.

While the others dozed, Ven took Garson's advice and wrote a letter to his family. Rather than it being a goodbye, though, he began to chronicle some of the most important things he had learned in the course of his journey east of the river. He had just begun to explain the most critical realization when the Crossroads Inn came into sight in the distance. Quickly he tucked the letter into the depths of his journal to finish later.

It was several hours before dawn when they finally approached the Inn, and they could see a long line of supply wagons offloading goods. Felitza and Nick were outside with Mrs. Snodgrass, ferrying in sacks and bushel baskets. Char and Ven looked at each other, rubbed their shoulders in sympathy for their friends, and smiled.

When they were almost to the crossroads, two streaks of fur leapt into the wagon.

"Yikes!" sputtered Ven as they landed on Amariel's lap. "Murphy! What the *heck*?"

"Didn't you miss us?" the orange tabby asked, puzzled.

"Uh—not really," Ven admitted.

"Hmmm. Not a good answer, I'd say. What would you say, Leo?"

The brown cat coughed. "Leo."

Ven's mouth dropped open. "That's very good," he said. "Did McLean teach you that?" The cat nodded. "Oh. Well, congratulations."

"She's up to four words already," said Murphy proudly.

"She?" asked Ven. "She who?"

Murphy rolled his eyes. "Leo."

"Leo's a girl?"

Murphy sauntered over to Ven and leaned in close.

"Leonora is her real name, but she hates it," he whispered confidentially.

"Why didn't you tell me?"

The orange tabby pursed his lips, an expression that looked very strange on a cat face.

"You were a little busy," he said. He sauntered back to Amariel and climbed into her lap again.

Mrs. Snodgrass was shouting orders to the drivers when the cart with the children and the cats pulled up alongside the Inn.

"Three more sacks of oats, please, Bill." She looked up from her clipboard. "And what are you deliverin'—oh! Oh, my! Look who's here! Well, welcome home, loves! How was your visit to Saeli's family?"

"Wonderful," Ven said. "She decided to stay for a while." He leaned out of the wagon and kissed Mrs. Snodgrass on the cheek. The portly lady blushed, then smiled.

"Well, what's gotten into you, Young Master Polypheme? Whatever it is, I like it!"

"Sense, finally, perhaps," Ven replied.

"Neh," said Ida.

"But whatever it is, I have to take it with me to town right away," he continued as Murphy and Leo climbed off Amariel's lap, stretched, and leapt out the wagon. "Thank you for being so wonderful to me, Mrs. Snodgrass. I really do appreciate it."

The innkeeper's smile faded slightly.

"Why? Where are ya goin' now?"

"Just to the pier," Ven said as Tuck prepared to go again.

"Oh, good! Because I do believe the Captain may make port today," said Mrs. Snodgrass. "He'll be happy to see you."

Ven smiled bravely. "I hope so."

"We'll be back soon, Mrs. Snodgrass," Clem said. "But we have to go now. Anything you need from town?"

"No—what I need is comin' on his own, thank you. See you in a bit, children." The innkeeper went back to her deliveries.

Ven waved to Nick and Felitza, then turned to Char as the wagon began rolling toward Kingston.

"Don't you want to get out—go say hello?" He nodded toward the kitchen maid.

Char sighed. "I do—but I'll go later. Right now, we all feel there's nothin' more important than gettin' both you and Amariel to the dock."

"Perhaps you might want to rethink that, Ven," Tuck said. "That gentleman with the parsnips looks like he could use a hand with those sacks." He nodded toward the door of the kitchen, where a tall man stood, wearing a straw hat and a grin.

"The king!" Ven exclaimed, then clapped a hand over his mouth as if to call the words back. He grabbed his knapsack and hurried into the Inn.

"That was subtle," called Ida as he ran through the back door.

Ven caught up with King Vandemere in the kitchen. "How did you know when I was coming home?"

"In the tallest tower of Castle Elysian there is a telescope," the king replied, looking around the Inn again in wonder. "It belongs to my chief Vizier, Graal, who has been away for quite a while. It can see *very* far. I've taken to looking through it each morning and evening whenever I can, and last night I saw you on your way toward the bridge. So I timed my arrival to coincide with yours."

"Is it an odd, twisty sort of telescope?" Ven asked as he led the king hurriedly into the main room to the hearth.

"As a matter of fact, it is," King Vandemere said. "How did you know?"

"It's a popular style among the many kings I know," said Ven, chuckling.

On the hearth McLean was quietly singing to himself. The Singer looked up and bowed as the king came near.

"Scat," McLean said to the air. It swirled amid a good deal of sniffing and spluttering as the Spice Folk, clearly offended, huffily left the hearth. "Hello, Ven—welcome home."

"Thank you. Will you do me a favor, McLean? It's important."

"If I can."

"I need to be able to give this gentleman my report—and I need to do it quickly." It almost seemed like the handkerchief was itching in his pocket. "Without anyone else hearing."

The Singer nodded. He took out his strangely shaped stringed instrument and began to play, conjuring up a tune that seemed to blot out all other sound in the room.

Ven turned to the disguised king.

"Do I have a tale for you." he said. "I only wish I had longer to tell it."

Kiran Berries, the Exodus, and the Day the Sun Overslept

I tried as hard as I could to capture Scarnag's voice as I told the king his story, but gave up quickly. There was no way a human or Nain voice could duplicate all the sounds, the hisses and growls and the deep music in a dragon's voice. The dragon book he gave me—the one with the words—says that dragons have no larynx, the voice-box that people have that lets them speak. Instead they use the wind, a little like Singers do, to make the sound of what they want to say.

I gave McLean permission to listen in on the story, because I thought he would understand it better than anyone else could. I remembered what Scarnag said about how once it was told, it would be like a bell that was rung, staying in the place that it was told forever.

I couldn't think of a better place than the Crossroads Inn to tell it.

YOU WANT TO KNOW WHAT CAN TURN WISDOM TO THE DESIRE to be a scourge, Nain?

There is but one answer: One day, the sun slept late.

That may make no sense to you. I'm sure you have never heard of a time when the sun did not come up in the morning. It is not something you ever think about, is it, Nain? Perhaps as you go about your life you wonder *when* the sun will come up, or whether the clouds will hide it when it does. But I imagine it never occurs to you to wonder *if* the sun will come up, does it?

Every being with a mind has something called Great Truths, whether he knows it or not. Great Truths are things we believe in without question, like knowing the sun will come up every morning. We ask ourselves *when* it will, not *if* it will. But if one day the sun were to sleep late, and leave the world in darkness until the next day, do you think anyone would ever take its rising for granted again?

It would only take one time for all of humanity to begin to question, to worry, to wonder if the sun was going to do it again. Right now it's something you believe without thinking about, isn't it? It's something you trust. That's the true meaning of trust, Nain—something you believe in completely without having to think about it.

So what happens when trust is betrayed?

But not just any trust—trust so deep that it is part of who you are. The betrayal has to be so immense that it is not only enough to change your name, it changes everything you believe about yourself.

You want to know what happened to Ganrax. I cannot tell you the tale as if it happened to me, because the being to whom it happened is long dead, as I told you truthfully when you first entered my library. So instead I will tell it to you from a distance, because that is how I see it. The distance of years, the distance of pain.

Ganrax, the young wyrmling you speak of, never knew any of his own kind, not even the one who gave him life. From the time of his hatching he was raised among your kind, not his own. Fed by hand, nursed when ill, comforted when frightened, kept warm near the fires within their mountainous lands when he was cold. The Nain were the only family he knew, and to dragons nothing is more important than family.

You have said the Nain believe this as well. Let me tell you why I know that is not true.

More than feeding and raising the young dragon, the most important task in his upbringing that the Nain tended to was his education. Dragons hoard knowledge. They think of it as treasure. So when the Nain gave the young one an unlimited supply of history and lore, science and stories, maps and globes and books, he felt more loved, more cherished than you could ever imagine. He saw these creatures with whom he shared the earth, who gave him food, warmth, comfort and, most important, knowledge, as his family. He trusted them the way you trust the sun to come up in the morning.

There was one more thing that the Nain gave the young dragon, something that he loved almost as much as he loved learning. You know of the kiran berry? Perhaps not, as you are upworld Nain. But those who live within the earth know it well. The kiran berry is a tart, hard little fruit, red like a blood ruby. Its skin is sour, but if one is patient enough to get past it, the flesh deep inside it is sweet as honey. The berries have a deep taste of earth about them. They grow on spidery bushes beneath the ground, in caves and tunnels where the sun never reaches. They are a favorite, therefore, of creatures who live in such places, like the Nain—and dragons.

Being a youngling, Ganrax loved kiran berries the way you or one of your human friends might love sweets. The Nain who raised him gave them to him as treats and as rewards for learning something well or behaving properly. Whenever the dragon child and his Nain family went for walks in the deep and winding tunnels of earth, the Nain would always bring along a pocketful of kiran berries to keep him from straying too far from the path. Ganrax was fascinated with the world around him, and often would scamper away to explore new wonders he saw. The Nain would bring his interest back by tempting and rewarding him with kiran berries.

So Ganrax's life was a happy one. He passed his days deep within the southern mountains of Northland, the vast continent to the north of this island. He did not know that he was away from his own kind, as most dragons live solitary lives anyway. He was well cared for, protected and encouraged to learn, everything that made his life blissful.

What the wyrmling did not know was the reason he had been given to the Nain from the time before birth, and why the Nain were raising him.

The continent of Northland is a place of great riches, immense cities, huge seaports. At the time of his birth, though Ganrax did not know it, a terrible evil was brewing in the cities and flatlands north of the Nain mountains. Slowly, over time, that evil spread south, choking out cities and villages, destroying everything good in its path and taking over what remained. But it moved slowly, to make sure that once it had taken over, it could never be uprooted, never be stopped.

And it has not been stopped to this day, Nain. It still grows, it still spreads. And one day it will come to this place. Remember my words, for it may happen in your lifetime.

The Nain had decided, long before Ganrax was hatched, that they needed to leave their mountain home, to flee to a place of safety on another continent and rebuild their kingdom. When this decision was made there was great suffering, because the Nain loved their home deeply, as all dwellers of the earth do, and did not want to leave. Even more terrible was the knowledge that they would have to cross the ocean to find safety, for as you know better than anyone, Nain fear the water and are afraid to travel on the sea. But there was no alternative, so the rulers of the kingdom came up with a plan.

They called the plan, and the leaving of their homeland, the Exodus.

First, they found three brave Nain who were willing to set forth as explorers and find a new, uninhabited land where they could rebuild their home. Because the evil was moving slowly, they had time to make careful preparations, and they did.

The tasks of the Exodus were also divided up. Some of the people of the mountains were responsible for taking apart and dismantling the things that would not be left behind. Others were responsible for buying ships to sail to the new world. Others were in charge of organizing how the population would be moved from deep inside the earth to those ships. It was a plan that took many years to achieve.

The Nain decided the most important thing they owned was their history. More than anything else, they feared losing all their legends, all the books about the past and the maps that brave Nain explorers had made, because Nain do not relish exploration and would hate to have to repeat it. Perhaps all creatures that live within the earth crave knowledge and value it. And the Nain knew that the best way to insure that their knowledge survived was to teach it to a being whose lifespan was vastly longer than any of their own, who had a great ability to learn it quickly and more completely even than they did, and who would guard that knowledge like a treasure.

So they decided they needed a dragon.

Not an adult dragon, however, because adult dragons have minds of their own, and their own knowledge. The Nain knew if they were to convince a dragon to adopt all their knowledge as its own, they would have to start with one who did not have any yet.

An infant. A hatchling.

I do not know how the Nain convinced the mother of the wyrmling to part with one of her eggs. The writings say that the dragon gave the Nain the egg willingly after they told her of the coming evil, and of their plans for the Exodus. I don't know if that is true or not. Dragons guard their children jealously, so it is possible that they killed her and took the egg, since it is hard to imagine that she would have given it up willingly.

The wyrmling was told that he was given to the Nain by his mother for both his own safety, to keep him away from the coming evil, and to aid in preserving the knowledge as his treasure. That part of the story is polluted, because once the trust was broken, the truth of the history is lost. This is the reason your Lirin Storysinger and everyone like him swears never to lie—because once falsehood enters the story, it is impossible to ever know what is true again. It destroys history, and all the world is weaker for the loss of it.

Whoever knew the truth is long dead. So I will never know the answer. And it haunts me. With every waking thought it angers me more. That anger seeps into my scales and turns them acid. Endless anger brings on endless pain—it is a cycle all but impossible to break.

I have strayed from the tale.

When the three Nain explorers set out to find a new land, they brought Ganrax with them. They also brought all of their most valuable books, maps, globes and charts—which you see here in this library—because the Nain rulers wanted to get those valuable things out first, in case the mountains were overrun before the Exodus.

The three Nain and the young dragon boarded a ship and set sail for the south, where they knew a great land mass lay. That land mass was this island, and in the north it had mountains even taller and more jagged than their own. They knew upon seeing them that those mountains would be the perfect new home, with untouched riches to plunder and great stone walls to protect them.

Neither the Nain nor the dragon enjoyed the voyage. All the Nain were seasick, but none so ill as Ganrax, who they feared might die. It's a miracle that they all didn't.

Finally, upon reaching land, the Nain were overjoyed. The northern mountains had many low foothills leading up to the High Reaches, which would provide a sturdier defense than they had back home. The riches they had anticipated—gold and silver, gemstones and coal, salt and potash, were plentiful and untouched. It was like discovering a treasure beyond price, and the Nain could not wait to get back to Northland to tell their fellow Nain about their new home.

Before they set sail, however, they built the dragon a library.

You stand within the structure now, a deep, winding tunnel leading down to a warm lair. In the lair they carefully stored all their books and maps and globes, all the documents of their history. They filled it with food and supplies, and made it as strong as a fortress could be, so that the dragon would be safe. They sculpted mazes and playgrounds for him to play in below the ground. They built everything they could think of to make him happy. They packed up their tools, told Ganrax to enjoy his new home, and that they would return as soon as they could with the rest of the population.

Then they bade him goodbye and walked away.

They had only gone about a hundred paces when the little dragon was beside them again. The Nain blinked in surprise, then led him back to the lair, explained that this is where he was to live, and they would return as soon as they could. Again they turned to leave.

And once again the dragon was beside them.

Now the Nain were worried. They had expected the dragon to understand the plan, being so vastly more intelligent than any of them were. They explained to Ganrax that he was being left in the fortress for his safety, and for the protection of their history. They reminded him how important his part in the survival of the Nain was. They lectured him about responsibility, and told him again they would return as soon as they could. Then they turned to leave one final time.

Only to find the baby dragon at their heels once again.

The wyrmling understood the plan for the Exodus. He understood his need for safety, and for the safety of the information in the library. He understood the threat in the mountains of Northland.

He just didn't care.

Because the Nain were his family. He was a child, an infant by dragon measure, and he did not wish to be separated from them for any reason. Dragons feel everything more intensely than men—jealousy, greed, loyalty, anger and love. Ganrax loved the Nain as much as his own life, and believed they loved him that much as well. It was his Great Truth. That was more important to him than his safety, than his mission, than his treasure.

So try as they might, the Nain could not get him to stay in the cave.

Finally, when it became clear that Ganrax's persistence would outlast their own, the Nain consulted with each other, and made a decision that started a war.

They returned to the mouth of the cave, playing chase and tag and other games with the wyrmling. Ganrax was excited, and happily took part in those games. Then, as a "reward" for winning the last of his games, the Nain took a handful of kiran berries and tossed them down the tunnel past the mouth of the cave. The baby dragon scampered after them, and while he was retrieving his prize, the Nain rolled an immense boulder over the opening.

Trapping him inside.

Then they went home.

I do not know if they could hear the bleating of the little dragon, the scratching at the rock walls that had been built to be a fortress, the cries and the wailing, as they walked away. It's hard to imagine that they could not, for the earth itself shook with them. Trapped alone, in the darkness of the tunnel, the dragon screamed and called and begged until the ground wept tears of moisture all around him.

Finally, when he was exhausted, the dragon fell silent, and waited, knowing in his heart that the Nain would change their minds and come back for him. He waited and waited and waited, as you would wait for the sun to come up if dawn did not break when you expected it to. But the only thing that came was silence.

And it has never left.

I do not know what happened to those three Nain explorers—whether they died on the way back to Northland or not. The Exodus took much longer than any of the Nain leaders had planned, and as a result, many years, centuries even, had passed before the population finally arrived in their new home. And when they did, none of the three who had built the lair were with them.

So at last when the Nain came looking for the dragon they had left behind, the guardian of their history, the keeper of their knowledge, instead of a joyful reunion they were greeted not with the wisdom they had remembered, but with the acid and fiery breath of *scarnag*, a scourge who now hated them. With each passing day the hatred has grown, Nain, until it fills the entire cave. It overflows.

That's what betrayal does.

Especially betrayal of a Great Truth.

Especially when the thing used to accomplish that betrayal is a token of love.

Like kiran berries.

So the Nain lost their history. And their honor. And their friend. They may not even know why.

The dragon lost more.

- 28 -

The Report

THAT'S A VERY SAD TALE," SAID THE KING WHEN THE LAST WORDS of it had died away. "And a very important piece of magic for the book we will write someday. Thank you, Ven."

"My pleasure, Your Majesty," said Ven. His nervousness was making his hands and feet twitch. "I'm sorry I can't take more time to tell the whole tale in detail of what happened, but I have something urgent I must attend to. If I could just hit the high points, however—"

"Hit away," said the king, smiling.

"Right." Ven took out the two dragon books. "I think you should keep these in that secret place in Castle Elysian where you have other pieces of the magic puzzle stored, sire. This one, with the writing, was a gift, so I would like to keep it for now, but this other—the one that's sealed in the gold-lined box—I think that's something you should definitely have under great protection."

"I agree. I will take it back with me."

"It's only on loan," Ven added. "One day it will need to go back."

"I understand."

Next Ven gave him the wooden box Alvarran had given him and told him the story of how it had been presented to him.

"I guess it's the sign that the puzzle you gave me is complete," he said when he had finished the story. "The dragon got what he wanted. The Nain got what they wanted. The Lirin got what they wanted. Hopefully this is what you really wanted. Alvarran may be 'the Intolerant' and 'the Unfair,' but I don't think he can add 'the Untrustworthy' to his long list of names."

The smile left the king's face, replaced by a look of wonder and nervousness. He broke the seal on the box with great care and opened it.

Resting in the middle of the blue velvet lining was a plain silver ring.

A smile warmer than the sun returned to the king's face, and his blue eyes glowed even brighter.

"Thank you, Ven," he said after a moment. "Thank you."

Ven felt relief wash over him. "So is that what you wanted?"

"No, but it's a good down payment on it."

Ven's curiosity shot through him like he had been hit by lightning. "If that's not what you wanted, after all that, what *is*? Please tell me—I won't tell anyone."

"You saw her," said King Vandemere. "She's the one that gave you this." He held up the box.

"That beautiful Lirin girl? Who is she?"

"Elspeth," the king said. His face went red. "Alvarran's daughter. The Lirinved princess. She and I met when we were very young. I was about your age, and I was wandering the world, learning as much as I could about the people I now rule."

"You told me about that," Ven said. "You went in disguise, so that you could look for the magic hiding in the world without anyone knowing it was you."

"Yes. In the course of my travels, I met a young Lirindarc woman who was wandering the world as well. We, er, fell in love, each believing the other to be nothing more than a young man or woman of common birth. Finally, when we admitted who we were to each other, she invited me home to meet her father, so that I could ask for her hand. But Alvarran would not hear of it. He forbade Elspeth from seeing me, even after he learned who I was. He feared that I would take her away from the Enchanted Forest, and he would never see his daughter again. But even though you can keep two young people apart, you can't change how they feel about each other—even if you are a king. We have waited for more than five years for Alvarran to change his mind."

"So that's what you meant when you said you would call Alvarran 'sire'," Ven said excitedly. "You didn't mean you wanted to give up your throne to the Lirindarc king—"

"Er—no. That wouldn't be prudent."

"You meant you would be his son-in-law, right? Isn't *sire* another word for *father*?"

"Indeed," said the king, smiling.

"And Alvarran has finally agreed to the marriage?"

"So it would seem. Apparently so has Elspeth—that's why Alvarran told you he could consider granting the request, but that he did not have the power to do so alone. Elspeth would have had to say yes as well."

Ven sighed. "How I wish I was going to have a chance to talk to you more before I go," he said. "I'd love to tell you more about the dragon, and hear more about the ring, and your engagement."

"Next time, perhaps. In the meantime, tomorrow you can see

the surprise I had made for you. Oliver Snodgrass should have brought it in by now."

Ven's hair almost blew off his head.

"Oliver brought it with him? Did it come from far away?"

"Very," said the king. "Tomorrow the suspense will be over, and I will give it to you."

"Thank you, sire." Ven scratched the wildfire in his scalp without even knowing he was doing it. Finally he handed the king the small sack of kiran berry jewels.

"I'm going to keep one of these, just to remember the dragon by," he said, tucking it into his pocket along with the jack-rule and the Black Ivory sleeve and buttoning it carefully. "But you can have the other two for your collection. That story is in my journal as well."

"Thank you for everything, Ven," said King Vandemere. "Come and see me tomorrow, will you? I think it's safe for you to come back to the castle now."

"If I can," said Ven, standing up to go. "I'll try—but I have something very important to do first."

"Have a safe trip to town," said the king. "And remember to keep your head down still. Just to be safe."

"I will," Ven promised. "Now I have to run a race against time—and I'm not liking my odds."

‑ 29 ‑

The Race Against Time

T HE RIDE TO THE ABANDONED PIER WAS SMOOTH, AND ALL THREE of the girls fell asleep on the way. Ven was too excited and too nervous to sleep, so he wrote more of his letter home and put it inside his journal, so that he could finish it and post it if and when Amariel was all right.

The sky was turning gray, almost a light blue, when they finally pulled up to the abandoned pier.

"Wait here," Ven said to Char as he opened the gate of the wagon.

"You sure you don't need help?"

"I'll shout if I do. But this might be ugly—and embarrassing— so I want to give her some privacy." Char nodded and leaned back against the wagon side.

Ven helped the merrow down from the wagon bed, then led her down the pier to its end. He pulled the cap from his pocket, then held it out to her.

At first Amariel just looked at him. Then, as the first ray of sun crested the horizon, lighting the rooftops of Kingston, she looked down at the cap. The same rosy color that had appeared a second before in the ray of sun caught in her cheeks. Her eyes opened wide, then took on a sparkle. She smiled, then looked at Ven.

"My cap! Where did you find it?"

Ven thought about avoiding the question, but decided he had learned enough about keeping secrets.

"Clemency had it," he said. His words began to tumble out of his mouth as the expression on her face started to change. "She didn't know she had it and she didn't know that you were a merrow and she didn't know what it would do and she didn't mean to hurt you and she's really sorry and—"

Amariel's face went black with anger. She seized the cap, put it resolutely on her head, then jumped off the pier into the water in the middle of Ven's sentence.

And disappeared.

At first, like before, there was no sign of her at all. Then, also like before, the bubbles began to roil, the water began to turn colors, ending in gold. The dress Mrs. Snodgrass had given her floated to the surface, spinning helplessly in the bubbles until the tide pulled it under the dock.

Finally the merrow's head popped above the surface.

There were gills in her neck, and webbing between her fingers.

And, even though Ven could not see it, by the way she was moving, he knew she was no longer without her tail.

"You look wonderful!" he called to the merrow. "How are you feeling?"

Amariel glared at him. "Wonderful," she said. "Just *wonderful*."

Ven sighed in relief. "I'm so glad," he said.

"I'm being sarcastic," Amariel said. "I feel like a fish who's been out of water for a very long time. I'm all *dry*."

"Is everything working all right down below?"

The merrow's eyes went wide in shock. "That's a very personal question," she said. "How about you? Is everything working all right down below on *you*?"

"I apologize for the phrasing," Ven said, delighted to see her vigor had returned. "I just want to know if your tail is back in working order."

"It seems to be," said the merrow, swimming around a little.

"Good."

"So where was it?"

"What?"

"Where was my cap?" the merrow shouted.

"Clemency had it."

"So you said. Where did she keep it?"

"Oh. In her pocket, in a handkerchief."

"Ugh," said the merrow. "That's disgusting. I'm going to have to get it cleaned now. Yuck."

"I'm really sorry about everything that happened," Ven began. "I tried—"

The merrow swam backward, her arms paddling wildly. Her eyes had recovered the fire they normally held, but it was an angry fire. Ven could see beyond it there was a good deal of hurt as well.

"Do you see now?" she spat. "Do you *see* why my mom, and all the other merrow mothers, insist that we *stay away* from humans? They warn us to avoid them, not to trust them—do you see *why*?"

"You have every right to be angry, Amariel—"

"Oh, well, *thank you*," the merrow said bitterly. "Do you think so, Ven? You told me you would watch out for me, that you would make certain nothing bad happened to me—and I even believe you tried. But even with all that protection, what happened? Was I safe?"

"No," Ven admitted. "I'm so sorry."

"Well, I guess you taught me one thing," she went on. "I guess my mom was right. She would probably appreciate hearing me say that, since I almost never do. Thank goodness I survived. I guess I can at least be grateful for that."

"They didn't mean to hurt you, Amariel. I know that's not much comfort—"

Ven's words were drowned in a splash of cold saltwater from her tail.

"Don't you dare make excuses for them," the merrow said. "It was in her pocket—she must not have looked very hard. And don't you dare apologize. I made my own decision to trust you, to believe what you said. I didn't have to give you my cap, but I did—and I knew the risk I was taking. I'm just sorry to find out that the horror stories they tell about humans are true—even the nice ones. Even the friends of your friends."

"What can I do to make this up to you?" Ven asked desperately. Amariel was floating farther and farther away from the dock, looking like she was preparing to dive.

The merrow paused in the waves. She took a deep breath, as if willing herself to calm down.

"There's nothing to do," she said. She sounded a little less angry, and more sensible. "There's no need. I guess everything we live through in life teaches us something, Ven—everything we survive, at least. This is what I learned: that even though there are nice humans, and Nain and Gwadd and whatever, people who live on land and people who live in water cannot really be friends, except from a distance. And even then, the risk may be too great. The dry world is an interesting place, but it's not worth risking my life for again. I will never set foot on land again, not ever— because I never again want to have feet."

"I understand completely," Ven said. "I don't blame you a bit."

"Good." Finally, for the first time since she had returned to the water, the merrow smiled slightly, though she kept her lips tightly closed. "Well, thank you for the adventure, I guess. I'm going to miss you."

"What are you going to do now?" Ven asked. His throat felt like it was closing.

"Are you *kidding*? I'm going home. I've been away from home, from my family, ever since I found you sinking during the shipwreck. I haven't seen my mom in so many turns of the moon I've lost count. Goodbye, Ven. I'm glad you lived, and I'm glad I met you, I guess. Thank you for showing me the dry world— even if it almost killed me. I'll never forget you—don't forget me either, or you will regret it." She chuckled as the last words came out of her mouth. "But then, I don't think a Nain ever forgets the first merrow he meets. It just would be wrong."

Ven fought back tears. "Please stay around a little longer," he said. "You just got your tail back, and you might not be up to your normal strength. You don't have to go home right away— you can stay in the shallows where you've been since you got here. Don't go out to the open sea yet. Wait until you're feeling better."

"I feel better than I have in such a long time," Amariel said. "I can't explain this to a land-liver, but I just feel the need to swim, swim hard and long. It will be good for me to get back to the depths, to get away from the land and return to the wonders of the sea. I'm sorry you'll never see them yourself, but I've told you enough stories about them to last you a long time."

"All my life," Ven said. The tears were winning, and he brushed them away roughly with the back of his hand. "I'll remember them—and you—all my life."

"I know," Amariel said. "I won't forget you either. Well, goodbye, Ven—take care of yourself. And stay away from humans."

"I can't do that," Ven said. "My very best friend is a human. Even if he disappoints me, or I disappoint him, we trust each other. We forgive and make amends. If there's anything I learned because of all this, it's that there's no point in living without trust. Without it, we're really just alone, no matter how many people we share the world, or the sea, with."

The merrow blinked.

"Well, I suppose there is something to that," she said. "Goodbye, Ven."

"Amariel!" he called as she prepared to dive. "Wait a moment longer. Please!"

She sighed. "What now? The tide is beginning to turn, Ven."

"I want to go with you."

The merrow blinked again. "What?"

"I'm going with you. Where is that fisherman you said could cut gills in my neck?"

"Asa? He lives in the village to the south," she replied. "But you don't need to do that, Ven. Haven't you learned anything from all this?"

"Yes. I've learned that you are very important to me, even more than I realized. You trusted me even though you were afraid." The urge to cry had gone, driven away by the burning itch of curiosity. "*I'm* a little afraid of the gill cutting thing, but I trust *you*. I have always wanted to see the sights you told me about when you were keeping me awake, keeping me from drowning while I was floating on that piece of wreckage. I want to see the Summer Festival, and the Sea King and Queen—after all, I'm supposed to be in the company of monarchs all my life. I want to see the hippocampus races, and the underwater city of Tartechor, and the sea dragons you told me about. I want to see the tallest underwater mountains, and the deepest trenches where the fish carry their own lights, and everything else in every tale you ever told me. But even if I can't see those things, I still want to go with you."

He thought back to what Scarnag had said about Black Ivory.

That is one of the things in all the world that can mask the vibrations that something, or someone, gives off in the process of being alive. It can hide something's true name, making it invisible even to those beings who can see things that are hidden.

What are some of the others?

The only one I can think of, the only one mentioned in the books, is the sea.

"Maybe that's why Madame Sharra said she could only see my footprints for a short distance into the future," Ven said. "Maybe this is where my path is supposed to lead me now—into the sea. It certainly will be a good place to hide from the Thief Queen, and anyone else who is chasing me." The merrow stared at him, confused. "Never mind—I'll tell you about it later. Can you—ocean dwellers, I mean—talk under water?"

"Of course."

Ven was growing even more excited. "Well, if the invitation is still open, I'd like to take you up on it. I want to come with you. I mean, if you're willing to have me, that is."

Amariel exhaled. "Are you sure?"

Behind him Ven heard a cough. He turned to see Char, looking forlorn and hopeful, waiting at the end of the pier. He looked back at the merrow.

"Completely sure."

The merrow smiled. "All right, then. Come along."

"Can you give me a minute," Ven asked, pointing to Char. "I have to say goodbye."

"Hurry up—the tide won't wait."

"Be right back," Ven promised. He ran back down the rotten boards of the pier, leaping and jumping over the holes, until he was standing on the sand.

"Char—"

"You decided ta go with her, didn't you?"

Ven exhaled happily. "Yes. And I can't stay long, because the tide's going out."

Char nodded. "All right."

"Will you say goodbye to everyone at the Inn for me? Especially Mrs. Snodgrass and McLean? Tell them I'll miss them— and take care of the others, especially Ida."

Char stared at him, thunderstruck.

"What the heck are you talkin' about?" he demanded. "I'm not goin' back to the Inn if you're goin' into the *sea*, for pity sakes! How many times do you need it said to get it into your thick head? I'm supposed ta keep an eye on you—*Captain's orders*. You decidin' to become part merrow, or whatever you're doin', doesn't change that. I'm goin' with you."

"Are you sure? You understand what it takes to do it?"

Char's hand went immediately to his neck, and he swallowed hard. "Yeah." He checked Ven's neck. "I hope that he doesn't slice off *all three* o' your whiskers."

"Three? There are *three*?"

"Yeah, looks like you grew another one."

Ven grinned broadly. "Guess my beard's growing in seriously at last. All right, then. If we're going with Amariel, you make sure she's willing to have you. Tell her I'll be right back."

He jogged back to the wagon, where Tuck was waiting patiently beneath his straw hat. Clem was sleeping peacefully in the back, but Ida was wide awake, watching him closely.

Ven climbed into the back of the wagon. He picked up the bundle with all his possessions in it, then stepped over the wagon board and sat down beside the Lirin forester.

"Thanks for everything, Tuck," he said. The forester nodded. "Will you please do something for me?"

"If I can."

He handed Tuck his journal. "Please give this to the king. Congratulate him for me, and tell him about all the things we saw together, especially the dragon's egg and the river of gold and—oh, everything you can remember! Everything I remember is in here, written up as best as I could tell it. I signed all my drawings with my initials so that when he is compiling his book of all human knowledge, he will know where some of it came from, just in case I don't get back to compile the rest of it for him."

"I will do so," said Tuck.

"And this," Ven said, handing him the dragon book. "I hope he will let me have it back one day—but there's no point in risking water damage. Will you give it to him as well?"

"I will."

"And please tell him that I appreciate whatever surprise he had for me, and that it will drive me crazy until I come back and find out what it is."

"Done. Travel well, Ven. It's been a pleasure being in your company."

"For me, too." Ven shook the forester's hand. Then he climbed back into the wagon bed and crouched in front of Ida.

"I'm going away for a while," he said to the Thief Queen's daughter. "I wish I could take you with me."

Ida snorted, but she smiled her crooked smile more broadly.

"I really do," Ven insisted. "I want you to be safe from your mother. So I'm going to lend you something until I get back."

"What?"

Ven patted the nest of Black Ivory where the dragon's egg had rested. "This," he said simply. "Sleep in it—you seem comfortable there. While you're in it, I don't think Felonia, her thugs, her spies, or anyone else can find you. Get someone to help you carry it into Mouse Lodge—it's *really* heavy. Stay safe and take care of yourself until I get back. Please. And take care of the others." He nodded toward Clem. "Mrs. Snodgrass, too."

"All right, get goin', Polywog," Ida said tartly. "You're the only one who thinks anyone's gonna miss ya."

Ven laughed. He gave the bony girl a quick hug and climbed out of the wagon before the look of shock left her face.

"Oh," he called over his shoulder. "By the way—you know that molten gold the Nain put in those pots to keep the egg warm? Well, it's solid now—and the egg's not using it anymore. There's plenty for you, and Clem, and Mrs. Snodgrass—so now you only have to pick pockets if you're bored."

He ran back down the pier, where Char and the merrow were staring awkwardly at each other.

"You ready?" he asked his best friend.

"Guess so," said Char doubtfully.

"Not too late to change your mind."

"You know better'n that."

Ven laughed. "I do. So let's not talk about it further." He looked down at the water, where the light of First-sun was spilling over the merrow, making her beautiful scales shine like a thousand jewels.

"We're ready, Amariel," he said. "Show us your world."

The merrow just smiled.

"Come along," she said. "Hope you can keep up, 'cause I'm not waiting for you."

ENDNOTE FROM THE DOCUMENTARIAN

This is where the last of the three journals of Ven Polypheme found in our archaeological dig site ends. Unlike his first two notebooks, there is no final comment. It just ends.

Inside it was a sealed letter with only the words *Polypheme, Vaarn, the Great Overward* written on the outside.

It had never been opened.

Our dig took place in what is believed to be the site of the city of Vaarn on the continent of The Great Overward, as it was called in ancient times. The dig unearthed several old dwellings and what appears to have been a factory. Its closeness to the harbor leads us to believe these sites may have been the Polypheme family home and shipbuilding factory. If this proves to be historically true, perhaps Ven sent these notebooks home to his family after the information in them was added to *The Book of All Human Knowledge*.

We hope that's the case, because if it is, perhaps there are more journals out there to find.

As of this writing, we have three more dig sites going in various places around the world, but alas, so far the search has turned up no more of Ven's writings.

The Book of All Human Knowledge, as well as the tome known as *All the World's Magic*, were both lost at sea long ago, so we don't know anything about them for certain. We know that Ven is credited in other historical texts for doing some of the research in these magical reference books, but whether he wrote a little, a lot, or all of them remains a mystery.

It is hoped that one day we may recover more of his journals, so that we may continue to look back in time to places where the magic he saw in his travels might one day be found. We have already found evidence that some of it has survived.

Just today, as I finished the last of my restoration efforts on this last of the journals, I noticed a rather large flock of black birds perched on one of the trucks we use in the archaeological dig. There were so many that they covered the entire vehicle. When I went outside to shoo them away, however, an enormous shadow passed overhead, and the ravens flew off.

I shielded my eyes and looked up to see if I could catch a glimpse of the bird.

I did not. It flew away too quickly.

But I did see a huge feather drifting down on the wind.

It was as long as my arm.

And now I am wearing it in my pith helmet.

I am off to work, hoping to find more of Ven's journals, and more of the ancient magic of the world recorded therein.

—Elizabeth Haydon

ACKNOWLEDGMENTS

In addition to the luminaries I thanked in the first two volumes, who still hold warm places in my heart (which I would like back when they are done with them, please), I would like to acknowledge the following helpful people for their contributions to our ongoing archaeological dig:

First and foremost, as always, Dr. Alexander Vandersnoot, Vaarn expedition leader, who has handled every aspect of the dig as well as updating our blog at www.venbooks.com.

T. L. Scott, noted camel guide, who, like other two-initialed authors such as T. E. Lawrence, T. S. Eliot, and T. H. White, entertained me with his writings as we were crossing the endless desert of Jyl on an unbalanced dromedary. (Hope your saddle sores heal quickly, Scott.)

Mr. "Woomph" Ralboosh, Expert in Everything, our expedition's concierge. (It may seem strange that an archaeological expedition *has* a concierge, but gracious living out here in the wastelands is a must among documentarians—we have so little else to live for.) That raspberry-scorpion sorbet flambé was the best I've ever had! Thanks mucho.

Dr. Swishy Humdinger, the dig's physician, who tirelessly tends to our sandburned fingers and sunburned skin. Swishy, get some rest. If you haven't got your health, then you haven't got anything.

Miss Jodi Rosoff, the expedition's communications expert, wherever she is. She was last seen atop a towering sand dune under the full moon, tapping Morse code into her cell phone receiver, trying to order carry-out sushi in the middle of the desert. The many reports of a hovering disc-like ship in the area have not yet been confirmed. Jodi, phone home!

Lady Beatrice Evelyn Voleny, for the loan of her giant flashlights and all her sage advice about how to sooth sand-flea bites.

Professor Baxter "Bax" McCracken, the group's slave driver, for keeping round-the-clock shifts going by blowing a screeching whistle into our tents every four hours like clockwork. Reports that he was buried alive in an unmarked sand dune are mostly false. (We *will* get you yet, Bax. When you least expect it, expect it.)

Technical guru Godeye Luft de Raideres, superhero of technology, hiding behind the persona of a mild-mannered New York skating instructor, for all his help untangling the strings on our transatlantic tin cans and using ground-penetrating radar to locate Ven's family artifacts (though I *still* don't believe his mother had a shaving brush, Godeye, no matter how much you insist).

Mistress Karen Barry, the world's foremost expert in kiran berries, for her kind assistance and support.

And finally, a cheerful shout of camaraderie to the talking sand-turtles of the Hishgigumbo oasis. The water might have been a mirage, but our conversation about world politics was one of the most meaningful I've ever engaged in. Many thanks, fellas, and stay wet.

—EH

A NEW NOTE FROM THE DOCUMENTARIAN

As noted at the end of the third of the Ven Polypheme Journals, *The Dragon's Lair*, the original dig site contained only three volumes of Ven's notes and drawings. Ongoing expeditions have been searching for more of the mythical lost journals, but as of yet we have not been able to definitively authenticate any more examples of his writing.

That does not mean we are not working to do so, however.

Recently, a new discovery was made in the jungle lands ruled by the ferocious Womba Looma tribe of the tropical island of Rompa Snizz. While it has not been officially confirmed as a genuine Lost Journal, because it was greatly damaged by sea water, our team has been working around the clock in an attempt to restore it. We hope to discover whether it is, in fact, a later episode in Ven's story of magical adventure or just a clever forgery. A third possibility exists in that it could be, in fact, the real story of someone else entirely, with friends who had miraculously similar names to Ven and *his* friends. In any event, there is a great possibility that whoever penned this journal might have met an unfortunate ending after writing it.

The Womba Looma are cannibalistic; or at least they were back in the Second Age of history, when Ven lived. Our archaeological team escaped intact, but one scientist did have his hat eaten.

We will not publish the entire contents of the journal, which is called *The Tree of Water*, until we are absolutely certain it is genuine. But here is a snippet of one of the stories that survived being buried in the jungles of the Womba Looma, which apparently takes place under the sea.

—Elizabeth Haydon

Elizabeth Haydon is now working
to restore the fourth volume of
The Lost Journals of Ven Polypheme,
The Tree of Water.

See below for a sneak peek for your eyes only.

S HHHH," AMARIEL WHISPERED. VEN COULD TELL BY THE SIZE OF her eyes that she was terrified.

He pressed himself up against the ghostly coral structure, its glowing formations hard as rock, though Ven knew it was actually a mass of living creatures. He tried not to shudder as something wiggled against his back.

Above them the stalagmites tapered up toward the surface, growing lacey and fragile as they reached up into the patchy darkness toward the hazy green light. The higher up they grew, the thinner and wispier their purple and green arms became. They reminded Ven of the frail threads of spun sugar that he saw from time to time in the Magical Confectionery in town.

Just then, the light disappeared, as an enormous black shadow passed overhead, blotting it out.

Megalodon, Ven thought. He had seen the giant shark once before, while aboard Oliver Snodgrass's ship, the *Serelinda*. The lookout in the crow's nest had shouted the name, and suddenly every sailor fell silent and stood utterly still.

Their eyes looked exactly as Amariel's did now.

The last time he had seen the beast, it was nothing more than a giant fin the size of the mainsail of the *Serelinda* and a shadow that passed beneath the hull. Now that he was in the water, feeling the pressure of its wake as it swam above him, it felt as if the moon itself had fallen out of the sky and was growing to crush them into the sandy ocean floor.

He could feel Amariel's hand slip into his own, the webbed fingers trembling. He could hear her voice, clear from being in the air, just before they had submerged.

And for goodness' sake, if we come upon a shark, hold still and don't make any noise or movement until I discover if it's one of my friends or not. They can tell where you are by your movements. And your smell, of course, especially if you're bleeding. Even my friends might eat you by mistake if you're bleeding—or even me. Blood in the water kind of cancels out any notion of politeness.

I don't suppose Megalodon is a friend of yours, Char had joked.

Amariel's voice in reply was as cold as Ven had ever heard it.

Megalodon has no friends. Even the pilot fish isn't his friend.

Ven took slower breaths, trying to keep his heart from beating too loudly. He looked as far to the right as he could by just moving his eyes, but he couldn't see Char. He could feel him, however, because the spidery fronds of the reef coral were shaking violently, just like Char did whenever he was really frightened. *He must be leaning against it*, Ven thought. *Good, then at least he's still behind me.*

After what seemed like forever, the hazy light appeared again. Ven looked up and could see the very end of the enormous tail fin, waving back and forth as the beast moved beyond the reef, heading out into the darkness of the depths again.

He squeezed Amariel's hand in relief.

"Thank goo'ness *he's* gone," he heard Char mutter behind him.

"No joke," Ven agreed. He smiled at the merrow, only to lose that smile an instant later when he caught the look on Amariel's face.

She was staring behind him, her eyes even wider.

He glanced over his shoulder.

At the edge of the light, he could see the giant shadow turning.

"The pilot fish," Amariel whispered. "It's seen us."

READER'S GUIDE

◦ The Lost Journals of Ven Polypheme ◦
THE DRAGON'S LAIR

ELIZABETH HAYDON

Illustrations restored by JASON CHAN

ABOUT *The Dragon's Lair*

The third installment of Ven Polypheme's adventures again features passages from his "recovered" journals as compiled by acclaimed fantasy author Elizabeth Haydon. Gifted with a highly curious mind, Ven travels through a world populated by myriad clans and creatures, from human to Gwadd to Lirin to Nain, and from dragon to mermaid. Each group possesses its own wisdom, and the discoveries Ven makes as he travels among them gradually fit together to create a fascinating, often deeply insightful worldview. Here Ven leads his friends, Char, Clem, Ida, Saeli, and Amariel, on an adventure to carry out King Vandemere's mission to stop a fire-setting dragon and end the feud between the Nain and Lirin peoples. With the Thief Queen in constant pursuit, Madame Sharra's frightening fortune troubling his mind, incessant squabbles among his friends, and a mermaid's secret tucked in his pocket, Ven makes the difficult journey and is rewarded with an amazing discovery about dragons, stories, and, most importantly, about the true meaning of friends and family.

ABOUT THIS GUIDE

The information, activities, and discussion questions which follow are intended to enhance your reading of *The Dragon's Lair*. Please feel free to adapt these materials to suit your needs and interests.

ABOUT THE AUTHOR

Elizabeth Haydon, the daughter of a U.S. Air Force officer, began traveling at an early age and has visited many countries of the world. She is a skilled herbalist, harpist and madrigal singer, an anthropology and folklore enthusiast, and a professional editor of educational literature. An accomplished fantasy author for both adult and younger readers, she lives on the East Coast with her husband and three children.

WRITING AND RESEARCH ACTIVITIES

I. Curiosity and Secrets

   A. Throughout the novel, Ven uses words such as "itching" to describe the curiosity that motivates his actions and ideas. Peruse the novel to find other words or phrases associated with curiosity. Make a brainstorm list of words, phrases, and images that suggest curiosity to you. Go to the library or online to find a definition of curiosity and a list of quotations related to this term. If desired, create a "curiosity collage" of words, quotes, drawings, and other relevant images.

B. Write a short essay describing a time when you were very curious about something, such as a birthday gift you thought you might receive or your grade on an important test. How did your curiosity affect your behavior? What was the outcome of the situation? Invite friends or classmates to share their curious essays.

C. Divide friends or classmates into two groups to debate the following question: Is curiosity a good and helpful quality or a dangerous thing?

D. As the character of Ven, list the pros and cons of keeping Amariel's secret from your friends. Discuss your list with friends or classmates. Vote to see whether most of them agree or disagree with Ven's actions. Ask them to explain their votes.

E. With friends or classmates, discuss some other secrets at play in *The Dragon's Lair* (Hint: What secret does King Vandermere keep from Ven?). How might secrets and curiosity play a role in real life?

II. Merrows, Kings, and Dragons

A. Use watercolor paints, colored pencils, or other art media to depict the interior of Garnax's cave, Saeli's hidden home, or another key setting from the novel. Make your creation as true to the text as possible. Share your results with friends or classmates. Discuss the similarities and differences in your visual interpretation of these settings with those of other students, being sure to consider choices in color, texture, organization, and scale of the works. Then draw what your "lair," hidden room, or secret cave would look like if you could make it anything you wanted.

B. Divide a sheet of paper into two columns headed "River King" and "King Vandermere." Create a comparison chart of the two kings, being sure to consider each man's style of leadership and their sense of commitment to those whom they rule. If desired, add other leaders to your comparison chart, like King Alvarran the Intolerant and Garson, the leader of the Nain. How are they different? How are they the same? Compare the characters of Mrs. Snodgrass, Tuck, and McLean the Storysinger.

C. Create a character guide to The Adventures of Ven Polypheme. Include characters from *The Dragon's Lair* and other books in the series, if you have read them. Design a page for each type of being, such as human, Nain, or Gwadd. On each page, list the names of characters of this kind, descriptions, sketches, and other information as desired. Make an illustrated cover for your guide.

D. What is the true identity of Scarnag? In the voice of the character of Ganrax, write the story of your first night alone in the cave. Or write about your feelings after your meeting with Ven.

E. Go to the library or online to learn more about the mythology of dragons or merrows/mermaids. Use your research to create an illustrated, informational poster about your chosen creature. Be sure to include a paragraph describing how Ganrax or Amariel is similar to, and different from, the dragons or mermaids from your research. If desired, add a reading list of famous dragon/mermaid stories and songs to your poster.

III. Journeys

A. As the character of Ida, Clem, Char, or Saeli, write a series of journal entries describing: Why you decided to join Ven on this adventure; your attitude toward his new friend, Amariel; your hopes or fears for the journey; your feelings at the journey's end. Then write similar thoughts from Amariel's point of view.

B. Imagine you live at the Crossroads Inn. Write a short essay including your name; your clan (human, Nain, or other); how you came to the Inn and whether you live in Mouse Lodge or Hare Warren; your feelings about the place, your housemates, and Mrs. Snodgrass; and your relationship to Ven. In the character invented in your essay, join friends or classmates in a role-play conversation in which you debate joining Ven on his mission for King Vandemere. What do you think of Ven? What has he told you about the journey? What are the risks of staying at the Inn versus joining Ven?

C. Like Ven, try keeping a journal in which you record interesting things you have learned. For several days or weeks, write down thoughts, discoveries, memories, and ideas you have about your school, community, and life in general. Compare your writings with Ven's entries throughout the novel. What conclusions might you draw about the act of keeping a journal?

D. Over the course of the novel, Ven learns important lessons about friendship and family. Make a list of at least three of these lessons, choosing those that seem most meaningful to you. Illustrate and post the list in your home or classroom.

E. Reread the epilogue. Write a short essay explaining why you think Elizabeth Haydon chose to include this information and what it might mean for the next installment of the series. With friends or classmates, create a brainstorm list of the adventures you hope Ven will next take and the questions, problems, or mysteries you hope will be resolved.

QUESTIONS FOR DISCUSSION

1. What does the preface of the story tell readers? How might these opening paragraphs lead readers to expect this book will be different from other fantasy stories they have read? Does the preface seem to provide fictional or nonfictional information? What gives you this impression? What do you hope to discover in the chapters which follow?

2. What does Ven tell readers about himself in the opening pages of Chapter 1? How is he different from other Nain? What are his thoughts about magic? How does Ven feel about adventuring? Who is the surprise visitor in Chapter 1 who changes Ven's thoughts about wanting some rest before his next adventure?

3. What task, or tasks, does King Vandemere assign to Ven? Whom does Ven decide to invite along? What are his reasons for inviting these friends on his journey? Who does he leave behind and why?

4. Why does Ven think Amariel ought to join his group? Had you been given Amariel's choice, would you have forfeited your cap for the chance to see life on land? Why or why not?

5. Ravens are a recurring image in *The Dragon's Lair*. What do these birds represent? What actions or plot elements of the story are affected by ravens?

6. Who is Madame Sharra? What does she tell Ven? What effect does her reading have on Ven's thoughts and actions? How would you feel if someone read such a fortune for you?

What special gift does the mark on his hand bring to Ven? Would you use such a gift? Why or why not?

7. Why doesn't Ven tell his friends the truth about Ameriel's identity? How do Char, Clem, and the others feel about the merrow? Have you ever kept a secret because you believed it was in the best interest of a friend? What effect did this have on your friendship with this person, and with others? What advice might you have given Ven about keeping this secret?

8. What does Ven carry encased in Black Ivory? What treasure of his grandfather's does he also carry in his pocket? How do these objects impact his journey?

9. In the opening of Chapter 9, Ven cites a Polypheme family expression "He's had one too many turns at the forge." What is the meaning of this expression? How does it apply to Ven? How does Ven's realization of his misunderstanding of the situation between Amariel and his other friends foreshadow the larger lesson about friendship and family he will learn from Ganrax?

10. How does Ameriel help the group when they encounter the River King? Does this change the others' attitudes toward the merrow? Why or why not? What does Ven learn about the dragon from the River King? What deeper lesson does the River King teach Ven?

11. What is Saeli's gift? How does she make the group vulnerable? How does she help the group make a discovery? What sort of wisdom do Saeli and the Gwadd folk impart to Ven?

12. After Tuck, Clem, and Char help some Lirin fight a fire, what does Ven learn about Lirin attitudes toward Nain? What is important about the Lirin man's comment at the end of Chapter 12 that states, "If someone asked me a few years ago, I'd have said that both dragons and Nain were nothing but made-up creatures in children's stories"?

13. In Chapter 13 Amariel finally smiles. How does Ven feel about this? How does this signal an unhappy change in the merrow? Whom do the ravens seems to most want when they attack the wagon once again? What decision does this cause the group to make?

14. As they head for the Gwaddlands, what is strange about the landscape? How does the milk taste? What is important about this experience? What has happened to the Gwaddlands? What do her friends think of Saeli's home? How does the food taste there?

15. Why is Ven finally forced to reveal Amariel's true identity in Chapter 16? Does this improve the relationship between Ven and his friends? Between Ida, Clem, and Amariel?

16. How do Ven's dreams affect his actions in the story? Are the dreams realistic or symbolic? How do the dreams help readers better understand Ven's character?

17. As they approach Scarnag's lands, what surprising reaction does Tuck have to Ven's removal of the dragon scale from the Black Ivory? What danger is posed by the Lirindarc?

18. What are Ven's thoughts on prejudice, or being treated badly, in his journal entry of Chapter 18? How do these observations help Ven to better understand Ganrax's struggles at the end of the story?

19. Describe Ven's encounter with King Alvarran. What bargain does he make with the king? What are his considerations about using his power to alter Time at this point in the novel?

20. What does Garson tell Ven about Scarnag? Is his story correct? What else worries Ven as he travels to the dragon's lair? How might these worries be related?

21. What truth does Ven realize about Scarnag's identity? What important gift does he offer the dragon? What does Ven receive from the dragon?

22. With what do the Nain entrust Ven and his friends? To whom does Ven deliver this object? What is the result of this delivery?

23. Why does Ven turn down the Lirin king's offer to visit the Enchanted Forest? What does this tell readers about the lesson he has learned from Scarnag? What important object does Clemency find in her pocket and what is the result of her discovery?

24. How does Ven tell Scarnag's tale to King Vandemere? Why does the dragon believe it is very important that stories be true? Do you agree? Who else does Ven know that also believes this?

25. Does everyone have a Great Truth? What might you consider to be your Great Truth?

26. When Ven returns Amariel to the sea, what does he realize might be the surprising meaning of Madame Sharra's ability to see his footprints for only a short distance in the future? What new adventure does he consider? Would you join him? Why or why not?

Starscape

Award-Winning
Science Fiction and Fantasy
for Ages 10 and up

STARSCAPE

www.tor-forge.com/starscape